Fingering The Family Jewels

Greg Lilly

Regal Crest Enterprises, LLC

Nederland, Texas

ISBN 1-932300-22-8

First Printing 2004

9 8 7 6 5 4 3 2 1

Cover design by Donna Pawlowski

Published by:

Regal Crest Enterprises, LLC
PMB 210, 8691 9th Avenue
Port Arthur, Texas 77642-8025

Find us on the World Wide Web at
http://www.regalcrest.biz

Printed in the United States of America

Acknowledgments:

I want to thank my wonderful friends and dedicated fellow writers Viki Cupaiuolo, Michelle Groce, Robert Herrin, Diana Renfro, and Jean Rowe for their advice, support, and wine. Thanks for allowing me the room to grow and to learn.

Thanks to my faithful first readers Kayleen Fitzgerald, Angie McCoy, and Tina Warholic who never shy away from a manuscript box landing on their doorsteps. Your encouragement is pure gold to me.

Thanks to Regal Crest's Cathy LeNoir and my editor Sylverre for their guidance and understanding.

Brad, thank you for putting up with me all these years and for helping me make time to write. And to the rest of my family, this is fiction. No one would believe the truth. I love you all.

To the memory of my grandmothers who showed me the true meaning of love and family.

Chapter One

"AUNT WALT IS dead." Mother's voice, strong and steady, struck my ear.

I switched the phone to the other ear. "What? She can't be." Walterene, a cousin of my mother's, was one of the few family members I liked. "I talked to her last week."

"Nonetheless, she died from a sudden stroke." Her simple statement stung from the lack of emotion, lack of sympathy.

My stomach cramped as if my breath had been knocked out of me by her words. "But..." I struggled to speak. "When?"

"Tuesday night." Mother always was short and direct.

"How's Aunt Ruby?"

"Ruby thought I should call you. Let you know about Walt."

"When is the—"

The phone clicked, followed by silence, then a dial tone. The Bitch had hung up on me. "Damn you." I slammed the phone down.

My roommate, Emma, sat on our third-hand couch, smoking a Marlboro and painting her toenails a glossy vermilion. Vermilion. She always joked that I couldn't name three professional football teams but could come up with fifteen names for red; this was a trait Aunt Walt had cultivated in me. Emma glanced over with sorrowful eyes. "Who?"

"Aunt Walt died Tuesday, and that was the Ice Bitch letting me know."

"Derek," she hobbled over to me on her heels to keep from smudging her nail polish and hugged me. "I'm so sorry to hear she's gone. She's in a much better place."

"Yeah, away from the family." I couldn't believe Walterene was gone, out of my life forever. Her strong will, her logic, her kindness, her openness, she had always loved me no matter what I did. It was an unconditional love that I didn't find easily or really believe in except from her or Ruby. I checked the clock. "Too late to call Aunt Ruby tonight; she's usually in bed by ten. Though I doubt she can sleep without Walt there."

Emma made her way back to the couch. Her skinny legs stuck out of her housecoat like two beanpoles. Trying to be a model, she threw up more than half of what she ate, living mainly on cigarettes, black coffee, and bananas. She had a beautiful face; of course that's what is said of fat girls, but it can be said of skinny, titless ones too. I liked Emma's black hair and blue eyes; she reminded me of an anorexic version of a young Liz Taylor. She dropped back to the couch and fanned her toenails. "Why do you hate your family?"

"Because they're fake." That about summed it up.

"For example?"

"They go to church because they have money, and in Charlotte, North Carolina, if you are rich and don't go to church, no one will do business with you. To them, it's a way to make business deals."

Emma smiled, casting her eyes up to me from her continued fanning. "Not because they don't like the idea that you are gay?"

"Like it? They tell me I'll burn in hell. Again, using religion when it's convenient for their purpose." I always became enraged talking about them; that's why I usually avoided it. Walking to the window, I noticed a young straight couple pushing a stroller up Hill Street; a cool mist was descending on the city. I turned back to Emma. "Do you know my dear mother told me she hoped I got AIDS and died? That way I would die out here in San Francisco, and no one in Charlotte would know."

"No?" Emma's eyes widened.

"Oh, yeah. She always let you know what she believed was the gospel truth. She ruled the roost, behind closed doors." I laughed to myself thinking about her in public. "But as soon as we would walk into that fucking Baptist church, she would fall two steps behind my father. Then, when we got home, she took over again, and Thomas shrank back into the background."

"If he's so meek, why did she marry him?" Emma lit another cigarette and leaned back.

"The Harris family is in the construction business. My great-grandfather, Ernest, believed that women should produce babies, not build houses. My mother grew up in the construction business and learned how to get what she wanted by yanking men around by their balls. She didn't want a power struggle in her marriage, so she married the weakest, meekest wimp she could find." My love for my father came from his affection for us kids, but I would have respected him more if he had stood up to my mother.

"Construction? You never told me that. Guess that's your attraction to men with tool belts." She smiled and tucked loose strands of hair back behind her ears. "You really need to get over these negative feelings toward your family." Emma nudged me on.

"I didn't feel like I deserved to be alive until I left that house. Aunt Walt and Aunt Ruby were the only ones in the family who gave me any encouragement. They were two old maids who lived away from the family, stayed out of the politics of running the business. Of course, as unmarried women, they didn't get much of a chance to participate."

"Typical, male-dominated society," she huffed.

"This, coming from a woman who wants to strut down a runway in the name of fashion?" I teased her because I could.

"I'm using men to get what I want. If I can be paid big bucks to walk in front of a crowd, I'll take it. Your aunts should have stormed the office and taken over—or fucked the construction workers and led a coup."

I couldn't imagine Ruby or Walterene fucking construction workers. Hell, they were in their sixties; maybe in their twenties, they could have had a hard-hat or two. "Oh, great, now I have a mental image of frumpy Walterene on top of a muscled, sweaty back-hoe driver, riding him like there's no tomorrow." I laughed. Emma could always make me smile.

"Go, girl. Go, girl," Emma chanted, waving her arm in the air like a broncobuster and thrusting her hips off the couch in a simulated fevered fucking frenzy.

"Enough." My thoughts went back to the fact that Walterene was gone. "I hate that she never got away from the family. There's so much more in this world than Harris Construction, and I'm not sure she ever realized that." The canary-colored walls of our apartment surrounded me, a happy shade to counter the gray fog pressed against the windows that framed the San Francisco hills. Walterene and Ruby had never ventured out to California to visit; in fact, none of the family had ever flown out to see me.

Emma sat up straight on the couch. "Just how rich is this family of yours?"

"Rich enough to not have to play by the rules." In the dust of the coffee table, I drew the outline of a skyscraper. "They helped build Charlotte, literally. Harris is on the names of streets, buildings, and neighborhoods all over town."

"So you must have been quite a catch in the gay bars."

"Hell, I was never allowed out of the sight of some family member." My thoughts went back to the first time I'd had sex with another guy.

I was fourteen and on a camping trip with my cousin Mark. At nineteen, he was the most beautiful man I had ever seen. Growing up, Mark and I had always been closest in age, but five years made a big difference. I had begged him to go to Grandfather Mountain on a camping trip.

"Kid stuff," Mark had huffed.

I thought he made the sun rise and set. I spotted his bench presses in his bedroom while he worked out for the upcoming football season at Duke. Going into his second season, he intended to be a starting wide receiver. The muscles strained in his chest as he pushed the barbell up, sweat trickled down his shirtless torso; he reminded me of Superman—broad chest, thin hips, flat stomach. A trail of dark hair snaked from his navel down past the waistband of his gray gym shorts where sweat had soaked the material to the color of a storm cloud. I glanced at the outline of his cock lying to the left, creating a bulge I wanted to touch. "Please, just overnight. My parents won't let me go unless you come."

He set the weights down and shook his head. "Not with a bunch of high school kids."

"No, just me and you," I pleaded.

"Okay, okay," he agreed.

After a day of hiking, we pitched the tent and fixed a dinner of beans and cornbread. We settled down by the fire and talked about college and football; I absorbed every word he said. Mark stood and stretched, then pulled off his shirt. I watched. He unbuttoned his cutoff jeans and they fell to the ground. His white briefs seemed to glow in the firelight. I looked for the familiar bulge that mesmerized me, then he pulled down his underwear. My heart about stopped; his dick looked twice as big as mine, thick and long. While he neatly folded his clothes, I followed his lead, believing older, college men always slept in the nude. When I pulled off my underwear, the warm July breeze hit my cock; that and the sight of Mark produced an erection. I tried to cover it, but I wasn't fast enough.

"Damn, Derek. What's up with the woody? A woody in the woods," Mark teased, standing on the other side of the fire bucknaked with his own cock twitching.

Embarrassed, I didn't know what to do except punch him like I always did when he teased me. He caught my fist in his hand and wrestled me to the ground. Wrestling turned into more, and for four years we were lovers.

After college, Mark decided he needed to find a woman to settle down with. I was devastated, and in my depression, I told my father I was in love with a man. I didn't say who; I knew the family edict on privacy. He and my mother decided it was best that I go away for college. They sent me to Jerry Falwell's prison in Lynchburg. I stayed a month. My sister, Valerie, came to get me. She gave me $10,000 and told me to go wherever I wanted.

I lived in Richmond for a few months, then DC; finally some friends I knew moved to San Francisco, and I followed. The past six years had swept by so fast, I'd almost forgotten why I'd moved west.

"NO. EMMA, I was never much of a bar person. I always felt I was better than bar trash. Funny, how being treated like trash makes you want to rise above it all."

Emma's large blue eyes pried into me. "You haven't been back in years."

"A couple of times, but the family doesn't want me around. That's clear. My parents never invited me to stay with them. I stayed with Valerie or Aunt Ruby and Walterene." The thought of Aunt Walt swirled around my brain, her smiles and laughter, her encouragement and interest in my life. Tears threatened to spill from my eyes, but I sniffed them back. If only she had been my mother, instead of the bitch named Gladys.

"Do any of them know about your new job?" Emma asked.

"Internet development means nothing to them. If it doesn't have anything to do with bricks and mortar, it's a hobby." I knew Walterene and Ruby would be proud of the business I had started with friends. *Walt. She's dead.*

The phone rang again. I let it ring. Emma answered, then handed it to me and left the room.

"Have you heard?" My sister Valerie, another old maid in the Harris family, asked.

"About Walterene?"

She sighed. "Yes, I wanted to tell you, but Mother just said she had notified everyone."

"Thank God, at least I'm part of everyone in her eyes."

"Derek, she loves you, like I do—"

"Oh, right." Mother never showed love to anyone.

"Listen to me." Valerie's voice grabbed me. "Mother is old, doesn't understand anything that isn't part of her world. Come home. If not for me, for Aunt Ruby; she needs us. She needs us all."

"Val, I can't. I just can't face them. I'll call Ruby tomorrow."

"If you need money—"

"I'm doing fine, thanks. When is the funeral?"

"I don't think..." she hesitated, "on Saturday."

"I'll send flowers."

"Derek, your family is here. Mother and Father, Tim, Laura and the kids, and I—"

"Yeah, I'll be in touch. Thanks for calling." I hung up before Valerie could start her routine on families working out differences before it was too late. But, it was too late. Walterene was dead. Ruby was alone. Valerie, an old maid at forty-one. Me, the shunned faggot son in San Francisco. All misfits in the kingdom of the Harris clan.

Emma came back into the room from the kitchen, munching on a banana. "Should I help you pack?"

"Hell, no."

"Won't you regret this later? Things you should have said? Things you should have done?"

"Last time I talked to Aunt Walterene, I told her I loved her, and she said she loved me. That is all that needed to be said." I settled back into the chair and turned up the stereo to put an end to the conversation.

"What about..." she yelled over the music, then grabbed the remote from me and shut off the receiver. "What about your Aunt Ruby? Doesn't she need you?" The penetrating look she gave me made me glance away.

I stared out the window; the fog had rolled in thicker and I could barely see two blocks down the hill to the BART station. *I could be on the BART, and on my way to the airport in thirty minutes.* "No." I shook the thought loose with a jerk of my head. "They banished me. I won't subject myself to them again. No family is worth their torment. Besides, I have my family here: you, Lindsay, Jeff, Kayleen, Jason, Bill—my family of choice. I don't need the hassle of my birth family." I looked back out the window, watching a seagull pick its dinner out of the neighbor cat's dish. "Fuck them."

She smiled at me. "What time will you be leaving?"

Chapter
Two

MY FLIGHT WAS scheduled to arrive in Charlotte at 3:05 Friday afternoon. I didn't really expect anyone to meet me at the airport. After a sleepless night, I had called Ruby, and then caught the next flight out of San Francisco. The flight seemed to take no time as I stared at the window reliving moments I had spent with Walterene, trying to convince myself that she was really gone. I felt numb, out of my body. The loss of her left me cold and vacant; my childhood home lost all warmth without her presence. The plane circled downtown to line up for its landing. Pressing my face against the cold plastic window, I strained to see the Charlotte skyline as a glimmer of sunlight blazed off the Bank of America tower. The town had expanded; which of those skyscrapers had Harris Construction done? It's bizarre to fly over something you know your family created, like they wield the power of God to change the landscape to suit their needs.

We arrived on time, and emerging from the corridor, I scanned the crowd to see if Ruby or Valerie had come to meet me. Ruby always had her hair dyed a deep red, her trademark. I think she was a natural brunette like the rest of us, but she wanted "Ruby Red" hair. Not a redhead in sight. Valerie, tall and thin like me, should have stood a little above the other women, but the crowd seemed squat and dull.

"Guess I'll rent a car," I muttered, squeezing through the happy reunions in the terminal.

My bags in the trunk of a white Camry, I drove away from the airport and onto Billy Graham Parkway. "Damn, things have built up around here," I muttered. Office parks lined the road where woods once stood. I rolled down the car window and the warm, heavy air stirred dust off the dashboard; deep breaths filled my lungs with the thick humid air of springtime. Traffic started and stopped until I turned onto South Boulevard; soon I pulled onto Sedgefield Road, lined with old elms and maples. Ruby and Walt's house sat on the corner. The emerald-green yard spread out cool and inviting.

"Derek." The door opened, and Ruby wrapped her arms around me in a bear hug. Her body felt spongier than I remembered, but her hair still held the ruby sheen she loved. She let go and pulled me into the den where the smell of years of fried chicken and Ruby's recently applied hand lotion mingled into the distinct scent of my aunts. "I'm so glad you came in. It's been too long. If only Walt could see you..." The dark circles around her eyes were new but expected.

"I'm so sorry I didn't visit sooner..." the words trailed into the sorrow I felt at Walterene's absence.

"No, no, you kept up with us more than nephews and nieces who live a mile away." She sat down in one of the two wingback chairs facing the television. A talk show was on, and she turned the sound down.

I hesitated before sitting in the other wingback, Walterene's regular seat. Her warm, calm essence settled around me as if she still occupied the chair. "How are you doing?" I asked.

"Okay," Ruby said automatically, then sat quiet for a moment. "I miss her. Hard to realize she's gone. We've been together all our lives. Now, an old woman like me has to start a new life alone." Tears streamed down her powdered cheek. "I don't think I ever cried as much as I have in the past couple of days. I'm sorry."

I knelt down in front of her and held her cold hand. "Don't apologize."

"You're such a good boy." She smiled and rubbed my head. "The baby of the family."

"Twenty-five isn't much of a baby."

"Derek, you will always be mine and Walt's baby. We never had babies of our own, but when you came into the world, we knew you were special. Gladys was so busy with Valerie and Tim..." She drifted off into her thoughts with a faint smile.

"I'll get my bags out of the car." I stood to leave.

"Oh, honey, someone should have met you at the airport. I didn't think to call Valerie or Tim."

"Tim? Do you see him much?"

"Your brother's busy with a new housing development up around the university area. I never seen houses thrown together so quick and sold at such a price." She shook her head.

I grabbed my bags, and she led me back to the guest bedroom. The house only had two bedrooms; the third had been turned into a reading room with their books. No one had ever made any remarks about Ruby and Walterene sleeping in the same room, the same bed. I hadn't thought much about it, that was just the way things had always been.

The guest room looked out onto the back yard. Walterene's love of plants showed in the clumps of tiger lilies, violet blue irises, climbing thorny roses, and shiny-leafed camellias lining the fence. She had a small goldfish pond near the cellar door; I noticed the small stone waterfall had been turned off. Two wrought iron chairs sat next to a table facing the pond. Everything about the house had shadows of two people. Ruby would have a hard time being here alone.

She stood in the doorway watching me.

"The yard looks great. I noticed the tulips at the corner."

"They're on their last legs. We usually start ripping them up about this time. Walterene wanted to put scarlet sage in that bed this summer." She looked down, then back at me. "Maybe you can help me with that next week."

"I'm not sure how long I'll be here, but I'll help all I can."

"Ruby," a voice called from the back door.

We went to the den and found Valerie carrying a casserole dish into the kitchen. "Derek? What are you doing here?" Her green eyes were wide with the question. "Oh, it's so good to see you. I didn't think..." She set the casserole on the stove. "I'm glad you came home." She hugged me hard. At forty-one, she still looked like the teenage big sister I remembered from childhood. She wore little make-up and kept her hair shoulder length; wearing a gray business suit, she looked the part of an accountant. She hadn't gone to Carolina, Duke, or Wake Forest like our brother or cousins, but instead went to the community college and worked her way up in a firm outside the Harris empire. She was a beautiful woman in her own way, independent, smart, and kind. "Aunt Ruby, Aunt Edwina sent this chicken casserole. I picked it up on my way home from work." She turned her attention back to me. "Derek, why didn't you tell me you were coming in?"

"Oh," Ruby interrupted, "that was my fault. I meant to call you after I talked to him this morning, but time got away from me."

"Don't worry about it." My sister hugged me again. The strength of her body, her arms, impressed me; she still possessed her high school cheerleader body. "I'm just glad he's here. Do you want to stay with me?"

"No thanks. Ruby and I will be fine here." I wanted to keep her company, especially with the funeral being the next day. "Hey, isn't there a visitation tonight at the funeral home?"

"Last night," Valerie corrected. "The Builders' Ball is tonight, so we had the visitation last night."

"You're kidding?"

"No, the family didn't want to make people choose between the two." Val looked out the window and wiped her nose with a paper towel.

Walterene's visitation, treated as just another item for the social calendar? No need to ask, the scheduling reeked of Gladys the Bitch. Or was my assumption too hard on our mother? Valerie and Tim didn't clash with her the way I did; of course they hadn't dropped the "I'm gay" bomb on her.

Ruby peeked under the foil of the casserole, stuck her finger in, and tasted. "Not bad. Edwina was never much of a cook, but this is one of her better dishes." The comforting aroma of chicken casserole filled the kitchen. "Valerie, stay for dinner. Neighbors and family have stuffed our refrigerator with food. We, I will never be able to eat it all before it goes bad."

Val looked at me, then to Ruby, and back to me. "I'd love to. I have too many Friday nights alone in front of the television. I'll go home and change. Back in twenty minutes." She hugged me again and kissed my forehead. "Derek, thanks for coming in."

"Sure, Sis." My eyes stung a little.

"REMEMBER WHEN TIM took you to that strip club out on Wilkinson Boulevard?" Valerie laughed and took another sip of her wine. We ate in the dining room with the lights dimmed and candles lit. "I was never so mad at him. You were way too young."

"I was fourteen," I explained to Ruby, "and Tim had asked me if I had ever seen a naked woman. Of course I hadn't, so he took me to this nasty little bar on Wilkinson."

Ruby frowned over her empty dinner plate.

"He had no right to do that," Valerie huffed, but then smiled again.

"The bouncer knew Tim," I looked at Val and snickered because, in his early twenties, our brother had stuffed most of his weekly salary into the G-strings of strippers, "and he made Tim take me into a private room so the other customers wouldn't see me."

"That Tim." Ruby shook her head. This seemed to be a habit with her when she thought about him.

"Anyway, girl after girl came into the room and danced. They teased me, rubbed their tits against my crotch, tried to take my pants off, and I fought them the entire time. I thought they were disgusting." I lowered my voice as if someone else might hear. "Apparently, in the private rooms, the girls can take off everything. One girl, a blonde, or at least at first glance a blonde, danced with her little G-string on until she noticed I had little interest in her talents. She hooked one leg over my shoulder and started to thrust her crotch in my face. God, the smell! That salmon and rose scent still comes back. She ripped off the G-string and there I was face to face with the ugliest thing I'd ever seen."

"Eeeww," Val cried out.

I leaned into the table. "It looked like a pulsating open wound with a beard of black hair. I almost threw up."

"Stop it!" Val yelled.

Ruby giggled.

"Well," Val defended, "a penis isn't the prettiest thing in the world."

"Valerie!" Ruby's face turned as crimson as her hair.

"Well, it's not," she laughed.

"I never met one I didn't like," I countered. "Besides—"

"Okay, that's enough, children." Ruby halted the conversation, although she still snickered. "Oh, it's good to laugh again."

I poured her another glass of wine, then got up to take away the dirty dishes.

"Quit that," Ruby ordered. "I can clear the table."

"No, let me. You sit there and relax. Enjoy your wine." I gathered up the plates. Valerie took the empty casserole dish and bread plate.

"This is good wine," Ruby giggled. "All this talk about privates has got me flustered." She fanned herself with her napkin. "Oh, Lordy me."

Val rinsed the dishes and handed them to me to place in the dishwasher. "She's so lively since you got in."

"More like since we uncorked the wine," I laughed.

"Nonetheless, it was thoughtful of you to come in. She needs us now." Val shook her head. "Aunt Walterene was upset with the Board. A lot of changes are happening."

"Did they do something to cause the stroke?"

"No, no, but," Valerie hesitated, "there is some stress among the family."

"How long was Walterene in the hospital?"

Over the spray of the running water, Valerie whispered, "She died on the way there. The paramedics wouldn't let Ruby ride with her; she blames herself for not being with Walterene during her last moments."

"I know what she means. I had friends beg to come home to die; they wanted to be out of the hospital, the constant noise, the smell of death and sickness; surrounded by strangers is no way to die." Losing friends to AIDS had tied me to the same mindset as people in their sixties, seventies, and eighties: facing mortality, planning wakes and funerals, strategizing how to die with dignity among friends and loved ones. "How's the rest of the family taking it?"

"Great-Aunt Ernestine says she should have gone first. 'No

mother should have to bury her daughter,' she told me." Valerie
wiped tears from her eyes. "Of course, Mother, Vernon, and the
other cousins are heartbroken, too. It has called a temporary truce to
their bickering over the business."

Ruby yelled in from the dining room, "What are you two doing
in there? Just set that in the sink, and I'll take care of it in the morning."

Valerie went to the doorway. "Aunt Ruby, we're almost finished. Can I get you some dessert?"

"No, dear. I'm big as a house. I can barely pull my girdle on
each Sunday."

I closed up the dishwasher. "We can talk about this after Ruby
goes to bed."

We said our goodnights to Ruby. She kissed us both and hobbled off to bed. Once she was gone, Valerie and I settled down on
the couch in the warm paneled den with more wine and cigarettes.
"So, tell me what is going on with the Board."

"Derek, it's such a mess. Uncle Vernon is grooming his boys to
take over so he can work on his Senate campaign."

"Vernon is running for Senate?" I couldn't believe it. Vernon
was Mother's brother and the oldest of the grandchildren of Ernest,
who started the business. Like past North Carolina politicians, he
wallowed in family money, but portrayed himself as a self-made,
hardworking, blue collar worker who had done well. Conservatism
to him meant family, no welfare, plenty of tobacco subsidies for the
farmers, catering to big business under the table, and everyone
should be white, Protestant, heterosexual, and preferably wealthy
men.

"Sorry to say it, but yes, he's running. City council and mayor
never satisfied him." She took a drag on my cigarette.

"Hopefully, the voters will see through his facade."

The look she gave me confirmed that Jesse Helms Republicans
still ruled the state. "If he doesn't make it this year, next election
will be a shoe-in."

"So, what's happening with the Board?"

"Vernon is trying to squeeze out any family who doesn't agree
with the boys taking over."

Retrieving the cigarette from her, I inhaled the sweet smoke as I
considered Uncle Vernon's sons Mike and Mark, and son-in-law Gerald. Mark's image drowned out other thoughts, his smile, his laugh,
the warmth of his touch. I wanted to see him again, even though our
secret relationship led to my mother sending me away. No one knew
Mark had been the reason I'd told my parents I'm gay, but I was glad
I did. Still, the hurt of losing him, of losing my family, burned deep.
No blame pointed to him or to my announcement to my parents; I

placed the fault on Gladys, her closed-mindedness, her concern for the opinions of Charlotte society, her need for social status.

"Edwina and Roscoe," Val continued, "have always kept their hands in the business. Mom and Dad let Vernon do things his way. Ruby doesn't really care, but keeps her shares. Walterene sided with Edwina and Roscoe." Val took another sip of wine.

"Sided?" I asked. "On what?"

"The direction of the company. The boys want to diversify by building the residential business that Tim works in. Mark pushes more uptown condo projects. Did you know he and Kathleen live in Fourth Ward now?"

"No." A sharp pain shot through my gut. "He's still the golden boy, isn't he?"

"Vernon doesn't really favor him over Mike, treats them both like Jesus Christ incarnate." She winked at me.

Does she know about me and Mark? No, no one knows, I reassured myself and ground out the cigarette. *Best to keep it that way.* "Wouldn't Walterene, Edwina, Roscoe, and Ruby have enough shares to take over the Board?"

"No, Vernon made sure he had Mom's and the remaining share-holders' backing before he started any changes. In fact, things got so out of hand at the last meeting, Vernon called the police to remove Roscoe from the building."

"Damn." I couldn't believe they had gotten so hostile. "Bet that pissed off Grandma."

"She hit the roof, mostly because it made the papers. She said Papa Ernest would have taken every one of them to the woodshed.

"It doesn't sound so bad to me," Val continued. "Mike and Gerald are focusing on commercial development; Mark wants to develop more upscale condominiums in Uptown and heads up subdivision development on the outskirts of town."

"So why the disagreement? Roscoe and the rest should be glad the company's branching out." I lit up another cigarette and poured more wine.

"Number one, it's riskier than commercial. Two, they aren't crazy about Vernon's sons taking over; we're all still viewed as children. Plus, it leaves little likelihood that their kids will get a piece of the company."

"Who'd want it? Constant fighting, family and business bound together, money and past hurts; it's a recipe for dysfunction." I noticed Val yawning. "I'm still on west coast time; I bet you're tired."

"Yeah, with the funeral tomorrow," she looked at her watch, "correction, today, I need to get to bed."

We stood up and hugged. This was what family should feel like:

open, safe, a place where things can be discussed without fear of backstabbing or harsh judgments. Of course, I only felt that with Walterene, Ruby, and Valerie. "Are you okay driving home?"

"Yeah, I'm just a couple of blocks up Park Road. Now you get some sleep. There will be a lot of family tomorrow. Mom will probably shit when she sees you." She laughed, then quieted herself. "Ruby's sleeping," she whispered.

"I'm not the one making all the noise."

Val grinned. "Get your beauty rest. It's going to be interesting."

Chapter
Three

"MOM WANTED TO come over to help get Ruby ready for church," Valerie had arrived early, "but I talked her out of it. I told her too many people fussing around Ruby would upset her."

I poured coffee for Valerie. "Good, I would rather see her in a crowd where I can avoid her as much as possible."

"Less stressful for the both of you," she agreed. "You know..."

"No, I will not try to mend fences with Gladys the Bitch."

"Derek! Watch your mouth." Anger flashed in her eyes. "Mom has tried to do what she thought was best for us. Sometimes, her plans didn't work out."

"What's best for us?" I fumed. "What's best? She threw me out of the house."

"No, she sent you to college."

"She wanted me away from Charlotte."

"She wanted you to grow up to be—"

"To be her puppet. A wife named Puddin' who's active in the church, children at Charlotte Country Day, me making contacts and climbing my way to the top, and a mansion in Myers Park. That's her dream, not mine."

Valerie shook her head. "No, she's lived that life. She wanted something better for you."

"Well, she should be happy; I have a better life than that. I have loyal friends and a job I love."

"That's what is important." Ruby startled us. She entered the kitchen in her plain black dress, ready for the funeral. "One more thing you need: someone who loves you." Tears welled in her eyes, and she picked up a small colorful porcelain elephant that sat on the corner shelf, next to dog-eared cookbooks. She patted it gently, and set it back in its place.

"Aunt Ruby," Val put her arms around her, "we love you; you aren't alone."

"It's not me I'm worried about." A faint smile trembled on her painted lips as she looked from Valerie to me.

A silence settled over us, heavy and thick.

Walterene's spirit hovered within the house; I sensed it coming from her gardening books, her chair, the pictures of family on the walls, and from Ruby. She stayed strong without Walterene, although I knew that was the hardest thing she had ever done. Walt had been the dominant one, the woman who could talk the car mechanic into a discount, not from argument, but with compliments and listening and winning him over. She beamed with the love and kindness and understanding of each person she encountered. Ruby was the flirtatious one. She batted her eyes and laughed at silly jokes; she cooked and cleaned and shopped, while Walterene gardened, fixed leaky faucets, and debated politics. The combination kept them together; they complemented each other.

Her spirit lingered. I wanted to wrap it around me, to be part of me, absorbed into the man I wanted to become.

A low, dull car horn blew outside, and Valerie checked out the window. "The limousine is here. Let's get to church." She set her coffee mug in the sink and took Ruby's hand to escort her out the door.

MYERS PARK BAPTIST, fairly liberal for a Baptist church in the South, was filled with Charlotte's finest citizens. The banks were represented by their chairmen, sitting on opposite sides of the aisle like it was Trade Street, Wachovia to the south and Bank of America to the north. The Belk department store family, represented by McKay and his Uncle John, sat just behind Ed Williams from the *Charlotte Observer*. In the front rows, I saw Mother and Father; Tim, Laura, and their two children sat behind them. Grandma Eleanor sat stone-still between Mother and Vernon. Next to Uncle Vernon was his wife Irene, and finishing out the pew were Mike and Sheila, Margaret and Gerald. Mark should've been with his brother and sister, but I didn't see him. Across the aisle, Walterene's mother, Great-Aunt Ernestine, sat flanked by Edwina and Roscoe on one side and Ruby's brothers, Sam and Odell, on the other. Ernestine cried so hard her thin shoulders shook. Ruby led us toward the seats next to Edwina.

As we approached the altar, I caught Mother's glance. Her head nearly snapped off when she realized it was me. She elbowed Father to get his attention; he smiled when he saw me, but she caught him. Tim and Laura looked, and their kids pointed.

Valerie and I sat down. Ruby crossed past Edwina and Roscoe to hug Ernestine. The old woman's gnarled hands gripped Ruby, and they both trembled under the weight of their tears. The organist started a slow hymn that sounded familiar, but I didn't know the title. I hummed a little to keep my mind off the reason we were there. I couldn't cry in front of these people. "Men don't cry," Mother had always taught us. Ruby sat between me and Valerie, holding each of our hands in her tight cold grip.

The casket sat in front of the altar, and from my position, I could see Walterene's powdered profile. How pale and quiet she looked. Nothing like the fiery, joyous woman she had been. The coffin held nothing more than a shell that had housed Walterene. Our Walterene had dissipated into each of the lives she had touched. I knew she lived in me. Tears blurred my sight. I tried to not blink to keep from knocking them out of my eyes and down my cheeks. I looked up at the ceiling and sighed.

As the pastor droned on, I looked at the family gathered around. Time had turned teenagers into parents, parents into grandparents, grandparents into humbled antiqued souls waiting for their turn before the altar. Old man Ernest's blood seemed to keep his surviving daughters, Grandma Eleanor and Great-Aunt Ernestine, stronger physically than their sisters-in-law. Great-Aunts Rebecca and Louise had both buried their husbands years ago, and I was honestly surprised they were still alive. Ruby's mother Rebecca lived in Sharon Towers under constant care. Today she sat humped in a wheelchair at the end of our pew, staring at a stained glass window. Louise sat behind her children, Edwina and Roscoe, rocking side to side with the music in her head. The only sibling left was Great-Uncle Earl, the youngest of the original children and the only male still alive. He lived in Manhattan and hadn't been seen in years.

My attention came back to the casket because Tim and Vernon's boys and several others had surrounded it.

There was Mark.

He stood next to his brother Mike and brother-in-law Gerald. He hadn't changed much since I last saw him, still the perfect Harris male. Thirty years old with boyish looks, thick black hair that wouldn't quite stay in place, wide eyes and thin nose; even in his black suit, I could tell he still had the build of a college wide receiver. They flanked the mahogany box that held Walterene's body. The men from the funeral home folded the satin trim inside the casket, and then closed the lid on her. I wanted to rush to it and touch her one last time, to say good-bye, to beg her to come back, to say how sorry I was that I wasn't with her when she died. Tears spilled down my face, and I wiped them away with my sleeve; I would never see her again. The pallbearers lifted the casket with slow movements and carried it down the aisle. We filed out behind it in silence.

The limousines took us to the rolling hills of Sharon Memorial Park. We gathered under a large green tent where I ushered Valerie and Ruby to seats, then returned to stand behind the family. Overly sweet roses, lilies, and lavender surrounded the dark hole where the coffin would be lowered; warmed by the morning sun, they gave off the sickening scent of a spilled bottle of vanilla. A carpet of white roses covered the lacquered box. I watched as honeybees and yellow jackets found the flowers and began their orgy in the arrangements. After more words from the pastor, a bagpiper in full, kilted, Scottish regalia played "Amazing Grace" as the casket was lowered. The family began to disperse, sobbing and dabbing their eyes.

I turned to find Mother standing behind me. Her narrow face held vertical lines from her frown. Red-rimmed eyes stared at me through Liz Claiborne bifocals, and her thin body acted as a hanger for her DKNY suit. She looked so fragile, but so does a scorpion before she strikes.

"You shouldn't have come," Gladys the Bitch said in a harsh whisper.

"I didn't come for you. I'm here because I loved Walterene." I stepped toward her, but she held her ground.

"Fine." She clipped the word. "So you'll be leaving today?"

Was it a question or a command? "No, I plan to stay with Ruby for a while. She needs someone around."

"There's plenty of family here to take care of Ruby." A tight smile appeared. "Derek, go back to California." She turned to walk away, but I moved in front of her, blocking her retreat.

"I am family, and I'll decide how long I stay. Gay or not, you can't control me." I stepped back so she could leave.

She turned to me with narrow eyes. "Don't be stupid, Derek. This part of your life is over; let it stay part of your past." Gladys the Bitch spun on her heels and left without another word.

As soon as she disappeared into the crowd, Tim appeared without his wife or kids. "So, little brother, how's life in Frisco?" He slapped me on the back and tried to get me in a headlock. I goosed his side to escape. His mannerisms still smelled of a frat boy grown old.

I had to smile because he never seemed to change. "The city is much more easy-going than here."

"Yeah, well, Charlotte's a moving town. I got a new subdivision in the works south of Ballantyne. It will make those original Ballantyne mansions look like Wilmore shacks." Tim held onto my arm as he talked. "Damn boy, you been working out. I better look out; you might kick my ass for all those tricks I played on you."

I slapped his belly. "Looks like you haven't been working out." I teased him, but he had honestly gained weight in his stomach and face, making him look older than he was. "Forty's coming up this fall, isn't it?"

He hugged me close to him, and whispered, "I may have a few gray hairs here and there, but I can get it up on command."

"Tim, you're not fooling around on Laura, are you?"

"Me?" He feigned innocence.

"Keep your dick at home. AIDS isn't just for us queers."

"Shit." He drew the word out into three syllables. "Hey, it's Saturday night. Let's go find a pretty young couple. You take the husband, and I'll take the wife."

The stern look I gave him must have shocked him.

"Just kidding, just kidding. Laura and I are the perfect pair. Oh, there she goes now. You staying with Valerie?"

"No," I called after him, "Ruby."

"I'll call you." He caught up with Laura. She eyed me and nodded, then herded the children and her husband toward their Mercedes.

Streams of people flowed toward the line of cars, and I saw Valerie helping Ruby back to the limo. Just as I headed toward them, Mark tapped me on the shoulder. I turned, and he pulled me to him and hugged me hard. We broke the embrace, but he held my shoulders at arm's length and looked me over.

"You look great, Derek." His faint smile faded. "I'm glad you made it in for the funeral. I'm really going to miss Walterene."

"I wouldn't have missed the funeral. I just wish I could have seen her before..."

"I know. I get so caught up in work; I can't remember the last time I stopped to see Ruby or Walterene."

I let the silence fall between us.

"I hope you plan on staying for a while." He brightened up some. "Kathleen and I would love to have you over for dinner."

"That would be nice," I muttered. Did he not have any feelings for me? "I hear you live in Fourth Ward."

"That's right. We have a place in the TransAmerica building. You wouldn't believe Uptown." He became his old happy self. "I love living in town. I walk to work and to the Uptown Y; restaurants and bars are popping up everywhere." A woman walking by offered her condolences; he nodded in return.

"Mark," I got his attention back, "I still have feelings for you."

"Come on, Derek, we were just kids fooling around."

"Maybe that was it for you, but it meant more to me." Seeing him again brought back the old emotions. I had never had a relationship that compared to what I had with Mark. Maybe it was the excitement of the first love, maybe the thought of cousins having sex—an incestuous relationship forbidden because we were related and because we were both men—but at that moment, I would have given up everything to be back in his arms. Love had eluded me

since Mark; the world never revealed another to take his place. "I-I...
I just wanted you to know that I still love you." My voice broke as I
said it.

His face flushed, and he led me away from the crowd. We stood
beneath a large willow oak surrounded by the gravestones of strangers; low-hanging branches shielded us from the eyes and ears of others.

"Derek, please let that stay between us. I've moved on; I'm a
different person now. Kathleen and I are very happy."

Who was he trying to convince? Then it hit me: Why bother?
There was nothing here for me. These people didn't want me
around. Mark wouldn't even admit to himself what an extraordinary
connection we had; the past was past. Love couldn't last through the
restraints this family put on its children—we would all be beaten
down, molded to the forms and principles set by Papa Ernest Harris.
Gladys the Bitch was right, although I hated to admit it. I smiled and
patted his shoulder. "That was the past. It's not worth bringing up
again. I'm staying at Ruby's for a couple of days. If I don't see you
before I go home, good luck with Kathleen and the job." I pushed
one of the low-hanging limbs aside and started to walk away.

"Derek," he called after me. "Maybe we'll see you during the
holidays?"

"Yeah, that would be nice," I lied.

THE LIMO TOOK us back to Sedgefield Road. Ruby wanted to
lie down for a while. Valerie and I opened a bottle of wine and nibbled from some of the covered dishes in the refrigerator. "Val, I'm
going back to California on Monday."

"We'll miss you," her voice dropped.

"Do you think Ruby will be okay?"

"I can look in on Ruby on my lunch hours and after work. She'll
be fine in a few days." Valerie forced a smile.

"It would be great if you and Ruby lived in San Francisco."

"Our lives are here." She wrapped up a dish and set it back in
the refrigerator. "Why don't you get some rest, too. I'll be back for
dinner." She hugged me good-bye.

I went back to the guest room and drifted off to sleep.

I WOKE TO the squawk of the attic stairs being pulled down,
and called out, "Ruby, let me help you with that." I grabbed the
cord, and helped her lower the stairs down into the hall.

"Just wanted to take a look at some things in the attic. Walterene was always good at packing away her memories. She even

kept old Christmas cards." Ruby ascended the steps; I followed. The sun warmed the asphalt shingles above, creating a mix of tar and musty smells. The floorboards creaked as she clicked on a bare bulb and maneuvered a path between boxes, rolled up rugs, old chests, and framed paintings. Two more lights lit the entire space. Christmas decorations and boxes of old clothes seemed to support the roof. I helped her move a few boxes until she found what had been on her mind. She opened a tattered cardboard box filled with crumpled newspapers and pulled out a stuffed toy—an elephant. "This was one of Walterene's favorites from when we were girls. She used to drag Willie around everywhere she went." More newspapers spilled out of the box as Ruby dug through it. "Oh, look." She held up a yellowed perfume bottle. "Mr. Sams gave this to her."

"Mr. Sams?" I took the bottle she held out to me. The thick glass felt heavy and warm in my hand. I smelled the top; the sweet aroma of the funeral flowers invaded my head again.

"Mr. Sams was an old black man who helped around the Dilworth house." She grabbed the bottle back, rewrapped it in paper, and stuffed it back in the box. "I need to go through all of this." She contemplated the cluttered attic, then glanced at me. "Will you help me?"

"Aunt Ruby," I tried to think of a good way to tell her, but it just came out, "I'm leaving on Monday to go back to California."

"No," she pleaded, "please stay awhile. We haven't had any time together. There's so much to be done. I don't know if I... I can't do it alone."

She pulled at my heart. "I guess I could stay a couple of days longer, but I need to get back."

"Yes, yes." She gave me a smile, the first I had seen on her all day. "Just stay for a few more days. There's so much to be done, so, so much to be done."

Chapter
Four

SUNDAY AFTERNOON, EDWINA and Roscoe stopped by the house to visit with Ruby. As twins, they always seemed to be together. Edwina favored flashy colors and had on a teal, magenta, and lemon-yellow nylon wind-suit that crinkled when she moved, whereas Roscoe wore black polyester Sans-a-Belt pants that had been buffed to a shine by years of dry cleaning and a short-sleeved white dress shirt with a too-short, too-wide navy blue striped tie. Apparently, that one chromosome that kept them from being identical twins skewed them into different universes, hers flashy and opinionated, his meek and agreeable.

"Derek, what is it you do out there in California?" Edwina spoke to me, but looked at the muted television as if I would appear on the news to answer her.

"Edwina?" I tried to catch her eye with a snap of my fingers. She refocused her attention to me with a lazy turn of her head. "Is there something on TV you want to see?" I sat up straighter in Walterene's wingback chair.

"Derek," Ruby scolded, "Edwina is a very visual person. She's looking all the time, but she hears everything you say."

"Right you are, Ruby. Young man, I'm waiting to hear about your job and," she glanced back to the television, "I'm looking to see if Vernon is going to be on TV shaking hands and kissing babies."

Roscoe perked up. "Vernon's good at shaking and kissing."

A rough, gravelly laugh erupted from Edwina like it was the funniest thing she had heard. Ruby looked at me and shrugged. "Vernon thinks," Edwina continued, "his next stop will be Washington, leaving those boys in charge of the company." With a crinkle of fabric, she folded her plump arms across her pumpkin body. "If he thinks I'll stand by and let him put my money in the hands of those wild boys, then he's got another thing coming." She ended the sentence with a sharp nod of her head, as if she had typed the final period with her chin.

"They're grown men," Ruby offered, "and they have been in the company all their lives..."

"Don't matter, don't matter one bit. Vernon has been president since Daddy died. Hell, Roscoe should take over if Vernon doesn't want to run it any more, not some snot-nosed kids."

I looked over to Roscoe on the edge of the couch, cleaning his fingernails with his pocketknife. "Roscoe, do you want to run the business?"

"Maybe," he glanced at his sister. "I could do better than the boys."

Tiring of this subject, I offered to go to the store for Ruby. I drove toward East Boulevard for the few groceries she had on her list. The dogwoods bloomed like white puffy clouds in yards along the way with burgundy and pink azaleas lining driveways and sidewalks. I pulled onto Dilworth Road—one of the neighborhoods where few of the aging old money of Charlotte still held on against the younger affluent banking executives. I passed Latta Park and rounded a corner to see my grandparents' home. A three-story brick mansion sprawled across an acre of green lawn and towering oak trees. Porticos flanked either side of the house. I remember the older kids, Tim, Margaret, and Mike, had claimed one side for their headquarters, leaving the other side for the younger kids, Mark, me, and a neighbor girl named Alice. The older ones claimed we couldn't steal their "magic geranium," but we did and ran as fast as we could around the house to the safety of our headquarters. That summer, the geranium must have circled the house from portico to portico at least fifty times.

My grandmother, Eleanor, still lived in the house, but Mother and Father had moved in "to take care of her." Knowing Gladys the Bitch, I wondered what taking care of her meant. A vision popped into my head of Gladys slipping strychnine into her mother's coffee, then grabbing the will, hopping on her broom, and flying out the attic window to the lawyer's office, cackling the whole way.

Deciding to come back to visit Grandma when I knew Mother wouldn't be there, I pulled the car back on the road and headed on to the grocery store.

EDWINA AND ROSCOE had ambled on to their next relative's house by the time I came in with the groceries. Ruby said Mark had called and she'd told him I was staying for awhile. "He said he and Kathleen wanted you to come over for dinner tomorrow night."

"I can't."

"Yes you can," Ruby insisted. "You need to see your cousins while you're here. Anyway, I already told him you would be there—

eight o'clock. They live downtown on Church Street in one of those new buildings."

"Ruby! I can decide if I want to have dinner with Mark."

"Go, go, you can't stay huddled up here with me the whole time. I'm okay. Go have fun."

Fun? Yeah, right. But I knew she had made up her mind, and I was a little curious about Kathleen.

THE NEXT DAY I drove Ruby to the lawyer's office to finalize some of Walterene's affairs. We had lunch with Valerie. She said Mother attended a book club on Monday afternoons, so Ruby and I decided to drive back to Dilworth to visit Grandma. I pulled into the circular driveway and parked in front of Grandma's door, then helped Ruby out of the car.

"I could get used to this kind of treatment." Ruby smiled as I offered her my hand up the steps to the front porch. Ferns swung in the warm breeze along the porch, near wicker chairs arranged in groups for evening gatherings after dinner. I rang the doorbell and Martha, Grandma's maid, answered.

"Mister Derek, how nice to see you." Martha had to be almost as old as Grandma. She had always been so sweet to all of us, even in the seventies when Margaret and Valerie tried to liberate her from white elitist dominance. Margaret had even convinced Martha to wear her hair in an afro; that lasted about one day before she combed it out.

We walked into the entrance hall, and I could still smell my grandfather's pipe and grandmother's Chanel No. 5. A staircase curved gracefully up to the second story. The living room to the right had the same furniture and pictures I remembered; even the carpet held the same straight tracks from the vacuum cleaner. Grandma hated to see footprints on the carpet.

"Your grandmother is feeling good today," Martha said. "She has her good days and bad days."

"Bad days?" I asked.

"Well, sometimes she gets stuck in the past." Martha led us back to the sunroom where Grandma sat reading the newspaper. Grandma's hair was thinner than I remembered, but she sat up straight with her diamond rings and in her designer dress, hose, and pumps as if she waited to go to a church luncheon. Her beige hose sagged around her ankles and her rings slumped on her thin fingers; they had been bought for a more robust Grandma than I saw seated at the wicker table.

"Aunt Eleanor," Ruby called as we walked in. "Look who is here to see you."

She turned and smiled. "My little Derek, come here."

I leaned over to hug her. She seemed so fragile and small, a far cry from what I remembered from childhood when she would chase me across the backyard being the "tickle monster." Mother and Valerie would sit on the back porch and laugh as I would turn on Grandma and run after her. "Grandma, I'm glad to see you."

"Little Derek," she patted my hand and winked at Ruby, "he's as big as Papa was, but he's still our baby."

"Yes ma'am," Ruby agreed, settling into a rattan couch; a potted banana tree's leaf hovered above her head.

I sat next to Grandma at the table because she still held my hand. "How are you feeling?" I asked.

She pushed the newspaper out of the way and looked into my eyes. "I remember the spring this house was built; Papa designed it himself." She stopped for a moment, lost in her memories. "Erwin and Edward helped build it while Ernestine and I took care of our baby brother Earl." She smiled a faint smile down at the table, then looked at me again. "You remind me so much of Earl. He moved to New York; you know he went to work for William Henry Belk as a buyer. I don't hear from him as much as I used to."

I couldn't remember if Great-Uncle Earl was still alive and didn't want to ask Ruby in front of Grandma, in case he wasn't.

Ruby added, "I remember Daddy talking about building this house. Derek, he met Mama that summer."

"Oh, yes," Grandma fired up, "Erwin was oldest and handsomest; Edward always tried to outdo him. Guess being the second boy is tough. Edwina acts just like her daddy." She patted my knee. "Erwin and Rebecca would sneak off to Latta Park and kiss on the bench that used to be behind some pine trees." She looked at Ruby with great concern. "Are there still pines in Latta?"

"I think there's a few," Ruby answered respectfully.

"Well, anyway, that was around the time of the war. Camp Greene was over on the west side." She looked at me and winked. "Many a young Charlotte girl was courted by a pilot trainee from the camp."

"Grandma," I acted shocked. "Did you date a pilot?"

"Lord no, I was way too young. I couldn't have been more than six or seven."

Ruby brought her back on track. "What about Daddy and Mama courting in Latta Park?"

"Oh, yes. Erwin must have been fifteen and smitten with Rebecca. She walked by every day while this house was being built to see him. In the late evening, he would go to her house to sit on the swing or walk to the park or ride on the trolley." She thought for a moment. "Do you know the trolley is running again?"

"Yes, ma'am," I answered.

"Us kids loved riding the trolley downtown with Papa and Mama. They took us to our first movie at the Academy—seems like it was about the Confederates and Yankees, and about the Klan saving a family from the Negroes."

"What?" I couldn't believe I heard her right. "The first movie Great-Grandpa Ernest took you to was *Birth of a Nation*?" I had seen clips of the historic film in a class I'd taken in San Francisco; technically, a groundbreaking film because of the director's innovations, but the subject matter was pure anti-black propaganda. *"Birth of a Nation,"* I repeated, not believing my great-grandfather would have taken his children to it.

"Scared the you-know-what out of me," she giggled. "I was sure a black man would grab me before we got back home, but Papa assured me that his friends—"

"Aunt Eleanor," Ruby interrupted. "Did you know that Mark and Kathleen have asked Derek to come to their house for dinner tonight? Derek and Mark always got along so well when they were younger. I'm glad they're still friends." She took a breath and continued, "And Derek will be here for a few days. He's been such a help to me. He mowed the lawn. We're going to replant the—" She turned to look back toward the door. "Oh, hi, Gladys."

Every muscle in my body tensed at the sight of my mother; I stood up quickly, ready for a fight.

Her eyes took in the three of us in quick jerky movements. "Mother, what nonsense have you been boring Derek and Ruby with?"

"Just talking about Papa and this house. What nonsense should I bore them with?" Grandma shot back, "I can always talk about you—that should bore them. Leave us alone, Valerie."

"Mother, I'm Gladys," she corrected.

"I know." Grandma seemed to be getting tired.

Ruby pushed herself out of the chair and grabbed my hand. "We should be leaving." She pulled me toward the door. "Goodbye, Aunt Eleanor. Bye, Gladys."

I wanted to stay and hear Grandma zing the Bitch again, but Ruby insisted on our leaving. I hugged Grandma and said, "I'll see you later. I love you."

She squeezed my hand and smiled.

I walked past Gladys without speaking.

I DROVE DOWNTOWN to Mark's condo in the TransAmerica building on Church Street. The building took up an entire city block; offices and restaurants faced Tryon Street, and the residential part lined Church Street. The building encircled a courtyard of fountains and sculptures. Even at eight o'clock on a Monday night, people still lingered in this space. I found Mark's condo on the top floor; a shimmering green marble hall echoed my footsteps as I approached the door. Sweat broke out on my upper lip, and I wiped it away before ringing the bell.

"Hey, Derek." Mark shook my hand with a firm grip and slapped me on the shoulder in the tradition of straight male bonding.

I wasn't sure what kind of home I had expected, but this one overwhelmed me. The columned foyer continued the marble flooring and led to a living area that soared two stories; floor-to-ceiling windows framed a view of the Charlotte skyline and Crowder's Mountain in the far distance with the last of the crimson sunset glowing on the horizon. Huge leather couches, a mahogany armoire, and flat-panel television on the wall caught my attention before I saw her. Kathleen stood in the doorway to the kitchen, wiping her hands on a kitchen towel. *My God,* I thought, *it's the Junior Leaguer from Hell*—heels, little black dress, gray pearls, and a silver Neiman Marcus-logo apron.

Mark guided me toward her. "Derek, this is Kathleen."

She extended her right hand, fingers drooping a little; I didn't know if I should shake it or kiss it. I reached out and held her delicate hand with both of mine, no shaking. "It's so nice to meet you, Kathleen. I wondered what kind of woman could tame this tiger."

She giggled, "Oh, Mark's a dear."

I giggled back, "Yes, he is."

She smiled.

I smiled.

Mark smiled.

"So," I began, "I see by the apron you've been cooking. You really didn't need to go to all that trouble."

"No trouble at all." Kathleen hugged Mark's arm. "We love working in the kitchen."

"You mean *cooking*?" I asked.

"Yes, exactly." She rubbed Mark's stomach. "Mark is getting so fat; he's losing all definition in his abs."

Mark pulled away from her. "I'll get drinks."

Fat? Mark appeared in prime shape to me. I scrutinized Kathleen; her black hair hung to her shoulders in sleek perfection; pale emerald eyes stared from beneath a long canopy of lashes; her thin face held no lines; her plunging neckline revealed her breastbone—no cleavage, her tits seemed no more than nipples. Her champagne-flute figure complemented their stylish penthouse decor.

"Mark looks like he's holding up well. How long have you been in Charlotte?" I asked her.

"Since college. We met at Duke. I'm from Charlottesville, Virginia. You know, where the University of Virginia is?"

"What made you choose Duke over UVA?" I asked, but didn't really care.

"My mother was a Delta Zeta at Duke when she met my father; I wanted to continue the tradition." She reached for a boiling pot on the stove, lifting her right leg as she leaned in. "Hope you like spaghetti, it's my specialty."

"Sounds wonderful," I lied.

Mark sat the wine glasses on the coffee table. "Come have a seat; Kathleen will be a little while."

"Yes," she insisted, "you boys relax. I'll be there in a jiffy."

Damn, why this walking, talking mannequin? I took a gulp of the wine before sitting down across from Mark.

"It's a Chianti. We bought a case when we went to Tuscany two years ago." He waited for me to say something.

"Nice," I took a sip this time, "very dry."

"Derek, how long do you intend to stay?" Mark asked.

"Not long." I took another sip of wine. "I just wanted to spend some time with Ruby."

Silence fell between us. I listened to Kathleen's high heels clicking across the kitchen tile.

"Dad's running for Senate." Mark smiled.

"I heard that. Democrat or Republican? Oh, dumb question, Uncle Vernon was always a big Jesse Helms supporter. So, who is he scaring the public with to get into office: welfare mothers, liberal democrats, social security fraud, released prisoners, gays?"

His look told me that "gay" had never been said in his palace. "His platform is to reform the tax system."

I took another swig of wine, and my head swirled like the wine settling back in the glass. "Great platform—a millionaire wanting to cut taxes. So, who's he going to cut funding from?" I counted on my fingers, "Welfare, education, the arts, AIDS research..."

"Maybe we shouldn't talk politics. Tell me about California." He filled up my glass again.

"I live in the Castro district with my roommate, Emma. Strictly platonic, if you know what I mean. She's a model." I leaned in and whispered, "Frankly, she's anorexic and just a couple pounds heavier than Kathleen."

"Kathleen's an athlete," Mark defended. "She runs marathons."

"Really?" I knew my sarcasm was out of control. Maybe it was the wine. Maybe it was seeing him in this perfect little life. Maybe I just hated everyone. "She cooks spaghetti and runs marathons, quite a woman. You did well."

"Okay, that's enough." I knew he'd reached his limit. "Kathleen is my wife; you show her some respect." His face flushed.

"Sorry." I meant it. "I didn't expect everything to be so perfect in your life. I'm working hard to make ends meet and so are all my friends back home, then I come here and everybody is rich and living the good life. And then, there's our history. I'm a little bitter about the past."

"A little bitter?" He laughed.

I had to smile, too. "Does it show?"

"Only when you open your mouth." He sat back and asked, "Do you think we are all without worries? Work is hell with the family feuding over every little decision; we can't get anything done. Dad's running for Senate, and reporters watch our every move and monitor everything we say."

"But," I had to ask, "how's your life?"

"Honestly? Confusing."

I waited for more, but he didn't continue. Kathleen walked up behind him and announced dinner was ready.

We dined on a pretty good spaghetti sauce and drank more wine. Mark relaxed, and Kathleen laughed at my jokes. We drank more wine. She kicked off her shoes, he loosened his tie, and I drank more wine. By the end of the evening, I genuinely didn't hate Kathleen. Or maybe it was just the wine.

Chapter
Five

I MISSED EMMA: her chain smoking, coffee drinking, sarcastic attitude. On East Boulevard sat a small shop called the Paper Skyscraper that sold cards, books, knickknacks of all sorts—things gay men and bored housewives love. I stopped in to get a card to send Emma; usually I would have e-mailed her, but Ruby didn't have a computer. Odd, how surprised I was when she asked, "What's e-mail?"

Scanning the racks of cards, I found the perfect one for Emma: a black and white art photo of a muscled and oiled naked man lying on the hood of a '57 Corvette, his arms back over his head, and one knee lifted just enough to cover the goods from the camera's prying eye.

"Nice," a deep male voice said over my shoulder.

Startled, I turned to see deep brown eyes shaded by thick brows staring at me as if he knew what I had been thinking as I looked at the erotic image on the card. A thick mustache covered his upper lip, but allowed his grin to stretch across his face ending in accenting dimples. He had to be mid-thirties, judging from the slight lines that gathered around his eyes. I had been cruised by the best of them in San Francisco, but I was caught off guard here; pulling my thoughts together, I said, "Yes, the card is for my roommate in San Francisco. She loves stuff like this." *Now, he knows I'm from San Francisco and I have a female roommate*, I thought, *that should be enough to clue him in.*

"Hi, my name is Daniel." He shook my hand and kept steady eye contact.

Not Dan or Danny, but Daniel. He's gay. I smiled, "I'm Derek."

"You in town long?" he asked. His brown curly close-cropped hair had hints of gray.

"Several days. You live here in Charlotte?"

"Yes, as a matter of fact, I live about three blocks from here."

Okay, the next logical step in a pick-up was for him to ask me over to his place. My palms sweated. I didn't want sex; I was just flirting. *Can't a guy flirt these days without a sexual panther jumping me and dragging me off to his lair?*

Maybe he saw the panic in my eyes, because he then said, "Derek, it was nice to meet you." He turned and walked away.

What? What went wrong? I was ready to turn him down, but he didn't ask. *Yeah, well, okay, I just want to see him find someone better than me.* I looked around the store. *I'm the sexiest guy in here. Maybe he was straight?*

With my ego bandaged, I took the card to the register. A pretty Greek girl took my money and thanked me. The bright sunlight blinded me as I walked outside; I turned my head and saw Daniel coming out of the door of an adjacent store.

"Hello again, Derek."

"Oh, hi." Icicles hung on my words. No one robs me of the chance to turn them down without good reason.

"I thought I might have a beer, would you join me?" Daniel was rather handsome and polite.

"Well, maybe one." I threw the card in the car and walked with Daniel to a restaurant a block away. As we strode down the sidewalk, I glanced at his khakis and short-sleeve white shirt and how he had rolled the sleeves to show his biceps. *Kind of a gay uniform*, I thought, *but he wears it well.*

We settled into a dark booth and ordered a pitcher of beer. The scent of hamburgers grilling and cheese melting helped relax me. The waitress seemed to know Daniel, so I didn't worry about my safety. I could remember more than one friend who got the shit beat out of him by leaving a public place with a stranger.

"Do you have family or friends in Charlotte?" Daniel asked as his chocolate eyes scanned me.

The waitress delivered the pitcher of a local brew, and Daniel poured it into icy mugs. His forearms flexed as he sat the beer in front of me.

"Family," I said. Leaning back in the booth, I placed both hands around the cold glass. "I grew up here, but this is the first time in years that I've been back."

"You grew up here?" Daniel asked. "It's rare to find a native here." He smiled showing his dimples. "I'm a native Charlottean too, where did you go to high school? Of course, it was probably years after I graduated." He sipped his beer and pulled out a cigarette.

Great. I sighed with relief now that I could light up a cigarette too. After lighting his, he reached across the table, offering the lit match to me. I looked into his eyes, took his hand and led it to the tip of my cigarette, inhaled, and then blew out the match with my exhale—something I'd seen in a movie, very sexy.

His dimples appeared again as he smiled. "So?"

So? What? Did I miss something? Did he ask if I wanted to go out? To his place? My mind scrambled for the question and the right answer.

"So, what high school?" he asked again.

"Oh," I tried to compose myself, "Myers Park. You?"

"West Meck."

"My sister Valerie went there, busing and the seventies and all that. My parents wanted us to go to the public schools. Mostly my dad's idea; he said it would make us learn to deal with all kinds of people."

"That's a liberal view. Most affluent families today send their kids to private schools."

"Affluent? Why do you say that?"

"Just the way you talk, the way you move, all signs of good breeding." He was a charmer.

"Mother wanted us in private, but somehow Dad won that one. We all did well in public school. Valerie was a cheerleader, Tim was quarterback."

He leaned forward. "Mason? Valerie and Tim Mason? Your brother and sister?"

"Yeah, you know them?"

"Tim is two years older than me. I remember playing football with him."

Shit, he knows the family. "Yeah, I'm the little gay brother no one talks about."

Daniel eased back into the booth and shook his head. "Damn, it must be tough with your uncle Vernon saying the things he does about gays."

"What? Remember, I haven't been in town long; what's he saying?"

"We have a committee trying to defeat him." He sat forward, gripping the handle of his beer mug. "He's spouting the usual crap about gays and lesbians converting children, tempting straight people, being the downfall of the family, and how religion can change sexual orientation. He's tried to block tax money from going to AIDS charities."

"Damn." I scratched my head, trying to help the disturbing information sink in.

"He led a protest of a play with a gay character, and has had books removed from the school libraries." Daniel rubbed his hairy forearms and sank back into the booth. "And to think he has a gay nephew."

Hearing this made my stomach churn. I took a gulp of beer hoping it would settle the acid climbing up my throat. "You know, in a way, it doesn't surprise me. The family is fucked up."

"How so?" Daniel ordered us another pitcher of beer.

"To begin with, Harris is my great-grandfather's name. Grandma Eleanor married a cousin named Harris, distant cousin they claim, but looking at Vernon, I'm not so sure. Vernon and Mother are double Harris blood. In fact, the Harris name is so important to them, we all have it. Tim is Timothy Ernest Harris Mason; I'm Derek Montgomery Harris Mason; Valerie is Valerie Amanda Harris Mason. It's a mess filling out my name on a form.

"Anyway," I continued, "when I realized I was gay, they shipped me off to college, I guess to protect the Harris name, so it wouldn't be stained with scandal."

"Being gay isn't scandalous, at least not these days. It took me years to come out. I was always scared someone would see me going into a bar, or worse yet, meeting someone in a bar I knew." Daniel chuckled.

"Yeah, that does seem odd to me. Especially after living in San Francisco all these years; if you aren't gay there, that's the scandal."

"Hey," his eyes sparked, "would you be willing to talk to the media about how this campaign affects you? The gay nephew of the conservative candidate, you know, refuting his points on gays and lesbians, that's the majority of his platform. Without it, he doesn't have any real platform."

I liked the idea, embarrass Vernon and Gladys and make them squirm. Gladys always tried to hide me, but what about embarrassment for Valerie and Ruby? "Maybe... But I don't live here, this isn't my election."

"You're still a story. Vernon Harris has a gay nephew that he disowned. We could show the voters how wrong that is."

"No, can't do it. I don't plan on staying here much longer."

Daniel cast his gaze down to the table and twisted the edges of his beer soaked napkin. "I really enjoyed talking to you; it's not everyday I meet someone like you: handsome, interesting, fun. I was hoping to see you again."

I sift through all of San Francisco for a guy like this, and then find him in a town I can't wait to get out of. My damn luck. "If you give me your number, I'll call you later. Maybe we can go out to dinner tomorrow."

He wrote his name and number on a matchbook; I slipped it in my pocket. *Maybe I'll stay a few more days. Charlotte might not be as boring as I thought.*

RUBY STACKED BOXES to one side, clearing a path through the attic. "I feel bad moving Walterene's things up here so soon."

"It's best to do it while you have help," I followed her across the dark dusty space, "and besides, it will help to stay busy. I can organize things up here; why don't you go downstairs and decide what can be stored away?"

She turned and went back to the stairs. "I just hate rummaging through her stuff. Not in the ground three days, and we're burying her life in boxes."

"We're preserving her memories," I corrected. Then I thought about how generous Walterene had been. "Oh, and Ruby, why don't you make a pile of clothes to donate?"

Ruby climbed down the rickety pull-down stairs, muttering to herself. I knew she wasn't crazy about packing up Walterene's clothes, but my experience with death in San Francisco was that there were enough reminders without seeing the deceased's clothes every time a closet or a drawer was opened. I started going through boxes and writing the contents on the side, and arranged some scattered books on shelves built between the studs of the gable. Then I saw a box stuffed with notebooks and girls' diaries, the type with little locks securing the contents from nosy brothers. *This could be interesting,* I thought. "My Diary" was imprinted on the front of a pink one and under that, in carefully blocked print, the name: Walterene Ethel Simmons—1946. I felt a little guilty opening it, but this was Walterene as a little girl; I felt she wouldn't have minded.

> January 26
> Dearest Diary,
>   Uncle Earl wrote from New York. He says I should come visit to see a play called Carousel. Blackie died. He was a good dog. Pa said he will go to heaven and keep a dead soldier company. Edith's father died in the war, maybe Blackie will be with him. Ruby said she saw Sam naked taking his bath. She said it was funny. I wish I had a brother.

I flipped through the pages looking for something more interesting. She was probably ten or eleven then. I thumbed through some of the other diaries—ones from her teenage years. I came across handwriting that seemed urgent and feverish; the first words on the page confirmed it:

> They killed him, no questions, no trial, nothing. Mr. Sams had always been so nice to us all. Gladys lied. I know she did. She was mad because Ruby and I teased her. But to claim that! How could she?
>   I went to the tree where they hanged him, made Ruby come with me. About a mile off Park Road in

the woods, an oak tree with high limbs still had the rope swinging in the breeze. I prayed for Mr. Sams.

I heard them go after him, of course I didn't realize what was going on last night, but I remember hearing the cars drive off and the hoots and yells from the men. I know he was with them, probably leading the way. I hate him. I hate Gladys. I hate them all. If it wasn't for Ruby, I'd go crazy. Mr. Sams—the only good and decent thing in my life, and they kill him.

Bet they took Vernon with them. Time to teach him to hate and kill people. Tomorrow, watch them hide their cloaks and hoods and join the rest of us in church. MR. SAMS WAS A GOOD MAN!!!

Murder. I couldn't believe it. I climbed down the stairs, and found Ruby sitting on the bed folding clothes.

"What happened to Mr. Sams?" I asked, holding the book out to her.

"That's Walterene's. Give me that." She snatched it out of my hand. "You shouldn't have read that. It's private."

"But someone hanged Mr. Sams, isn't that true?"

"Yes, but that was a long time ago." She held the diary close to her.

"It was the Klan, wasn't it? Was Vernon part of it?" I had to know. If he was, I had to stop him from being elected.

"What? No, no Harris ever did anything like that," she defended.

I knew she didn't want to talk about it, so I let it go. "I just saw that one page about Mr. Sams being killed and Walterene mentioned that they might have taken Vernon with them that night."

Ruby started to cry.

Easing down on the bed next to her, I tried to comfort her. "I didn't mean to upset you."

"Mr. Sams did yard work for Grandpa at the house on Dilworth Road. He had worked there as long as I could remember. When us grandkids came around he would tell us stories of old plantations and ghosts." She sniffed back the tears. "As we got older, he still treated us like children, patting us on the bottoms as he said goodbye. Gladys took it the wrong way and told Grandpa Ernest. He fired him on the spot. After more than thirty years, he was fired. The next day, someone found him hanging from a tree. He took his own life. In fact..." She stood and led me through the house and out the side door. She pointed to a towering oak next to the driveway. "That tree, Mr. Sams died on that tree."

"You make it sound like suicide. Do you think he killed himself for losing his job?"

"Thirty years is a long time to work for one family, and then to be fired. I always thought he took his own life. Walterene swore it was a lynching." She still stared into the soaring oak.

"But," I had to ask, "why this tree?"

"Oh, the house wasn't here then. A few houses had been built around, but Sedgefield Road had just been paved and houses were being built. That next spring, the foundation was laid for this house. Walterene and I were so afraid the tree would be cut down during the building, but it survived. She swore that she would live in this house one day, and years later she and I bought it because it had Mr. Sams' tree."

"That's a little morbid, Ruby. Wanting to live in a house where a lynch—"

She gave me a sharp look.

"Or a suicide," I added quickly, "happened. Why?"

Using the handrails, she guided herself down to sit on the brick step. "It was to honor his memory, the last place he was alive; no matter what those last moments were, they were still his."

I sat down next to her and held her hand. The branches of the oak reached across the driveway just a few feet above the tops of our cars. A few hanging baskets swayed in the breeze from the lower limbs, macramé hemp cradling lacy ferns. I imagined Mr. Sams, instead of the fern, swinging back and forth from a knotted rope.

"You know," she inhaled a deep breath, "this was the place where Walterene had her last moments. It will be where I have mine, too."

I couldn't relate to being so tied to a place. In all the world, one small plot of land and house that held her past and future so tight that she believed it would be the spot where she would draw her last breath. We sat there in silence.

THE NEXT MORNING, I woke to the soothing smell of brewing coffee. From the bathroom, I heard the doorbell ring. *Who the hell comes by at seven o'clock in the morning?* I thought. *Maybe Valerie on her way to work.* I shook it twice, tucked it back in my boxers, and flushed. Coming into the kitchen, I overheard Ruby trying to calm Mark's angry voice.

He spotted me and shoved the newspaper in my face. "What the fuck is this?" he demanded.

"Mark!" Ruby scolded.

I dropped to the couch. A bold headline read:

    Vernon Harris Scorns Gay Nephew

Chapter
Six

"I DIDN'T DO it." I knew Mark was too upset to believe me.
"No one, I haven't talked to...Oh, shit." Daniel, it had to be, but I
didn't agree to talk to a newspaper. Did he go to them?

"What? Who did you talk to?" Mark paced across the den.

Ruby settled into her chair and read the paper. "Says here that
Vernon denies knowing Derek is gay, and that he 'loves the sinner,
but hates the sin.'" She looked up with a sneer. "What a bunch of
bull; whose Bible is he reading from? I could tell Vernon a thing or
two." The phone rang, and she answered it with a short, irritated,
"Hello?"

Mark sat down on the couch and put his head in his hands. I
took up his pacing.

"Oh, sorry Valerie." Ruby leaned back in the chair. "Yes, we
saw the article. I don't know. Yes, I'll tell him. Okay, see you then."
She hung up the phone, and said Valerie would be by at lunch.

"May I see the paper?" I asked. Ruby handed it over. I checked
the byline: Daniel Kaperonis. He was a reporter. How fucking stupid could I be? "I know the guy who wrote the story," the words
squeaked out.

"What?" Mark bounded off the couch. "You talked to a reporter
without clearing it with Dad's campaign manager?"

"Hold on." I slung the paper to the floor. "I don't have to clear
anything with anybody."

He got in my face again. "Listen, in this town, what you say can
cause a lot of trouble for the family."

"Fuck the family." I spit the words back at him.

"Boys!" Ruby tried to separate us. "I can't stand this fighting."

"Ruby," Mark led her by the arm, "Derek and I need to talk.
Would you please sit down here? We'll go in the living room."

I stormed through the kitchen and dining room to the little-used
living room and turned, ready to fight, waiting for him to follow me,
but realizing I still wore only my boxers, I felt at a disadvantage

against Mark in his business suit. I went to my bedroom and pulled on jeans and a T-shirt. When I came back in the room, Mark sat in a chair, tapping the rolled up newspaper on his knee.

"Have you calmed down?" he asked.

"Me? You're the one who tore in here waving that damned paper around, accusing me."

"But you said you had talked to a reporter."

"I didn't know he was a reporter." I told Mark how I had met Daniel and what we talked about. "So, you see, I wasn't intending to talk."

Mark scanned the story again. "He didn't use any direct quotes from you in the article, but when he went to Dad, he did, just to get a reaction out of him. Dad all but admits he knows you're gay. Says here:

> Vernon Harris commented on rumors by acknowledging his nephew, Derek, left Charlotte to attend college, and now resides in San Francisco. Harris said, "He was always rebellious and young people go through a lot of experimentation." When asked about his own youthful experimentation, Harris only said, "I never did anything worse than sneak a cigarette or bottle of beer from my grandfather." Harris' grandfather was Ernest Harris, the founder of Harris Construction, philanthropist, and former Mayor of Charlotte. Vernon Harris, a US senatorial candidate, bases his campaign on the traditional family, and relies on several conservative churches for support. "The good God-fearing people of this community know I wouldn't endorse the homosexual lifestyle in this city, and especially not in any member of my beloved family." Harris concluded his remarks with the following: "I love the sinner, but hate the sin."

"What a dickhead," I said it before I could think.

"My father isn't a dickhead," Mark corrected, "he may act like one sometimes, but he means well."

"Means well? He's spreading hate and misinformation. What right has he got to stand up in front of the public and talk about homosexuality? Is he a doctor? A psychologist? A professor? No! He runs a construction company. What the hell does he know about me?" I looked into Mark's eyes. "And what the hell does he know about you?"

His face flushed, and in a low tone, he hissed, "He knows nothing about me, and it's going to stay that way. If you so much as mention to anyone that we had sex, I'll deny it and claim you're just trying to make trouble."

"Mark," I tried to keep my voice calm, "all his slurs and insults are not just directed at strangers, they're aimed at me. And you."

"I am not gay." The statement hung in the air like he had dropped the final curtain on that part of his life.

"Be completely honest with me. We spent a lot of time together years ago; I think I knew you pretty well." I took a deep breath. "Do you have any erotic feelings for men? I don't mean acting on them, just fantasies."

"No!" He stood as if ready to fight.

"Okay, okay," I tried to calm him. "I just mean, sometimes it's not so black and white. Many studies say that sexuality is a spectrum, and it changes in degrees. Maybe what we had was—"

"We were just kids." He sat back down, seeming more relaxed.

"Right. Lots of guys have some attraction to other men: hero worship of a sports star or a close, loving friendship." I smiled at a thought, "Of course, there is a difference when I look at Jeff Gordon—I'm not thinking about what a great NASCAR driver he is, I want him, sexually. But Darrell Waltrip—no way!" I laughed a little at my joke, and he finally gave way to a smile.

"He is cute for a NASCAR redneck," Mark grinned. "You know, we all have to make choices."

I nodded in agreement.

"You made yours to live your life as a gay man. I decided to live my destiny."

I couldn't keep quiet. "It's not a choice. I couldn't live any other way—"

"Willpower is all you lack."

"Bullshit, Mark, I will not deny my nature just because you do." I knew I was pushing him too far again. "I can't live my life sneaking around, jerking off with fitness magazines, or having an occasional anonymous encounter in a public park."

He didn't say a word. Head bowed, he didn't look at me.

Braced for his verbal or physical attack, I waited. The silence between us thickened.

Mark stood, and I readied myself with clenched fists. He walked to the window and stared for a while, then turned back to me, voice breaking. "This isn't San Francisco. People can't and won't accept what they feel is so wrong. Not everyone has the freedom to run off and do what their hormones tell them. Some of us take up the responsibility handed to us."

"My mother sent me away when I told her I was gay. I didn't run off. She didn't want other people to know—"

"The scandal would be too much."

"This is the scandal. Now, everyone in Charlotte knows I'm gay and that my uncle doesn't like it. Look," I beat my chest with my fist, "I'm still standing; the world has not stopped; it didn't kill her, and it didn't kill me."

"But you don't have a wife; you aren't vice-president in the company; you don't have business contacts all over the state." He leaned against the window frame, staring into the front yard.

"That's right, but I'm happy. I'm honest about who I am, and for the most part, people respect me for it." I walked to him and put my hand on his shoulder.

He pulled away from me. "That's easy for you to say." He picked up the paper again and waved it. "This is not a minor issue. This is sex; this is what brings careers to an end, but it will not ruin Dad's campaign. I'll see to that."

"Mark, Vernon has nothing to do with my life. Hell, I haven't talked to him in eight years; he probably wouldn't be able to pick me out of a lineup." I sat down on the old feather-stuffed sofa, sinking into it. I didn't want to tear apart the family any more than it was already. I didn't want to hurt Mark by pushing him to acknowledge his own desires. I didn't want to be here. Life had become too complicated; I wanted to go home.

Mark sat down next to me. "Will you talk to Dad's campaign manager? Maybe he can come up with a way to turn this around."

I still loved him. For some odd reason, at that moment, I couldn't deny it. I had broken into his emotions and rediscovered the person I knew all those years ago. He wouldn't admit his desire; the price was too high. It kept him bound to the life he'd built, to the life planned for him. The young prince who felt obligated to grow into the king everyone expected—that was Mark. "Yes," I said, "I'll do what I can. Maybe this will help soften Vernon's stance on some of the social issues."

"Don't even try," he warned.

I felt like I should at least attempt it, but I knew the old bastard would rather kiss a black man square on the lips during a news conference than change his long-held right-wing views.

GLADYS APPEARED ON Ruby's doorstep a few minutes after Mark left. The phone rang nonstop, family members wanting to congratulate me or condemn me depending on their relationship with Vernon. So, as Ruby fielded the phone calls, I was lucky enough to open the door to Gladys the Bitch.

She pushed her way through the door. "Why did you do it?"

"Just to piss you off." I followed her as she circled the den before lighting on Walterene's chair next to Ruby.

"Well, you did a fine job. The whole town is talking about it. My phone has rung all morning," she said.

I pointed to Ruby talking on the phone next to her. "Join the club, Gladys. I didn't realize I was talking to a reporter."

"So, you just tell your life history to a total stranger? I thought you had better sense than that." She appeared more haggard than usual. Her eyes were sunken into her thin tight face, hands with road map veins fiddled with the strap of her leather handbag. She looked as fragile as I had ever seen her. "You know people are trying to make Vernon fail, and this gives them plenty of ammunition."

"Why are you so concerned with Vernon's campaign? Isn't the family fortune enough for you?"

"Vernon is moving this family beyond Charlotte. Grandfather knew we would achieve great things here, but Vernon is taking them to the next level."

"But that's Vernon," I said, "what does that do for you personally?"

"Nothing for me, but it puts Tim and Vernon's boys in the national market. The business will expand to compete with firms from Atlanta, Washington, and New York. That is, if this mess you've started doesn't affect his campaign. Why on earth did you tell them you were part of this family?"

"Because I am, and I'm not ashamed of it, no matter what you do." I waited to see if she was listening.

"Ashamed of us? Why, you ungrateful fool. If it wasn't for me, you wouldn't be here."

Oh, so now I owed her for being brought into the world. "Yes, I know you gave me life, but how long do I have to keep repaying you for it?"

Ruby hung up the phone and shot Mother a disapproving look. "I get off the phone with one cranky old lady and have to listen to another one in my own house. Gladys, relax, it's not the end of the world." She nodded her head toward the phone. "That was Edwina. She's not quite clear on what 'gay' means. I assured her that didn't mean Derek wore women's clothes." She winked at me, and reached across the side table to playfully punch Mother's arm. "What a hoot Edwina is; could you imagine our big handsome boy here wearing a skirt and blouse? Lordy, Lordy, that would be funny."

Ruby with the giggles got me laughing. I looked at Mother; she sat stone-faced. "Oh, lighten up, Gladys. Vernon's evil plan to take over the world is still on track."

"You two deserve each other—both crazy as loons." She pointed at me. "You need to get down to Vernon's campaign office to straighten this out."

I decided to give her this one and not tell her I had already promised Mark I would go. "If you really think I should, I will."

Her suspicious gaze told me she doubted my sincerity. "I'm serious, Derek. You have to work with them to get this back on track."

"Mother, I said I will."

She seemed stunned, fumbling for her car keys. "Well, thank you, Derek. It's the least you could do."

Damn, she just can't let it go. "No, Mother, the least I could do is nothing. But I'll talk to his camp; I'm not saying how far I'll go for them, but I will talk to them."

After she left, I went back to the bedroom to find the book of matches with Daniel's phone number. I wanted to confront the jerk who'd caused all the trouble.

Dialing the number, I composed my message for his voicemail, but to my surprise he answered on the second ring.

"This is Derek Mason. What the hell do you think you're doing? Do you know how much trouble I'm in?"

"Hold on, hold on," Daniel tried to calm me. "I reported what I thought was public knowledge. You told me these things without hesitation."

"I didn't know you were a reporter."

"You didn't ask, and I wasn't talking to you as a reporter; I thought we were just getting acquainted over a beer, then I realized who you were, and I saw a story." He tried to make it sound so innocent. "Listen, have dinner with me tonight—as a way for me to apologize."

"You've got to be kidding. I wouldn't trust you to take anything I say off the record." I sat on the bed and flipped open the matchbook, then lit a match, letting it burn down.

"Right, I understand you feeling that way, but honestly, I would like to see you again, strictly 'off the record.'"

I took a pen off the bedside table and wrote *asshole* over his name on the matchbook. "Sure, what about your place, tonight? You could at least fix dinner for me. What's the address?" Like I ever intended on showing up.

"That sounds great," Daniel gushed. "How about eight o'clock?"

"Fine."

"Take East Boulevard to Euclid, south two blocks, then left on Tremont. The third house on the left. It's a beige house with a green shutters."

"Cool, see you then." I hung up, smug with my little payback. I called him; he didn't have my phone number or where I was staying.

When I walked back to the den, Valerie had stopped by. Ruby

fixed chicken salad sandwiches in the kitchen.

"I hear you've had an exciting morning," Valerie said as she glanced at the tattered newspaper. "Looks like this paper has had a lot of handling."

"Yeah, Mark, Ruby, me, Mother, we've all taken our aggressions out on it. So, how's your morning at work been?"

"Not this exciting." She looked impressive in her olive business suit; her black hair had a few strands of gray, but it made her appear more serious, more mature, like someone I would want to do my taxes. "So," she began, "how'd this happen?"

I sighed, and started into the story I had recounted over and over, but with Valerie I added the part about how handsome Daniel was. I even included the payback, no-show dinner I had set up with him.

"Derek, that's not nice. This poor guy will be cooking all evening, then waiting for you to show." She frowned at me and shook her head side to side like Ruby does when she talks about our brother Tim.

"Well, he deserves to be stood up, after what he did to me."

"All he did was talk to a cute guy, then find out you were related to a jerk running for Senate who verbally bashes gays. I don't know if I wouldn't have done the same thing." She thought for a moment. "But I guess I would have talked to you about the article first."

Ruby yelled from the kitchen, "That's not nice, to stand up a date."

"It's not a date," I yelled back, then to Valerie I said, "I just wanted to hurt him back..." I realized how juvenile it sounded as I said it. "Okay, I'll call him and let him know I won't be there."

"That would be the right thing to do," she smiled in a motherly way. Too bad she never had kids. She would've made a great mother. I wondered where she got that from, not Gladys the Bitch.

Ruby called us in for lunch; we gathered around the table, and then the phone rang.

"I thought I had that thing off the hook," Ruby huffed. "Derek, it's for you. Bill Robertson, Vernon's campaign manager."

"Shit," I stood to get it, then decided to wait. "Tell him I'll call him after lunch."

Ruby came back to the table with his name and phone number scribbled on the back of an envelope. "He sounded like a nice man. Maybe you should take Valerie with you when you go."

"No way," Valerie protested, "I would never get involved with someone working on Vernon's campaign. He's bound to be a Republican, and I'm a Democrat." She smiled at Ruby. "It would never work."

"All I said was that you might go with him," Ruby exclaimed, "and you were all ready to pick out china patterns."

We finished lunch, and I called Mr. Robertson back. I agreed to meet with him and Vernon later that afternoon. My thoughts went back to Daniel and the dinner. Maybe I should go; it wouldn't be nice to stand him up. Besides, I've always thought it best to keep a close eye on people I shouldn't trust.

Chapter
Seven

VERNON'S CAMPAIGN OFFICE sat on a corner of Providence Road near the Manor Theater. I pulled off the busy road and parked behind the low brick building. The office had huge glass windows plastered with Vernon's campaign posters. As I walked in, the receptionist glanced up from her phone call and motioned me into a wooden chair near the door. She didn't smile at me or to whoever spoke to her over the telephone; instead, she scratched her scalp with the end of her pencil and stared at a *People* magazine. Each scratch moved her sprayed-stiff helmet of hair about one inch to the right and then back to its original position. I watched to see if anything fell out. Her face reminded me of a damp dishrag, drooping and sagging around her eyes, nose, and mouth. About the time I started to guess her age and weight, she hung up the phone and asked how she could help me.

"I'm here to see Bill Robertson. I'm Derek Mason."

"Oh." She inhaled the word. "Let me check to see if he's in his office."

She scurried off down a hall. I studied one of the posters; Vernon hadn't changed much from what I remembered, same thin white hair, dark eyes, wide mouth, and not many wrinkles for his age. He probably could stand to lose some weight, but most men in their sixties have accumulated a few pounds over the years.

"Mr. Mason?" the receptionist yelled from the end of the hall.

I walked back to where she pointed to an open door.

Vernon sat on a leather couch along with Mark. Across a desk, Bill Robertson, a tall, lean man, stood and offered his handshake. Vernon and Mark kept sitting.

"Come on in and take a seat," Robertson pointed to a side chair next to his desk. The three men stared at me.

"Why do I feel like I'm on trial here?" I asked.

"No, no-o-o," Robertson soothed. "We want to work together and turn this into a positive for the campaign."

I looked to a fidgeting Vernon. "Hello, Vernon."

"What were you thinking? I should kick your—"

"Dad," Mark interrupted, "Derek's here to help us."

"That's right, Vernon," Robertson added, "he can help us reach voters who may have not considered you before now. This isn't damage control; this is an opportunity to gain votes. Of course, we don't want to seem too liberal and isolate our core supporters."

Like a child having to share his candy with a sibling, Vernon twisted on the couch. "All right, damn liberal paper makes me look bad cause I don't like queers."

"Hold on," I fumed. "This redneck jerk just lost my coopera- tion." I looked from Robertson to Vernon. "Vernon, it would be a danger to have someone as ignorant as you in public office." I pushed my chair back and headed for the door. A vision of Vernon yelling "queer" and picketing a gay bar chilled me, but then my mind made a more startling picture: a young Vernon tossing a rope over a tree limb to string up Mr. Sams. *Did he do it?* My mind tum- bled the possibilities of allowing a racist, a possible murderer, to run for the United States Senate.

"Derek." Mark grabbed my arm. He pulled me to the side of the hall. "Please come back and talk to us. Dad's not used to watching his mouth around family; he doesn't think of you or me or Bill as someone he has to be politically correct around."

"This man is running for the Senate; he shouldn't have to act."

He tried to make excuses for his father. "Dad's just upset about the article. Publicly, he's a sensible conservative, but he goes off the deep end when he blows off steam. That's all he was doing, blowing off steam. Come back in and talk with us, please."

I relented like I had too many times before. The animated con- versation between Bill Robertson and Vernon stopped when I walked back in.

In a hushed voice to Vernon, Robertson said, "Of course, you're right."

What have they cooked up? I looked Vernon straight in the eyes. "You treat me with respect, and I'll do the same for you."

"Fair enough," he agreed and stuck out his hand to shake on it. I squeezed his hand as hard as he squeezed mine.

"Wonderful," Robertson sat back down behind his desk, "let's talk about how a young, smart, gay nephew can benefit Vernon's campaign."

"Now that's a question," Vernon grinned at Robertson.

Silence filled the room as we all strained to think of a way to integrate a gay relative with a conservative campaign; left and right, open and closed, opposites till the end.

"Inclusion." Robertson looked at me, then at Vernon. "Our

campaign is the campaign of the people, all people: white, black, His-
panic, Asian, straight, gay, whatever."

"Is that true?" I asked.

"Sure, it's true." Robertson answered before Vernon could open
his mouth.

"So, where are the blacks, Hispanics, and Asians working on his
campaign?"

"Oh, we don't have any directly working with us, but we have
their support—"

"But if you say this, you need to have diversity on the team—"

"Mom's girl, Martha," Vernon piped in.

"Yes?" Robertson asked.

"Martha's black. Mom's maid, she supports me." He turned
and smiled at Mark.

"But, Dad, what they're saying is we need more visible association from different people."

"Hell, I know what he's saying. I just don't want minority opinions clouding my positions. I have to have a clear and easily under-
standable stance on the issues. If I need to add a few tokens, then
they had better be of my ideology." Vernon sat back and lit a cigar.

"Mark thought for a moment. "We can find some minorities. I
can check with some of the guys that work for the company. In the
past few years, we've hired a lot of Mexicans to work on the construction crews."

"That's fine and dandy, Mark," Vernon leaned forward, "but I
want to know exactly what percentage of registered voters fall into
each category. I will agree to having representation equal to the voting public. If fifty percent of the voters are Mexicans, then half my
campaign workers will be Mexicans." He got up and paced the floor.
"Hell, we'll all eat tacos and hug." Stopping in front of me, waving
the cigar, he asked, "Is that okay with you?"

"Sounds cool to me. I like the idea of shadowing the makeup of
your team from the diversity of the state."

"Young man, I can tell you that this state is mostly white, then
black, then the rest of you. I get a couple of black guys in here—"

"Women? What about women?" I wasn't going to let him slip.

"Women aren't part of diversity."

I rolled my eyes at Robertson.

"Yes, I think they are," he corrected.

"Damn, will I be the only white man left on this campaign?"

"Now, Dad," Mark said, "I'll get the demographics information,
and we'll know what we're really talking about." He left the room to
find his reports.

Vernon sat back down on the couch. "I guess since this uproar
was over you being gay, you would need to be on this team."

"I don't live in North Carolina. But I'm sure you can find some-one else to work with you." I thought for a moment. "Thanks for ask-ing."

"Sure. I just don't know any other gay people. You guys got a newsletter or something? Maybe a directory?"

I imagined Vernon placing a gay personal ad for someone to work on the campaign: *WCM (White Conservative Male) looking for energetic gay man to assist in US Senate run. This would be strictly physi-cal—no emotional or intellectual ties required.* "No, but I think there are some organizations around town where you might find some inter-est."

Mark came back with his demographics report. "State Board of Elections posts this on their Web site: Democrats 49%, Republicans 34%, Unaffiliated 16 %."

"See," Vernon said, "I'm already a minority; damn state is full of Democrats."

Mark continued, "White 78%, Black 19%, Indian 0.8 %, Other 1%."

"Where am I going to find an Indian?" Vernon chuckled.

"Male 45 %, Female 55 %. Sounds like the women have us out-numbered." Mark handed his father the printout.

"Doesn't say anything here about gays versus normal people." Vernon flipped the page over to look at the back. "No, no gays here."

"We're mixed in with all the other categories." I looked at Rob-ertson. "Most estimates I've heard place gays and lesbians at 10% of the general population."

"What are the political issues?" he asked while taking a pen and tablet in hand.

"I'm not exactly politically active—"

"Until you came to Charlotte," Vernon quipped.

"I guess the most basic is to be treated fairly and with respect." I stared at Vernon. "What everyone wants: no discrimination."

He flicked the ash off the end of his cigar onto the floor.

"That would work for all the minorities," Mark said. "Dad, wouldn't you agree that no one should be judged solely on their skin color, nationality, religion, gender, or sexual orientation? That should be a positive to work into the campaign."

Vernon looked at Mark, then to Robertson.

"Yes, Vernon," Robertson said. "That would be a positive. Do you believe in it?"

"No."

"No?" Robertson repeated. "But we agreed we needed to make some concessions."

"Whose campaign is this?" Vernon roared. "I agreed to add some minorities, and I'll agree to treat everyone in a Christian way, but I won't spout some ACLU crap about non-discrimination. Discrimination is against the law. I stand by the law."

"There's not a law on discriminating against gays and lesbians."

"There isn't a law about discriminating against Republican senators either," he shot back.

I didn't have the energy to try to win the point.

"Dad," Mark ventured, "let's just say we're against discrimination of all kinds."

"But what happens when the gays want to be added to the list?" Vernon puffed the cigar. "Everyone wants special privileges."

"Right," I said, "like I had the special privilege of being banished from the family because I said I'm gay."

"You didn't have to broadcast it. You could have kept it to yourself." Vernon snuffed out the cigar on the bottom of his shoe.

"Fine. I'm hitting a brick wall. No discrimination, and more blacks and women on the campaign." I summed it up.

"Okay. I can live with that." Vernon turned to Robertson. "Bill, what will this do to my other platforms?"

"We'll talk through all the possibilities, Vernon." Bill Robertson stood and turned to me. "Thanks for coming in, and please no more reporters?"

"Yeah, at least he seems a little more open than before." I shook his hand and left.

Mark followed me out, closing the office door behind him. "Derek, thanks for talking with us. I think you did Dad some good."

"A little more of an open mind." I shrugged. "Hopefully, he will add some diversity to his campaign; it wouldn't hurt him to get some new ideas."

Mark patted me on the back. "So, what's Ruby cooking for dinner?"

Dinner? I had forgotten to call and cancel dinner with Daniel. "Oh, I don't know, I guess I'm going to meet an old friend."

"Kathleen said she would like to have you back again before you leave town."

My mind swarmed around Daniel and dinner. "Yeah, that would be nice. I'll talk to you later." I hurried out of the office and drove through Myers Park to Sedgefield. Pulling into Ruby's driveway I saw her weeding flowers under the big oak, Mr. Sams' oak. What if Vernon did it? Had I just assisted a murderer's campaign?

A FEW MINUTES after eight o'clock, I parked in front of Daniel's house. The setting sun stretched shadows across his carefully maintained lawn. Several large azaleas weighted down with scarlet blooms lined the foundation of the house, and a pin oak

stretched its massive limbs showing off its new tiny thin leaves over
the house. Through the warm humid air, the spicy scent of charcoal
and steak drifted from the back of the house. I climbed the stairs to
the long porch and rang the doorbell.

"Hello, Derek, come in," Daniel greeted me at the door. "I
wasn't sure you would come, but I'm glad you did."

"Well, I said I would, didn't I?" The front room looked like
where he spent most of his time, television and stereo in one corner
with a large sofa and chair facing them, one wall covered with bookcases stacked with books and magazines; the paintings on the wall
revealed an interest in classical architectural drawings and Greek
mythology, the twins Artemis and Apollo flanking his fireplace.

"Can I get you a beer? I have steaks on the grill." He led me to
the kitchen and handed me a Michelob.

"Thanks. Nice place you have here." I wanted to get things out
in the open. "Daniel, why did you write that article?"

He leaned against the counter and took a swig of his beer. "Like
I told you on the phone, I didn't know you being gay was a big family secret. It intrigued me how Vernon Harris dealt with having a
gay nephew, especially with his history. I'm sorry I stirred up trouble for you; honestly, I would not have written a word about it if I'd
known the story would affect you this way."

"Everything said tonight is strictly off the record, right?" I
asked, but still wasn't sure if I trusted him.

"Of course, yes, I'm off duty as a reporter."

"Most of my family is very distant to me, but there are a few I
love dearly." I thought about Walterene, Ruby, Valerie, and Mark.
"I came here for the funeral of one of those few."

His dark brown eyes cast down. "Sorry to hear that."

"Anyway, I had a talk with Vernon today, and I think we both
feel a little better about what's happened."

"How so?"

I smiled at his question. "Thought the reporter hat was off
tonight."

"It is, sorry. Let me check on the steaks, medium-rare okay? I
thought we'd eat outside." He walked out the kitchen door to a large
private patio set up with an intimate table for two in candlelight.

"Wow, you went to a lot of trouble for not being sure if I'd
show."

"I hoped you would." He flashed a bright smile framed with
dimples. "So, you and Vernon are okay?"

I thought for a moment. "As okay as can be expected. I have a
question for you. How far back does the newspaper keep copies of
each edition?"

He took the steaks off the grill and added them to plates with baked potatoes and steamed vegetables. "How far back are you looking to go?"

"Late forties or early fifties."

"Yeah, on microfiche. You looking for something?"

I took a bite of the steak. "Wonderful, you're a good cook."

"My family had a restaurant a few years back, I helped the cook after school. Now, what went on in the late forties that has you so interested?"

I didn't trust him enough to reveal my suspicions about Mr. Sams' death, but I wanted to see if anything had been in the paper about it. "Just researching some family accomplishments. You know plenty about my family, what about the Kaperonis clan? They owned a restaurant; what else?"

Daniel sat back in his chair, smiled, and said, "Typical Greek family: we all lived close to each other, tried the restaurant business for a while. My mother and father live in Madison Park, just below Woodlawn Road. I have two brothers and a sister."

"Where are you? Youngest, oldest?"

"I'm the middle boy. David and Emily are older, then me, then Theo. In fact, David works for your family. He's an architect working with your cousin Margaret's husband, Gerald."

"Does he like it?" I waited for him to finish chewing.

"Sorry, yeah, Gerald's a good guy. I hear Margaret's a bit of a bitch, if you'll excuse me being so blunt."

"No, that's fine, I want honesty." I remembered Mark's sister as being very opinionated and headstrong. "What seems to be the reason for her bitchiness?"

He grinned with his eyes sparkling in the candlelight. "Now this is all hearsay, I don't know anything firsthand."

"Go ahead, forget the disclaimers." I moved my leg against his under the table. *Why not? I'm only in town a few days.*

"David says Gerald has a place in town. He doesn't make the drive down to Ballantyne each night like a good husband should." He looked down at his plate as if he wasn't sure if he should be telling me this.

"No big deal. Maybe they're going through some rough times? What about the kids? They should be teenagers by now." Margaret had two of the most beautiful little blond boys, always laughing and hanging onto their father's hands.

"Guess the family doesn't keep you up to date in California. Jerry, the oldest, got caught shoplifting at Southpark. Vernon pulled strings and had all charges dropped, but not before little Jerry cussed out the security guard in the middle of the food court. Racist little shit, too; he used the N word when a black police officer arrived. They threw him in jail overnight just to scare him."

"Margaret must have had a fit."

Daniel shook his head. "Old man Vernon handled everything. He was the one who told them to leave his grandson in jail."

Some things never change; they all stand back and let Vernon, and before him, Grandpa Ernest, handle things. No one ever questioned their decisions, offered alternatives, put up a fight; right or wrong they had the last word. I looked up at the shadow of the towering pin oak over Daniel's house; a vision flashed in my mind: a limp body swung from a strong limb in the darkening spring sky.

Chapter
Eight

DANIEL TALKED ON about the politics of Charlotte and of North Carolina, but my thoughts kept returning to the hooded gang chasing an old black man through the woods. Men leaving their elegant homes in Dilworth and Myers Park, banding together, and crossing the railroad tracks into the Wilmore neighborhood to dispense justice. Sedgefield was probably little more than two or three miles back over to the "white" side of the tracks from Wilmore. Back then, it must have looked like a refuge of forest for a fleeing man, or maybe it was the horror of death for a captive man drug into dark woods full of potential gallows.

"Derek, are you okay?" Daniel asked.

The sound of my name brought me back to the present. "Oh, yeah, I was just entranced by the size of that tree. I forget how lush and strong trees get back here. San Francisco trees are battered by the Pacific winds and odd climate; they don't get big unless you get away from the coast."

"San Francisco is a great city, not a tree city like Charlotte, but it has lots of other things. Do you get energy from the outdoors?"

My thoughts went back to that first time with Mark on our camping trip. "Yes, I believe I do."

"Me too," Daniel agreed. "I love being outside with the trees, working in the yard, feeling connected to the earth..."

"That's a Southern thing," I kidded, becoming more attracted to him by his rustic pleasures—*no pretentiousness here.* "Southern literature has a common theme of special ties to the land."

Daniel sat back and considered it. "But Western writing has that too. Northern, Eastern literature? I don't get that much from the New York writers' club. The center of their universe is that little island up there."

"That's why they're in New York. They get energy from people, lots of people and activity," I said. "Southerners and Westerners get a charge out of the land, the history. I always thought that appreciation for our surroundings came from the Indians; sorry, Native Americans."

He smiled at my political correctness. "Being of Greek descent, I never thought about that. My family left Greece, their land..." His thoughts took over, then he brightened. "Hey, you look like you might have some Indian in you, dark hair, prominent cheekbones, tall, wide shoulders, narrow waist..."

"I've heard Cherokee blood ran with the Harris blood, but don't put that in the paper," I warned. "I can just imagine the uproar: not only is he gay, but he's a half-breed."

"Don't worry."

"Oh, did you know that about one percent of North Carolina's voting population is Native American? That surprised me," I said. "I didn't expect it, I thought everyone here considered themselves black or white."

Daniel stood up to gather the plates and put his hand on my shoulder, then whispered in my ear, "The world is not all black and white, my young friend." He kissed my neck, and a trembling volt of electricity shot through my body.

I stood with shaky legs. *Wow, he's a lightning bolt.* I steadied myself with the back of the chair and then helped clear the table.

We settled on the living room couch with soft smooth jazz music and a bottle of even smoother merlot. Daniel told me about his work, but my thoughts drifted back to Vernon. He seemed too willing to give in to my suggestions. Why did they care if I felt included in his campaign? Was it just to shut me up? I didn't intend to give any more interviews. How would Vernon turn the article around to win votes?

He spouted religious doctrine as second nature, but I hadn't heard him say anything about homosexuality being against his personal beliefs. Votes, that pushed the conversation along; how to keep votes, how to win votes. The religion angle had to be just a ploy to gather the conservative Christians into his camp. I took a sip of wine and tried to catch up on Daniel's story.

"... I made the editor's changes even though I didn't agree with her, but it turned out that my source couldn't come up with concrete proof the husband was with his mistress when the wife was shot." Daniel kicked off his shoes and put his feet on the coffee table.

"How would you investigate an old crime? Something where most of the witnesses would be reluctant to talk?" I watched his dark eyes dart back and forth as he thought.

"How old a crime are we talking about?"

"Maybe, fifty years or more."

"Fifty years? Anyone still alive that was involved?" he asked.

"Well, probably." I didn't want to get into details.

"Okay, first you get in real good with a handsome reporter." He scooted closer to me.

The spicy scent of sandalwood, sage, and the lingering aroma of mesquite, charcoal, and sizzling steaks drifted around the warm heat from his body. "And?" I led him on.

He positioned his right arm around the back of the couch, resting his hand on my shoulder, and moved his left hand across to my waist. "And, you close your eyes..."

I did. Pulling my body close, he gently brushed my lips with his. His mustache tickled, and I smiled. He whispered, "Then, you relax."

I felt his kiss again, this time stronger, more urgent, more passionate. My desire grew, pulling at the roots of my lust. Excitement surged to every nerve ending. I could hear the rhythm of my pulse beating in my ears as he nibbled my earlobes and ran the tip of his tongue down the side of my throat. My hands caressed his broad back, pulling his shirt loose from the waistband of his jeans. A rush of cool air brushed my chest as my own shirt fell to the floor, then a warm, safe sensation flooded me as Daniel's hairy chest pressed against mine. I reached to the side table and clicked off the light.

WHEN I WALKED into Ruby's house the next morning, she shook her head and sipped her coffee. "And you wanted to stand him up."

"Well, he turned out to be a nice guy. In fact, a really nice, great, incredible guy." I knew I gushed, but I had just had blue-ribbon sex, the type of passion that only comes from crossing the line from repulsion to desire. Twenty-four hours before, I had wanted to kill him; now I wanted to go back to his bed and sleep the day away.

Ruby poured a cup of coffee for me and guided me into a chair. "Is he coming over?" She smiled. "I'd like to meet this young man who has you in such a daze."

"You will, you will." I picked up the newspaper, hesitated, then looked at Ruby.

"Oh, yes. Vernon has made a statement."

On the front page, Vernon's picture had a caption: *Vernon Harris agrees to help nephew overcome battles.* I scanned the short article, not written by Daniel, that said Vernon realized I needed help "to deal with certain issues." The old man kept everything vague, and the reporter didn't push him for specifics, almost as if Bill Robertson had written the article himself. I let it drop on the floor. "There's no getting through to him."

"That's for sure," Ruby seconded. "Oh, Gladys called to see when you were going back to San Francisco. I told her I wanted you to stay, to move back."

"Bet she about had a hissy-fit over that." I drank the hot, sweet coffee and entertained the idea of living in Charlotte: Daniel, Ruby, Valerie, Mark, Grandma... the entertainment value lessened... Vernon, Gladys... "No, I don't think this is the place for me." I glanced at Ruby's soft face full of mixed emotions, obviously still grieving the loss of Walterene. "Why is it some family members are so close and others can't stand the sight of each other?"

"That's the family bond," she explained. "We get thrown together because of family ties, and like any bunch of people, some will get along and some will grate each other's nerves. But we keep together because we're tied together by blood, love, and duty."

"Duty? Mark talks about duty." I tried to make that fit into my life. "My duty is to be true to myself."

"Mark sees something larger," Ruby said, pouring us both more coffee and heaping sugar into it. "I think he puts himself after his father's happiness and Kathleen's, and his brother's and sister's. Guess that isn't always the place to put yourself, but sometimes you don't always come first."

"What is your duty?" I asked.

"As a young girl, it was me. To be happy. Papa Ernest would tell all us grandkids what we should be doing, what our mission in life was to be. Of course, the girls were to get married, have children, and take care of their husbands. Walterene and I never cared for that." A faint smile played across her lips. "But I think Mark still believes that a Harris takes care of the family first, then worries about the individual."

"Do you think I'm being selfish?" I felt self-centered talking about my own happiness before all else.

"Lord, no," she said. "You have to be at peace with yourself before you can even think of other people. Are you at peace?"

I sighed and thought. "Yes and no. My biggest unease is still my mother. Why does she not want me around? If family is so important, why am I being asked constantly when I'll leave?"

Ruby looked down at her lap. "Gladys is an odd bird."

"She hates me because I'm gay; she's ashamed of me. But I don't get it; she's not that religious, and her church isn't as conservative as most. What's her personal disgust with me?" I could feel tears welling up in my eyes; was it from anger or something else?

Reaching over to hold my hand, Ruby said, "Honey, Gladys doesn't hate you."

The tears spilled down my face.

She continued, "People don't want to be reminded of things they see in themselves, things they don't like. You're as stubborn as she is, and as proud. You two are like a mean old blue jay attacking his image in a window. His own reflection makes him want to fight."

"Was she like this as a girl?" I asked. I couldn't remember her ever being a loving, caring mother; she had always seemed distant, like children inconvenienced her.

Ruby frowned. "Honestly, I never played with Gladys as a child. She didn't care for me or Walterene, or for that matter Edwina. The boy cousins got along much better than us girls."

The diaries, I thought, *could Walterene's diaries have something about Gladys, something that turned her into "Gladys the Bitch"?* I also wanted to read more about Mr. Sams. Maybe that was it. Walterene had accused Mother of blaming Mr. Sams for something—molestation? Had Mr. Sams sexually abused her, and Vernon taken revenge for his sister? I wanted to get back to the attic and search the diaries. "Ruby, I still have some straightening up to do in the attic."

"Now, don't throw out anything else," she warned.

"No, I just want to get it organized for you. Bet you don't know half of what's up there." I grabbed a pencil and pad from the kitchen drawer. "I'll make a little inventory of what you have and put the things you need the most closest to the stairs."

"My, someone's got a lot of energy for being out all night," she joked.

I washed out my coffee cup and headed to the attic. After clicking on all the bare light bulbs so I could see better, I finally settled next to the box of books. First, I sorted the diaries from school textbooks, notebooks, and *Mother Earth News* and *Southern Living* magazines; then, I checked each one for a date and lined them up in chronological order. Several time gaps appeared, and I wondered if there could be another box buried under the eaves. On my notepad, I made a list of the years accounted for and then the missing years. Walterene had chronicled more than forty percent of her life, up to her college years. I paged through the diary with the passage on Mr. Sams, and found another entry from a month later:

> Ruby and I went to Mr. Sams' Oak tree and cut down the piece of rope that still hung from a branch. I buried it, and we sang Amazing Grace and cried. No one talks about him anymore—like he never existed. I saw his daughter downtown the other day. I waved, but she just turned her head. Maybe she didn't recognize me. All I wanted to do was tell her how I missed him, but she went into one of the colored stores, and I was afraid to follow. I wonder how they're getting along without their daddy.
>
> Grandpa Ernest took the boys hunting up near Asheville. I wonder if they wear hoods to scare the

deer, too. He's such a mean old man. I hope he dies soon.

Mama wants me to go to the dance Saturday night with Aaron Walters. I can't 'cause the girls at school kid me and say if I were to marry Aaron, my name would be Walterene Walters, and they start calling me Walla Walla. Anyway, Aaron and I would never marry. He's too much like me, neither one of us like that boy-girl dating stuff. He reminds me of Uncle Earl, sweet and caring, a confirmed bachelor. I'm a confirmed bachelorette.

"Aaron was gay," I said and flipped through the pages looking for more on Mr. Sams. "He had a daughter, maybe I can find a name. She might still be around." I wondered what I would say to her if I found her. *Hi, I think my uncle killed your father. What do you think?* No, that wouldn't be the way to do it.

I ran out of pages in that diary, and the next one started up over a year later. The one that came before had its little lock rusted shut. I worked it some, but it didn't give. I hated to break it, but no key could be found. Finally, I took a finishing nail from the toolbox and jiggled it in the lock; it popped open. Flipping through the pages, scanning for names, I found a passage about Gladys:

Gladys told Edwina that she thought Ruby and I had "an unnatural affection for each other" and that cousins shouldn't be so close. She's just jealous 'cause no one likes her. She thinks she's so pretty, always wearing new dresses and having her hair done every week. Aunt Eleanor takes her downtown to Belk and buys her a new dress about every other week. She parades down Tryon Street with those dress and hat boxes like she was the Queen of Sheba.

At Sunday dinner, she sat there all prettied up, new dress, hair perfect, rouged cheeks, and Papa Ernest looks at her and says, "Gladys, what are you all made up for? You look like a hussy with your face all painted up like that." She got up and ran out crying. I thought it was funny at first, but then I felt a little sorry for her, just a little. I never know when Grandpa might say something mean to me in front of everybody. Aunt Eleanor stormed out after Gladys; she was mad at Grandpa, too. He just chuckled at them both. "More food for the rest of us," he said.

Gladys isn't all bad. She's had a hard time. Vernon is Grandpa's favorite, and her being his sister, she gets the short end of the stick all the time. The rest of us are lucky we don't have to be around Vernon and Grandpa together.

Ruby says Gladys is young and just trying to find her fit in life. I wonder what my fit in life is? Maybe it's not here, maybe it's in New York. Uncle Earl says that's the place to be.

I sat back and thought, *I'm not the first in the family who didn't feel I belonged. Old man Ernest was a crusty, harsh guy; it must have been hard growing up different then.* I heard Ruby calling me, so I boxed the diaries back and went downstairs.

"Come in here, it's almost lunch time. Valerie called to say she was stopping by." Ruby herded me toward the bathroom. "Take a shower, you look like a Saturday night whore on Sunday morning." She playfully slapped my butt.

"But I feel like a morning angel," I kissed her plump cheek, "and you're my sexy cherub."

"Get washed up before I call your mother on you to settle you down," she mocked sternness.

I got in the shower and realized I hadn't thought about going home since yesterday afternoon. *Wow, I might actually start liking it here.*

Chapter
Nine

VALERIA ARRIVED ABOUT a quarter after noon. Her eyes looked puffy, and she walked with dog-tired sluggishness; her starched business suit seemed to be the only thing holding her up. Ruby busied herself in the kitchen preparing fried chicken and mashed potatoes. I told Valerie about my meeting with Vernon, Mark, and Bill Robertson.

"You don't believe anything will change?" she asked.

"Did you see the paper this morning? No, apparently nothing I said sank in." I lit a cigarette and exhaled the smoke away from her. "I don't know why they even bothered."

She thought a moment. "Maybe they sized you up to see what kind of threat you might be."

"That's right, I'm from out of state and don't have any contacts here." I sighed at the track my mind took. "I hate thinking about him and his campaign."

"Good," she agreed. "Don't let him get into your life. He dictates too many peoples' lives as it is."

"Val, you look tired. You okay?"

"Just not sleeping well." A faint smile flickered on her lips as if she were apologizing for her appearance. "I have too many things—"

"Lunch is ready," Ruby yelled from the kitchen. She fanned the scent of the crispy chicken, buttery potatoes, and biscuits smothered in gravy toward us with her apron. "It's getting cold."

We converged on the table like vultures on roadkill; Ruby talked of planting her flower garden and of the neighbors' gossip. I didn't think to ask Valerie again about what was keeping her up at night.

The phone rang, and Ruby got up to answer it. "Derek," she called from the den, "it's for you."

The thought of Daniel rushed me toward the phone. "Hello?"

"Is this Derek Mason?" a scratchy male voice asked.

"Yes. Who is this?"

"Never mind who I am. I have a piece of advice for you: Get the fuck out of town. We don't want fags here."

Recovering from the shock, I replied, "Go to hell, you mother-fucking redneck."

He laughed, and I slammed down the phone. *Who knows I'm here? My name was in the newspaper, but people couldn't find me from that.* Only one thought came to mind: family. My relatives knew where I was. I walked back to the dining room trying to decide who would do such a thing.

"What's wrong?" Valerie asked.

I didn't want to upset her or Ruby. "Nothing, just a wrong number."

"But they asked for you." Ruby piled more mashed potatoes on my plate. "I thought it was your young man."

Valerie brightened. "You went to dinner with him after all? What was his name?"

"Daniel, and yes, I went to dinner."

Ruby grinned, and I knew she intended to tell Valerie about my all-night date if I didn't.

I rolled my eyes at Ruby, and turned to Valerie. "Yes we had dinner, and I ended up staying the night. I came in this morning."

"Well, well," Valerie shook her head and smiled, "you have Tim's knack for making friends."

The women let it drop at that, and I gladly changed the subject to Valerie's job at the accounting firm. I didn't want to think about Daniel while I still had the sound of the caller's voice in my head. The good part of Charlotte had just been eclipsed by its dark side. Every city housed bigots and small minds, no matter how much money and culture the corporations pushed in. I wondered if a caller like that could be capable of violence.

The scene before me, of Valerie and Ruby laughing and talking, disintegrated as my imagination saw white-hooded figures spin their pickup truck to a stop in the front yard and rush the door. After kicking it in, they pushed Ruby and Valerie to the side, and wrestled me to the floor, their putrid whiskey breath in my face, fat round hands tying my arms and legs, carrying me to the oak. I could feel the rough rope tighten around my neck, the knot to one side to ensure strangulation, then the tug as they pulled the rope down over a branch, bringing me up to my toes. A quick strong yank lifted me off the ground and my feet kicked as I fought to get free.

"Derek, what's wrong?" Valerie brought me back.

"Good Lord, boy, you're sweating." Ruby felt my forehead. "Cold and clammy; you need to lie down."

Valerie and Ruby guided me out of the chair and toward the bedroom. "I'm okay. I just..."

"Lord, I hope it wasn't the chicken." Ruby looked to Valerie. "Do you feel all right?"

"Yes, Aunt Ruby," she replied, "I'm fine. The chicken was wonderful. Derek should feel better after he gets some rest."

The voices started to run together as they reached my ears. The last thing I heard before blacking out was Ruby saying, "No wonder, out all night with some boy I don't even know; I should have been properly introduced before..."

THE SUN'S RAYS stretched long and warm across the room as I woke. I ran my fingers through my hair and joined Ruby in the den.

"Feel better?" she asked.

"Much. I guess I needed some rest."

She smiled and said, "Your young man called."

A chill sliced through my stomach; had it been the scratch-voiced man? "What did he say?"

"He said he would love to meet me. I told him I wanted you to stay, and he agreed it would be nice."

"Did he leave his name?"

"Derek!" she scolded. "I can't believe you spent the night with someone and don't know his name."

"I know his name; it's Daniel Kaperonis."

"Yes, that's it. Guess he's a Greek boy."

The tension melted away. "Did he leave a message?"

She grinned. "He said he had to work tonight, but to give him a call. He left this number." Ruby handed me a grocery receipt with his name and number written on the back.

I dialed the number.

"Daniel Kaperonis," he answered.

Warmth surrounded me with the sound of his voice. "Hello, Daniel. This is Derek."

"Sleeping Beauty wakes," he kidded. "Ruby said you were sleeping after, how did she put it? Oh, yeah, after 'tomcatting around all night.'"

"That's me, the tomcat." I winked at Ruby.

"I'm at the newspaper office; I have a deadline at midnight. You mentioned something about checking out the morgue?"

"The what?" *Did I hear him right?*

"The morgue, the back issue files. I thought maybe you could bring in dinner for us, and after a romantic desk meal, I'd show you how to look up old articles."

"That would be great." I looked at Ruby and put my hand over the receiver. "Have you started dinner yet?"

"Again?" she asked. "You eat out more than a cockroach in a

Chinese restaurant."

"Daniel is working late and wanted me to get take-out and join him for dinner." I could hear the excitement in my own voice, so I knew she wouldn't object.

She pushed herself out of her chair and took the phone from my hand. "Daniel, do you like home cooking? Well, I have a roast in the crock-pot; I'll send some over with Derek. You boys need to eat right and get more rest. Okay, bye."

She handed the phone back to me and went into the kitchen to check the roast.

"Daniel?" I asked to see if he was still on the line.

"Sounds like we'll have a good meal," he said. "I'll just have to keep the other guys in the office away from it."

"What time?"

"How about an hour? You know the Observer building? Have the night watchman call me when you get here."

"Sounds great." I almost jumped out of the chair with anticipation thinking about seeing him again. "Can I bring anything else?"

"Maybe your toothbrush, if you want to go home with me when I finish up."

A tinge of guilt cut through my gut as I looked at Ruby digging out containers for our dinner. "That would be great, but I need to spend the night here with Ruby."

"I understand."

"Tell him he can come over here if he wants; I still haven't met him," Ruby yelled from the kitchen.

"Are you listening to my conversation?" I asked.

"Of course," she said.

"Daniel, I'll see you in about an hour."

"I'm looking forward to it." His voice soothed me like warm milk.

Ruby cut a couple of pieces of carrot cake and wrapped them in waxed paper. "Don't worry about me, I'll call Valerie for dinner. Us two old maids can sit here and watch television."

"Yeah, the two of you will put on your dancing shoes and be out bar-hopping before I make it out the driveway," I kidded.

"That's an idea," she said and batted her eyes. "Maybe I can make some money like those girls in the strip clubs." She shook her chest and waved her arms, stirring spoon in hand.

DANIEL CAME DOWN to meet me at the front desk after the guard called to tell him I was there. I had an uncontrollable urge to kiss him in the elevator. His lips tasted of coffee, his face rough from beard stubble.

"Glad you could make it," he smiled, flashing dimples. "I thought about you all day."

The rude caller came back to mind as I reviewed my day without him. "I'm so glad to see you. I had a strange call around lunch time; it unnerved me a little." The elevator doors opened to a large room of gray office cubicles with ringing phones and clicking computer keyboards.

"Who called?" he asked, and led me down a narrow hallway to his cubicle.

I sat in the side chair. "Some asshole. He just said the usual stuff gay-bashers say behind the safety of an anonymous phone call." I placed the containers of food on his desk."What gets me," I considered if I should reveal my suspicions. "I know my name has been in the paper and that opens me up to a lot of crazy people, but only family knows I'm staying with Ruby. How could a stranger get that number?"

He voiced what I hadn't. "Maybe it wasn't a stranger."

My mind whirled through the suspects. Gladys the Bitch came first, but could she pull off a good imitation of a male voice? Vernon? Why would he bother? Maybe someone on his campaign?

"Does Ruby have Caller ID on her phone?" he asked as he poured sweet tea from a jug Ruby had provided.

I took a sip. "No. Hey, she only got a push-button phone because her dial one broke last year."

"Hopefully he won't call back. If he does, press *69 to get the number of the last caller, then report it to the police."

"Good idea." I sat back and watched as Daniel ate roast, potatoes, and carrots. His eyes sparkled as he talked. How he pulled it off, I don't know, but he looked incredibly sexy under the fluorescent lights of the newspaper office.

We finished our desktop picnic, and Daniel took me down to the basement. "An appropriate place for the morgue," he commented. Elevator doors opened to a brightly lit floor with high shelves of boxed microfiche. The only differences between this floor and Daniel's office floor were that the shelves replaced the cubes and there were no windows. Or people. In a corner, several old computer terminals lined the walls. Our footsteps broke the silence.

"This is the morgue," Daniel announced.

"Smells like it," I quipped.

He motioned to the computer terminals. "Those CRTs are connected to the AS/400 that houses information on each back issue."

"Doesn't the public library have the same system?" I asked.

"Close, but we have a better index. You can search not only on dates, but also on names or keywords. Do you know Boolean structured queries?"

I smiled. "You're talking my language now. I've programmed computers in VB, COBOL, Java, C++, even in PASCAL; I can handle a simple query."

"The computer will return a code that corresponds to the shelf and bin where the microfiche is. The viewers are behind those shelves." He pointed to the far end of the room.

"Easy, easy stuff," I laughed. "No problem."

"Go to it, computer boy." Daniel patted my butt. "Come back up when you're done." He turned and disappeared into the elevator.

Silence amplified my breathing to a gusty breeze. I settled next to one of the old 5250 CRTs just like the ones I'd used on my first job out of school. *What was the date Walterene wrote that entry? Of course, I forgot to check, rushing out of the house to get here.* I searched for the name "Sams" and found nothing. Broadening the search to include anything with the letters SAMS didn't help—over sixty thousand entries returned. To get as specific as possible, I played with different combinations of queries: with a date range, the letters for SAMS, and keywords "obituaries" or "death" or "murder" or "suicide," I ended up with thirty hits. I printed out the list and headed for the shelves to gather the microfiche.

Once I found the first two, the codes made more sense to me. The first character in the code told me which area to search, the second character which aisle, the third, shelf unit, and so on until I located the box where the fiche was supposedly in chronological order. Since I'd have to return these to their proper position, I decided to view three, then return them and get the next three until I discovered... *Well, I'll know it when I see it.*

In the far corner away from the elevator, the microfiche machines sat in the shadows. Several light bulbs had been loosened in the ceiling's fluorescent lighting fixtures, allowing the machine users to better see the black and white images displayed on the screen. Loading the second issue into the machine and finding the correct page, I found only another dead-end. *This is going to be a long night.*

A door slammed somewhere on the basement floor. I whirled through the filmed pages, found my destination, and then stopped to read. The silence of the air around me wormed its way into my mind. *Where's the person who just came in the door?* No footsteps. No keyboard clicking. No shuffling through boxes. I turned to look toward the elevator and staircase, but all I could see was a forest of shelves. Maybe they'd turned and gone right back up the stairs. I dismissed it.

My third microfiche brought up nothing. I gathered the other two up and re-tracked back to their proper locations. I decided to pull ten of the issues to cut down on time spent roaming the maze of shelving. As I pulled down a box from the top of a corner shelf, a shadow moved in my peripheral vision, but when I turned to look I saw nothing. *You're paranoid,* I thought, moving on to the next fiche code on my list.

I couldn't hold the five microfiche rolls in hand and needed to drop them off at the reader station. Turning left, I hit a wall of shelving; to my right, I followed the path I thought I had taken, but again I came to a dead-end. "This is stupid," I said aloud, disgusted with myself. "How can a grown man get lost in a basement?" I decided to look at the labels on the shelves, to follow them back in the right direction.

"Damn it." I kicked a shelf. The index card labels on each unit didn't follow a logical order. 5SG came before 2WR, which was not right, and not how it had been five minutes before. "Okay, Daniel," I yelled, "the joke's over."

Silence.

"I see you switched some of the tags."

No response.

"I admit it; this isn't as simple as I thought." I heard my voice shake. I put the rolls of film down, and climbed one of the shelves to look over the top. Just as my foot left the floor, the lights went out. Blackness surrounded me. I could feel the cold metal of the shelf next to my cheek, but I couldn't see it.

The scratchy voice sounded as if he stood three feet away. "Die, faggot."

Chapter
Ten

THE VOICE RANG in my ears. I held my breath to try to hear his movements. The basement held a dead calm. No sounds except the thunder of my own heart pounding; I was positive he could hear the deafening beat hammering in my chest. I inched my way off the shelf, my foot searching for the concrete floor.

"No use running. I got you." The voice came from my right.

Inky blackness tightened around me. My hands groped and gripped invisible shelving to the left, away from the voice. I tried to slow my rapid breathing, quiet and deliberate.

My left foot trembled as I lifted it and listened, then took the next step. My right foot rubbed a shelf. Listening, I adjusted and positioned my foot down for another step. Then again, trying to take each step a little quicker. *A misstep could cost my life;* I froze in mid-stride at the thought.

I stopped to listen for him.

Nothing.

Feeling my way using the shelving, I slipped down the aisle. I reached the end of the row, hands out in front of me, searching for something to use as a guide. My hand hit a metal shelf with a thud. I froze.

The scratchy voice spoke again. "Where do you think you can go? No escape for you, faggot." He was still only a few feet away.

A seed of rage sprouted somewhere in the dark corners of my mind. *The son of a bitch isn't going to hurt me, not without a fight. A weapon; I need something to defend myself with.* I tried to think of anything useful to be found among the boxes and shelves, but I didn't know who or what I would be up against. Maybe he had a knife, a gun, a baseball bat.

My trembling hand fumbled the shelving again, quietly, and I followed it until it ended; another shelving unit was not in arm's reach.

Metal scraped across the concrete floor, from my left, about ten feet away. Was he trying to move one of the shelves? I waited for more movement. How could he see?

I checked my pockets for a weapon: cigarettes, lighter, pencil, car keys. I pulled the keys out of my front pocket. They clanged together in a frightening rattle.

Footsteps rushed toward me.

I tried to arrange the points of the keys between the fingers of my fist—a trick Emma had taught me—instant brass knuckles.

The full force of his solid weight hit my right shoulder. He let out a surprised grunt at our contact. We both plunged into a shelf and dropped to the hard, cold floor. I still had the keys clenched in my fist.

"Bastard, son of a bitch," I punched at the body on top of me.

His rough coat absorbed the blows. He grabbed my wrist and pinned it to the concrete floor. The odor of charcoal and cigarettes clung to his clothes, reminding me of a place, a place I had been recently, but I couldn't lock onto it. He tried to grasp my other arm.

I wiggled under him to stay free. His face pressed hard against my shoulder, each hand pinning my arms. One more of Emma's survival tips: I kneed his crotch with all the force and rage I could rally.

He rolled off me with a sharp yelp.

Grabbing the opportunity, I scrambled to my feet to run, but he gripped my right foot. I fell and kicked at the darkness until I hit something hard and solid, hopefully his face.

He released me.

With my hands groping in front of me, I found my way to a solid wall. *If I can just follow this to a door or a light switch...*Again, I stopped to listen for him, his breathing, his steps.

No sound came from the darkness around me.

I pressed my back against the cold wall and groped along no more than five feet before I felt a metal shelf abutted against the wall.

Damn. I retraced my silent steps; this time I traveled farther before finding another shelf blocking my progress. *Now what?* I hugged an outside wall, but the shelves boxed me into a dead end.

I slid down the wall to sit in the corner. Where was he? I strained to listen. A shuffling noise caught my attention. It came from somewhere out in front of me. He had to be on the other side of the shelves. *Maybe I can just wait him out?*

Boxes crashed, slamming onto the floor, microfiche scattering across the concrete with a squeal. Scrambling to my feet, I bolted out of the corner, climbing up a shelf and falling down the other side. Directly across from it, I hit another shelf, so I ran down the aisle, hands searching in front of me, away from the wall, hoping to find an exit. At the end of the row, I lost contact with the shelving, hands out, trying to find something in the blackness.

More boxes fell behind me, and I fumbled forward and discovered another solid wall. This time, I let my hand glide over the wall as I hurried to the left. I found a corner and swung around it and kept following the cold cinderblock wall.

A faint red glow in the distance welcomed my eyes as I tried to focus. An exit sign illuminated a stairway door.

Running at full speed, I didn't care about my echoing footsteps. I hit the metal door with force, slamming it back against the stairwell. Bounding up the steps two at a time, I ran up to the main floor; bright light spots and starbursts almost caused my eyes to miss the entrance to the lobby.

I burst through the door.

With surprise, the night watchman looked up.

"Someone," I panted, "tried to kill me!"

"What?" The old man came around his desk. "Calm down, son. What's going on?"

I tried to catch my breath, but couldn't. "In the morgue. Someone cut off the lights. Chased me."

He guided me to a chair. "Stay here. Let me take a look." He took the stairs down to where I had just come from.

I sat there watching the stairway door, wondering if I should go back down to help the night watchman. But my mind couldn't settle long enough to make a decision. Glancing at the elevator, I saw the floor indicator over the door light up the B. The sound of the motor told me it was moving up. Someone was coming from the basement.

The ding of the bell sounded, and the door slid open. Without willing it, I moved to the stairwell door, silently opened it, and crept inside, peering through the glass to see who got off the elevator. From my vantage point I couldn't see the elevator door for a potted ficus tree, but a shadow emerged.

He seemed to hesitate, then retreated back to the elevator.

I opened the door again as the bell dinged the door shut. Cautiously, I checked around the plant to see the elevator stop on the fourth floor. What floor was Daniel on?

I went behind the desk to look for a directory. *Which floor is he on?* Gendron, Groce, Herrin, Johnston, Kaperonis...*Fourth? That's where the elevator stopped.* My mind jumped to conclusions. *But why? Why would Daniel do something like that?*

HANDS STILL TREMBLING, I got off the elevator and looked around the cubicles. Two men and a woman stood in a small circle talking, laughing. Daniel's cube seemed quiet; I walked to it, but he wasn't there. His computer still showed his article on its screen, stopped in mid-sentence. I looked around for him. *No. No way. He couldn't; he wouldn't. Why would he?*

"Hey, you finished already?" Daniel's voice made me jump. He walked into the cube and sat down, smiling.

My eyes searched Daniel for signs from our struggle. Nothing out of place, no scratches, no bruises, no dirt or dust on his white knit shirt. I heard a sigh escape from my lips. *He couldn't have done it.* "I got run out," I said trying not to sound too scared, but failing.

"Run out? What do you mean?" he asked. His pursed eyebrows and the concern in his voice, reinforced his innocence.

"Uh," I started, "I was in the shelves collecting microfiche and the lights went out. I heard a voice, one I had heard before."

"Voice? Who?"

"Today, on the phone, someone told me to get out of town and that faggots don't belong here." I watched anger redden his face. "Then tonight, after the lights went out, I heard that same voice telling me he was going to kill me."

"What?" He leaned forward in his chair. "Are you sure? Are you okay? Did you see anyone?" he asked, running fingers through his thick hair.

"Daniel, he killed the lights; it was completely black down there. He chased me. I'm lucky I made it out."

He stood up, banging his chair into his desk. "I'm going down there."

"Hold on, I told the guard in the lobby. He went to take a look."

"What did he find?"

I felt stupid now for not waiting to see if he had found anything. "I came back without waiting around. I saw the elevator go from the basement floor to this floor, so I followed it."

"This floor? You think he's here?"

"I thought, at first, it might..." I looked down at my dusty shoes.

"Me? You think I would threaten you?"

"No," I corrected, "at first, for a split second—I just didn't think anyone here would know who I am."

He held my shoulders firm and looked square in my eyes. "Derek, I would never hurt you or threaten you. I don't want you to leave Charlotte; far from it, I want you to stay. I want you around as long as possible."

I felt his electricity move through his grip and sear my body. I wanted to hold him, to not let go, to feel safe in his arms.

"I'm going to check this out." Daniel headed toward the elevator, then stopped and looked at me. "It stopped on this floor? You'd better come with me."

Once the elevator doors closed and we had privacy, I wrapped my arms around him. "Thanks for not thinking I'm crazy."

He returned my hug. "You aren't crazy, just a little queer." He winked and laughed.

"Funny. Is that Charlotte gay humor?" I bumped his chest with my shoulder.

"Just trying to lighten up the moment." He pressed the lobby button and then the basement floor button. "I want to check with Harold to see if he found anything in the morgue. You can stay there in the lobby while I check the basement."

"No way. I'm going with you."

The doors opened to the lobby. Daniel walked around the corner to the front desk while I held the elevator. He came back. "Not there. Maybe he's still downstairs."

We rode down to the bottom floor. When the door opened, the florescent lights illuminated the floor like mid-day. I searched the rows of shelving, looking for evidence of the struggle, overturned boxes, scattered microfiche, but I found nothing. Everything seemed to be in perfect order. *Where was I?*

"Harold, you down here?" Daniel called.

I glanced back to see him checking the stairwell.

"Hey, Harold, it's Daniel, you here?" He closed the door. "Guess we missed him. We can check the front desk on our way back up."

Walking back to the work area with the terminals, I checked for any sign that someone had chased me. I found the terminals; all was in order, my notes still there. But, turning a corner I saw it. A shelving unit leaned against another; boxes and microfiche littered the concrete floor. "Hey Dan—"

"Derek, come here, quick." Daniel's urgent voice carried over the high shelves.

When I found him in a remote corner of the morgue, he squatted over the limp body of the night watchman.

"Run call 911, he's still breathing."

Chapter
Eleven

AFTER THE POLICE finished asking all their stupid questions, I turned to Daniel. "Is there any way this will stay out of the paper? I mean, here in the Observer building?"

"Everyone's already asking questions." He looked around at some of the other reporters who had gathered in the morgue. "The police record is open to us."

"Great, just what I need. More publicity. I want to go home." I turned to leave, but he didn't follow me.

"Harold will be fine. Don't worry about him." His voice slapped me.

I turned back to see pain in his eyes. "Sorry." Embarrassed, I tried to cover my selfishness. "I'm concerned about him, but you have to remember I was the one stalked and threatened; I—"

"All you think about is yourself. That's so like the Harris family." He turned and walked toward the elevator.

"Wait a minute. What upset you?" Anger boiled up in my throat. "Excuse me, but I did have my life in danger, maybe you wanted that to be me on the floor."

Daniel jerked around to look at me. "No. That's not what I mean. I just..." His voice trailed off. Swallowing hard, he bit his lower lip. "I'm worried about you. Why would anyone want to hurt you?"

"You mean besides being Charlotte's token faggot?"

Daniel turned away from me.

I knew my words had hit him hard. "I didn't mean it was your fault."

"But," he said without looking at me, "this wouldn't have happened if not for my article."

I didn't have the strength to try to comfort him. The voice of the stalker haunted my mind; I needed to be back at Ruby's, somewhere, anywhere I might feel safe. "Daniel, let me know how he's doing."

Facing me again, he asked, "Do you want me to drive you

home?"

"No, thanks. I'll be fine." I pushed my way through the police officers and newspaper workers, glad to be leaving the morgue alive.

I DIDN'T TELL Ruby what had happened; instead I headed straight to bed. "Be sure to lock up," I called with my toothbrush in my mouth.

"What?" Ruby yelled back.

"Make sure you lock the doors."

"Honey, those doors are always locked." She appeared in the bathroom doorway. Her crimson curls corralled in a hairnet, an emerald quilted housecoat wrapped tightly around her buxom form, for some reason she brought to my mind Miss Kitty from *Gunsmoke* reruns. "You okay?"

"Yes, ma'am." I rinsed the toothpaste out of my mouth. "The newspaper article makes me a little nervous."

"A lot has happened since yesterday morning." She handed me a towel. "Don't worry about a thing. Walterene and I have a Peter Beater under the bed."

"A what?" I watched her go to her bedroom, crouch, and pull a baseball bat from under the bed.

She held it with both hands as if ready to bash the lamp. "My Peter Beater. Any man who tries to get in here will get his peter beat with this bat."

I winced and grabbed my crotch. "Invited men get to keep theirs, right?"

"Don't worry about your little thing."

"Hey!" I protested her choice of adjective.

"Nothing will happen to us with this nearby."

I pushed the bat down to her side and kissed her cheek. "Goodnight, Wonder Woman."

BEFORE BREAKFAST, I decided to take a run around the neighborhood. The cool breeze and brightening sunshine would cleanse the memory of the past night. I wished it had been a dream. Picking up the *Observer* from the driveway and scanning its pages for any mention of the incident in its own basement, I found nothing and set the paper inside the door for Ruby. "I'll be right back," I yelled to the kitchen. "I'll only run a couple of miles around the neighborhood."

"Don't go too far. Breakfast will be ready soon," Ruby replied.

Closing the door, I stretched in the driveway. Several cars and a school bus drove by—Friday morning rush hour in Sedgefield. I jogged up Wriston Place under the sheltering branches of oaks and elms, their new spring leaves bright in the rising sun. Their roots had buckled the old sidewalk, so I kept my focus on my path. The street ended at Dorchester where Saint Paul's Methodist Church kept a steady eye on the neighborhood. Beyond its steeple, the Bank of America tower presided over downtown Charlotte's skyline. Jogging over to Poindexter, I cranked up my speed to a steady run.

More cars traveled Poindexter, so I made sure I stayed on the sidewalk. *One week*, I thought, *one week and all this shit has come down*. Walterene's funeral had been bad enough, but seeing Mark made being back harder than I expected—although Kathleen had turned out to be okay. How would she react if she knew?

My mind went back to those summers with Mark home from Duke. His sister Margaret was married and out of the house, so was Mike. Aunt Irene and Uncle Vernon never seemed to be at home, so Mark and I would sit on the back porch of Vernon's Queens Road mansion and drink beer and smoke pot, and talk. We talked forever on those humid nights; he told me about college and how he wanted to travel around the world. The plan we made was that he would graduate and get a job somewhere in the Northwest, maybe Oregon. Then, he'd build a cabin in the woods—a Harris dream always included building something. As soon as I graduated from high school, I'd join him. There, we could be free from our parents and be together.

As I neared South Boulevard, I stopped to catch my breath. Hands on my hips, I walked and sucked air; sweat rolled down my face. *Got to stop smoking so much.* Looking back down the road I had just traveled, I decided to walk a little more, and then broke into a jog back toward Ruby's house.

Oregon, shit. I laughed out loud at the thought. Mark was all talk back then; he still was. He'd fallen into line when his time came, just like everyone else.

The city skyline rose above the oaks and elms as I ran down Poindexter, and I wondered if he was in his office this morning. As soon as I pictured Mark working at his desk, Daniel's image overtook my mind. I smiled. *I'll call him when I get back.*

My thighs ached, and my stomach cramped as I hit the distance when I knew the run was doing me good. Approaching Dorchester again, I decided to stay on Poindexter to extend the run. I liked the little brick houses and jade green yards of Walterene's and Ruby's neighbors. Azaleas bloomed thick and bright while tulips drooped their heavy heads; oaks stretched across the road to touch branches with elms; maples pushed their own bushy branches into the canopy as if they where missing out on what the bigger trees had going.

These oaks are massive. Mr. Sams' oak. The thought almost tripped me. That poor man, hanged from that tree outside Ruby's door. I tried to imagine Vernon and Mother, Walterene, Ruby, Edwina and Roscoe, and the various other cousins living in this town that Grandpa Ernest ruled from behind his desk. Did they lynch him?

I stopped running in front of a towering pin oak. Maybe the newspaper article had nothing to do with last night; maybe the scratchy-voiced man wasn't a gay-basher, but knew that I knew about Mr. Sams. Had he said anything about Mr. Sams? No, but a killer wouldn't reveal his motive to his victim, would he?

"I was there looking for information on him," I explained to no one as I walked and caught my breath. "If they did have something to do with his murder, it couldn't come out now, not with Vernon's campaign in full force." A woman jogged past me, and I smiled at her, but kept on talking to myself. "Who knows what I know?" I took a step for each name, "Ruby, for sure; Mother? Valerie? Mark? Vernon? No I haven't mentioned this to any of them, unless Ruby has told them."

I began to run again. The low rumble of a car approaching from behind caught my attention. Turning onto Sunset Road where there was no sidewalk, I stayed to the right. The car still followed me. *Go ahead and pass me, dickhead.* I jogged closer to the curb. *Why is he following me?* Not wanting to look back at him, paranoid thoughts clouded my mind. I looked for other people along the street. No one. I was alone on the street, and a strange car followed me. From the corner of my eye, I saw the dark car creep up beside me.

I looked for an escape.

"Excuse me," a squeaky voice said.

Terror strangled me.

An elderly woman asked from the passenger side window of the Chevy sedan, "Can you tell me how to get to Park Road?"

Letting out the breath I had held, I almost laughed at myself. Squirrelly fear mocked my usual reason. After pointing them in the right direction and looking around to gauge how far I was from Ruby's house, I turned and ran back.

"GET IN HERE," Ruby scolded. "Your breakfast is getting cold."

I went straight to the sink for a glass of water. After gulping it down, I asked, "Who knows about how Mr. Sams was killed?"

Ruby stopped dishing out eggs in mid-spoon. "Who said he was killed? People said it was suicide."

"Walterene's diary said it was a lynching."

"She wrote that because she was mad when he got fired. Looking back now, I'm sure it was a suicide." She shook her head as if to get rid of the memory. "Now, why are you thinking about a thing like that on this beautiful morning?"

"Who else knows about him?" I asked.

She sat my plate on the table and shooed me toward it. "Eat before it's cold."

"Who else?" I asked again.

"Well, everyone," she sighed. "He was Papa Ernest's gardener for years. We all grew up with him there."

I considered it. "Who knows I know?"

Ruby leaned back in her chair and sipped her coffee. "I mentioned it to Valerie and your mother."

"When? When did Mother find out?"

"Wednesday night when you were at your young man's house." She winked at me. "Gladys called while Valerie was here. I told her you had a nice time at Mark and Kathleen's house, and she asked what else you had been doing. I didn't want to tell her about your young man, so I told her we had been talking about family.

"She wanted to know what I had said about the family. She's so odd about that. But I told her we talked about Walterene and Mr. Sams giving her the stuffed elephant. Gladys got all huffy about me telling you anything, so I hung up on her." Ruby smiled.

If Mother knew, then Vernon knew. Would he have someone try to scare me away? How much did Mark know?

Chapter
Twelve

"I'M GLAD YOU called." Mark shook my hand as we walked into his office. "I ordered lunch. It should be here in a few minutes." The room we entered reminded me of old-money San Francisco. The walls were paneled in mahogany and trimmed with brass. Small gold tiles with the Harris Construction big H logo were embedded in the conference table. Persian rugs covered the marble floor, and the scent of leather from the couch and chairs mingled with Mark's spicy cologne.

I took a deep breath; memories of us surged in my brain. "Nice view," I commented as I walked to the wall of glass to the left of his desk. The sky's cyan blue contrasted with the brown-rose stone and aqua windows of Wachovia's jukebox-shaped building; clumped behind that arched structure stood its brother tower of the same stone and glass but crowned with slanted clear glass panels that created prisms of sea blue and emerald green in the sunlight. In front of me and beyond the bank, Duke Energy's squat tan concrete and Ericsson Stadium's silver and deep blue underscored the distant airport and its swarming 737s.

Mark placed his hand on my shoulder from behind me. I shuddered. His hand rubbed the back of my head. "Your hair is so short."

"Yeah," I said turning to look at him, but he kept his hand there. "I wanted to—"

Pulling me closer, he kissed me. My mind exploded with confusion, desire, anger, and pleasure. I didn't pull away.

He stepped back. "I've been thinking—"

"What the hell was that?"

"Hold on," he smiled. "Seeing you again has brought up old feelings."

"Feelings?" I couldn't think. "What about—What about Kathleen? What about your future? What about the family?"

"Whoa, Derek. I just kissed you. I missed that; in fact, I've wanted to do it since I first saw you." He sat down on the couch with one arm draped across the back.

Choosing the chair across from him, I asked, "Are you saying you're gay now?"

"Just because a man kisses another man doesn't mean he's gay."

I laughed out loud. "It's a damn good indication."

"I'm open, fluid, maybe," he smiled, "in my attractions."

"Why are you telling me this? What's changed?" I hadn't decided if I should be happy or pissed off by his display.

"I just didn't want you to think we were over." Mark sat forward on the couch. "We can still get together like old times, if you want."

"Have you developed multiple personalities? What is this shit? Just two days ago in your father's campaign office, you were as straight as he is."

Mark bit his lower lip. "That's professional, political; this is me."

"And Kathleen and your reaction to the newspaper article?" Daniel flooded my mind.

"Again, I have parts of my life that are separate."

"Have you been having other," I searched for the right word to use, "relationships behind Kathleen's back? That can be dangerous to the 'other parts' of your life."

"Honestly? No. The risk has been too much, but you know me; you know how it is, and what's at stake."

I finally got it. "So, I'm your whore. The safe lay who knows to keep it a secret."

Marks face flushed. "No, that's not it."

"I know a fuck-buddy proposition when I hear it. No, Mark, that's not what I want. I'm a person who wants respect and love, not something hidden in the shadows that is never mentioned because of shame." I stood up and walked back to the window. Even after what he had proposed, I knew it would be difficult to tell him about Daniel. "Besides, I met someone here in Charlotte; someone I like a lot."

He came to me. "Who? Damn, you just got here a week ago." There wasn't anger in his voice; he was almost acting like a friend.

"A guy named Daniel. He works for the *Observ*—" I stopped myself, but it was too late.

"That reporter? The one who wrote the story?"

"Yeah, but he didn't mean for it—"

"Derek, what the hell are you thinking?" He plopped back down on the couch.

Before I could answer, the secretary knocked on the door and brought in a tray of food. "Lunch," she announced. In a half curtsy, she gently laid the tray on the conference table and placed the plates and drinks.

Mark and I were silent in her presence.

She finished her preparation and smiled. "Will there be any-thing else, Mark?"

"No, thanks, Becky." He walked to the table and sat down.

Becky closed the door behind her.

"Come, eat," Mark commanded.

"Daniel didn't mean to stir up trouble for me," I started. The plates of grilled chicken pasta and glasses of sweet iced tea looked enticing—new Charlotte meets old Charlotte, sweet tea served with everything.

"Forget Daniel Kaperonis for a minute," he said. "I hear you had a little trouble at the Observer building last night."

I froze. What? How did he know? *Could he be the one?* Compos-ing myself as he stared at me, I knew he waited for me to admit or deny it. "Yes I did. In fact, I find it interesting that you know. Was it one of your goons?"

"Goons?" he laughed. "No, I don't have goons."

I drank some tea. "Having my life threatened and being assaulted isn't something I find funny."

"I'm sorry, but the story I heard was that you got locked in the basement by accident, and someone turned off the lights, then you ran into a bookcase and panicked." He grinned like it was all some big joke.

"Well, Mister Harris, your sources are wrong. My life was threatened. A man called Ruby's yesterday and told me to get out of town, and that faggots weren't welcome here. Now, in my book, you are part of the faggot family too, so don't act so smug."

The grin left his face.

"Then last night, when the lights went out, I heard the same voice telling me he was going to kill me. How would you like to be in pitch black and have someone come up behind you, saying that?"

He dropped his fork on his plate as if shocked. "Are you sure someone was actually there?"

"Mark, he tackled me to the ground; I barely got away. I've got the bruises to prove it. That asshole put the security guard in the hospital."

He sat back and shook his head. "I can't believe it. I'm sorry, that's not what I heard; I thought it was your imagination going wild. Just you being a drama queen."

"Drama queen? Where the hell did you hear that term?"

"I watch television. I know how gay men talk."

I laughed in spite of myself. "You are too much." My mind clicked back on the subject. "How did you hear about last night?"

"Charlotte's a small town at heart. I hear a lot of things." He picked at his pasta, thought a moment, and then asked, "Who do you think it was?"

"You tell me. You seem to know quite a lot. Back to my question: Was it one of your goons?" I watched his face for the truth.

He didn't falter. "No. I had absolutely nothing to do with it."

"What about Vernon?"

"Dad? No way. You couldn't do anything to hurt Dad's campaign. The gay issue is a non-issue."

I wasn't sure if I believed him on that. "But, what about Mr. Sams?" I watched him again for signs of recognition.

"Who?" he asked, obviously oblivious.

"Our great-grandfather's gardener. He was lynched?"

He shook his head. "I don't know what you're talking about."

"I found some of Walterene's old diaries..." The words flowed out: Mr. Sams' death, Vernon's possible involvement, and the research I had attempted in the basement of the Observer building. A dam had burst. Relief washed over me now that I didn't have to keep everything to myself.

He rubbed his forehead and pushed his plate away from him. "That's insane. Dad would never do anything like that, and I can't believe Papa Ernest would either."

"I would like to think that, but I can't get by his bigotry—"

"Derek, you're talking murder; worse, you are talking a lynching of a black man, I can't—"

A hurried knock at the door interrupted him. Becky came rushing in. "Sorry, but it's Allen Harding again. Gary's on his way up to talk to you."

"Thanks, Becky. Show Gary in as soon as he gets here." Mark went to his desk and dug through papers. Becky cleaned up lunch.

"I guess I better go." I helped Becky with the plates.

"Sorry, Derek, but Allen Harding is a pain in my ass. He's threatening to sue the company for firing him; he claims we cut corners on codes and paid off building inspectors. If we don't settle, he says he'll go to the city, county and state inspectors to report us."

As Becky closed the door behind her, I walked over to his desk. "Did you?"

"Hell no, but this type of publicity would be far worse than a gay nephew for Dad's campaign. Those diaries of Walterene's were written when she was just a girl; who knows what really happened? It isn't possible that things happened that way." He stopped his search through papers and pulled me close to him. "Derek," he whispered, "what we talked about today goes no farther than here. I admit I'm jealous of you seeing someone, but I'm not willing to make the sacrifices to get to where you are with your life."

"Mark, don't worry. You're always safe to talk to me about anything." I hugged him hard.

Becky's crisp knock on the door brought in Gary from the legal department. I excused myself and walked down the hall to the elevator.

Our history, our lives bound us like brothers; he needed someone to be himself with. I had loved him once, and I had to admit I still had strong feelings. His split personality confused me, but one side would eventually win the conflict, and I was betting desire trumped duty.

BEFORE I LEFT the building, I decided to drop in on Tim. Searching the electronic directory, I found "Tim Mason, vice-president." *Impressive for a big dickhead like my brother*, I thought.

Tim's office was considerably smaller than Mark's and on a lower floor. He had no secretary, so I knocked on his open door.

"Squirt," he yelled from behind his desk, "get your butt in here."

"Hey, Tim. I thought I might just drop in to say 'hello.'" I held out my hand to shake his.

"What's up with the handshake?" He grabbed me in a bear hug. "Come sit down and visit." He dropped back down in his chair and kicked his feet up on the desk. "It's Friday afternoon, and the weekend's calling my name."

"You sure are in a good mood," I commented. On his wall hung his fraternity paddle and an autographed photograph of Charlotte's good ol' boy radio team, *John Boy and Billy.*

"Fridays mean I get out of this hellhole for a couple of days; you bet your ass I'm in a good mood." He grinned and shot a rubber band across the desk at me.

"You don't like working here?" I shot the rubber band back at him.

"It's a job, and I get paid well, but Vernon doesn't let me do much with the commercial side—that's where the big deals are. That's reserved for Mike, Mark, and Gerald."

"Gerald?" I asked. "How does Margaret's husband get better assignments than you?"

"Son-in-laws outrank nephews."

I almost repeated Daniel's rumor about Gerald running around on Margaret, but decided better of it. "What about that development you're doing out past Ballantyne?"

He straightened up in his chair and smiled. "You remembered that? Shit, Laura doesn't even remember my projects."

"You mentioned it at Walterene's funeral, said it was big."

"Yeah." He leaned back. "That residential development could make me millions."

"Don't you mean, make the company millions?" I prodded.

He leaned forward. "I get a percentage, that's part of my salary."

"Now, Tim, I wasn't implying anything else."

"Shit," drawn out in three syllables, "I keep my nose clean. I'll prove to Vernon that I can do just as well as Mike."

"What about Mark? How does he do?" I wondered how other people saw him.

"Pretty boy? He walks on water in Vernon's eyes, but he never gets his hands dirty in the actual building business like me. Hey, you had dinner the other night at his place. What do you think about that hot little number he married?"

"Kathleen doesn't do a thing for me," I winked at him.

"Oh, yeah," he laughed, "I almost forgot the gay thing." He pulled up a company directory on his computer. "There's a guy in accounting who's gay, you want to meet him?"

"No, but thanks for thinking about me."

"That's okay. How's Ruby holding up?"

"I've seen her crying from time to time, but overall, Valerie and I are keeping her busy."

Tim scratched his head. "Yeah, that's tough for her; those two old maids depended on each other all their lives. I just hope Val doesn't end up like that."

"Valerie seems to be doing well for herself," I said, but I wondered if she was really happy; I hadn't had much time with her alone to talk about her state of mind.

"Yeah," Tim agreed.

"Yep," I couldn't think of much else to say to my brother, so I started to stand. "I better let you get back to work."

"Okay. Oh, has Mom said anything to you about Dad?"

The visual in my mind of Gladys the Bitch and me talking made me cringe. "No. What about Dad?"

"He's retiring and there's a party tomorrow night. You going?"

Damn her. "I wouldn't miss it. Do you think it would be okay for me to bring a date?"

Tim grabbed the phone. "You want me to call Jonathon in accounting?"

"No, I'll get my own, thanks."

I DROVE TO the Observer building to see if Daniel was in. Chills prickled my neck as I stood in the lobby waiting for the receptionist to call Daniel. He wasn't at his desk, so I decided to call him later.

Back at Ruby's, I asked her about Dad's retirement party.

"I haven't heard anything about it," she admitted. She folded her newspaper and set it next to her chair. "Of course, I'm not on everyone's guest list."

"Call Valerie. She should know about it." I wanted to go; why, I wasn't sure. Maybe to ruin Gladys' party, maybe to prove to everyone I was part of this family, or maybe just to see my father. He wasn't the most forceful man, especially with Gladys, but he'd always loved me. I knew that. The day Gladys the Bitch had banished me to Virginia, Dad had stuffed a note into my coat pocket. I found it once I settled into the dorm. He made sure I had his office phone number and a credit card. I never used the card, but knowing it and my father were available for me helped during some lean times.

Ruby punched in Valerie's work number and handed me the phone.

"Hey, Val, it's Derek. I saw Tim today, and he mentioned Dad's retirement party. Am I invited?"

"Well, it's not my party to invite... Yes, you are. It's tomorrow night at eight o'clock, 40th floor of the tower. You want to go as my date?" she asked.

I thought of Daniel and what a great spectacle we would make, but I didn't want Valerie to go alone. "That would be wonderful. What about Ruby? She didn't—"

"No, Derek, no," Ruby waved her hands at me. "I don't feel like any parties."

"Never mind," I told Valerie. "She's not up for it."

We made our plans, and I told her we would talk again the next morning. Those were my Saturday night plans, but I wanted to spend some time with Daniel. I called him at work to see if we could have dinner. His voicemail picked up.

"Hey Daniel, this is Derek. Just wondering if we could have dinner tonight. I'd love to see you." I left him Ruby's number and hung up.

She smiled at me. "You really like him, don't you?"

"Sure. Last night was hectic with him working and me, well, I spent some time looking at old newspapers." I didn't want to worry Ruby over my near-death experience. "But, I would like to spend some quiet time getting to know him better."

I WAITED. THE phone didn't ring. As the afternoon wore on, I checked the phone to make sure it still worked. I considered calling again, but thought it would look too desperate. Finally, about five o'clock, I called his house to leave the same message.

I waited. The phone didn't ring. Ruby and I decided to fix dinner for ourselves. Was he mad at me? Maybe he had a deadline. Maybe he had been kidnapped by the scratchy-voiced man. He'd better have a damn good excuse.

Chapter
Thirteen

THE NEXT MORNING I still had not heard from Daniel. I considered calling him again, but thought I would let him make the next move. As Ruby and I finished breakfast, the phone rang. I almost knocked Ruby off her chair getting to it. "Hello?" I answered the ring.

"Hi, Derek." Valerie's greeting disappointed my ears, which were tuned for the tenor of Daniel's voice. "Do you have a suit to wear for tonight?"

"I only brought the one I wore to the funeral. It's a little dark for a retirement celebration."

"Oh, that will be fine," Valerie assured. "I was a little nervous about getting you and Mother in the same room, but this morning it seems like a great idea."

I felt a devilish smile creep upon me. "It's a perfect idea."

"I'm going to get my hair done for tonight. I'll stop by and let you and Ruby see the transformation later this morning." She seemed almost giddy with excitement.

"You're wound up about this party, aren't you?" I asked.

"It's for Dad. It's his night. He's worked all his life to make a better life for us, and I'm happy he's finally going to get time to rest and enjoy himself." Right, as always, she knew the base reason for any event, and that was what she focused on. It could have been the sinking of the Titanic, and Valerie would have talked about the passengers who made it to New York; she never focused on the distractions. I guess that single-mindedness makes a good accountant. I, on the other hand, loved the sub-layers that flow under the surface. My mind couldn't stay focused on the main point. I couldn't wait to see Gladys the Bitch's face when I walked in, or how Mark would react with both Kathleen and me there, or if Tim would behave himself after a few drinks.

"You're right, Val," I said. "It's Dad's night. I'm glad we'll all be there."

I hung up the phone and decided to call Daniel. The phone rang until the answering machine picked up. "Hey, Daniel, it's Derek. I just wanted to say 'Hello,' and see if you wanted to get together sometime. I have a party to go to tonight, but I would love to see you this afternoon or tomorrow." Running on too long, I summed up, "Anyway, call me; I—"

"Hello? Derek?" He picked up the phone. His voice sounded hoarse.

"Well, I knew if I talked long enough, you would eventually get home."

"Just getting out of the shower," he explained.

The mental image of him naked and dripping on the other end of the line made me feel uncomfortable in front of Ruby. Of all the campy things that went through my head, all I came back with was: "Need any help?"

He laughed. "Yeah, come on over."

"You serious?"

His husky voice purred in my ear, "I'll leave the door unlocked, come on back to the bedroom."

"I'm on my way."

The phone cord hadn't stopped swinging before I grabbed my keys and opened the door. "I'm going over to Daniel's to help him with a project," I called to Ruby as I slammed the door shut.

HE LEFT HIS front door unlocked as promised. I walked into the front room; the closed window shades allowed a few rays of sunlight to stream through, but for the most part, the house was cool and dark. I stayed quiet, playing into the mood he had set.

I glanced around the room; the quiet stereo, the blank television, the still computer, the folded Saturday *Observer* appeared as if no one was there. The dark hallway beckoned me with the enticement of Daniel at the other end.

I pulled my shirt over my head and unzipped my jeans when the thought hit me: *Was that really Daniel's voice on the phone?*

A shiver slid up my body. Dark visions of the *Observer's* morgue invaded my brain. Had I seen his car out front? My mind blurred. A rustling sound came from the back bedroom.

Without taking another step down the hallway, I tried to look into the room. Shadows shrouded everything beyond the doorway. Sweat trickled down my chest, chilled by the cold breeze of the air conditioner.

Pulling my shirt back on, I inched closer for a better look. Someone lay in the bed, covered with a sheet; his face, turned away from the door, didn't give me the opportunity to identify him as Daniel or not. How horny was I? Enough to risk the possibility that this was the scratchy-voiced man waiting to ambush me?

I moved forward.

Far enough away to run, I ventured calling out to the person, "Daniel?"

He rolled over onto his back and pulled the sheet off.

Yep, that's Daniel. I smiled at the silhouette on the bed.

"SO, WHAT PARTY are you going to?" Daniel handed me a glass of tea and crawled back into bed.

I leaned against his shoulder and sipped the iced tea. "My father's retirement party. Oh, do you have a tie I could borrow? The one I brought for the funeral is too gloomy."

"Sure, I have a closet full. I was thinking that maybe we can get together tomorrow," he offered. "I thought we could drive up to Asheville for the day."

Sunday. For some reason, I felt I had an obligation. My life, my job, San Francisco... "My return flight is tomorrow. I changed it from last Wednesday to tomorrow." I didn't want to leave, not just yet.

He sat up. "Can you change it again for later in the week, or maybe next week, or..."

"Cancel it altogether?" I finished the idea for him.

"Well, yes, I don't want to put pressure on you." He thought for a moment. "No, forget I said it. You do what you need to do."

"We could e-mail each other, talk on the phone, visit..." I knew if I left, that would be the end of this relationship. He seemed to realize it, too.

I wanted more time: time to really know Daniel, time to reconnect with Valerie and Ruby, time to find out if Vernon had helped lynch a man, and if so, stop him from becoming a senator.

"I've got more vacation time," I said. "Where's the phone?" I crawled over him and grabbed the phone book and phone. Extending my return trip a week wasn't difficult, but we both knew it was just delaying the inevitable separation.

VALERIE ARRIVED TO pick me up for the party at 7:30. Her dark hair framed her face in soft wisps; her make-up took ten years off her appearance, and her simple cobalt dress showed off her shapely figure.

"You look amazing," I yelled.

Her cheeks bloomed with color. "Miracles can happen, that is after $130 for hair and make-up and $120 for a new dress."

"Stop being an accountant," Ruby teased. "You look great, just say thank you."

"Thanks," she beamed. "Derek, you look pretty good yourself. New tie?"

"Borrowed," Ruby answered for me, "from his young man."

My turn to beam. "Yes, this is Daniel's tie." I had picked a yellow silk with a pattern of pale green vines and burgundy grapes.

Ruby grabbed her camera and stood us against the fireplace for pictures.

WE ARRIVED DOWNTOWN and took the elevator from the parking deck to the fortieth level. The executive dining room covered half the floor; a podium towered on a stage with long tables flanking its sides. I whispered to Valerie, "Hope we're not up there on the stage."

"No, I think the executives and Dad and Mom are up there. Let's find our name cards." She guided me through the small crowd.

"Looks like there are more tables than people," I said.

She glanced around. "Supposed to be about eighty people; it's still early." We found the place cards: Valerie Mason and Guest.

Tim and Laura's place cards were at our table too, along with several other names I didn't recognize. I scanned the room for Mark.

Kathleen appeared first. She held herself with the air of royalty, gliding from group to group like an experienced hostess. In a corner, I spotted Mark talking to his brother Mike and sister-in-law Sheila; they laughed and sipped their drinks. No sign of Dad or Gladys the Bitch. Knowing her, she would keep him out of sight until everyone had arrived so she could make a grand entrance.

"Derek," Kathleen called as she crossed the room. She slid up to us in a whiff of Neiman Marcus' Eaude. "I'm so glad you made it." She hugged me with strong arms. "Valerie, you look fantastic. Where did you get that dress? It's beautiful."

Valerie giggled at the attention. "Belk at Southpark."

"I'll get us some drinks." I excused myself from the girl talk. I wanted to avoid Mark, at least for now. Tim and Laura arrived, so I made my way to them.

"Squirt," Tim laughed. I walked up to him, and his bear hug gripped me again.

I smiled at Laura; she looked as if she had just caught the scent of a sweaty Frenchman. "Hello, Laura, good to see you again."

"Derek," she acknowledged. She looked around, saw something apparently very interesting, and walked away.

"She's so warm and friendly," I winked at Tim.

"I want a girl, just like the girl that married dear old Dad," he sang.

"So, it's not just me?" I asked.

"Nope, Laura and Mom are two of a kind. Where's the beer?" He pulled me toward the bar.

Mark caught my eye as Tim and I ordered drinks. He smiled and started toward us. He had the confidence of a man who knew the room belonged to him; as he moved through the crowd, people shook his hand and slapped him on the back like he was the politician, not Vernon. I turned back to Tim. "You and Laura are seated at our table."

"You brought a date?" he asked.

I felt Mark's hand on my shoulder. "No, I came with Valerie."

"Hey guys." Mark, between us, had his other hand on Tim's shoulder.

This time, it was Tim who smelled the sweaty Frenchman.

Mark continued, "This is a wonderful evening for Uncle Thomas and Aunt Gladys; all the executives are here. He has been such a big part of the company; we'll really miss him."

"Another twenty-five years and that will be me." Tim chugged his beer.

I felt Mark rub my shoulder under his grip. "Tim, let me steal your little brother; I want to introduce him to a few people." Mark led me away.

"I need to drop this drink off with Valerie."

Mark followed me to Valerie and Kathleen; their group had grown to include Mark's mother, Irene. Kathleen grabbed Mark's arm as we joined the circle. "Mark, I have been looking for you for ages—Mom's wearing the pendant we brought her from Paris."

We all leaned in to look at Aunt Irene's chest. A hummingbird of multiple rubies and emeralds sparkled from her left tit; I immediately thought of the nipple rings popular in certain circles, and imagined Aunt Irene proudly modeling the hummingbird drooping from her nipple for a leather-clad Vernon.

I turned away to stifle a laugh. The women resumed their conversation. "I need another drink," I told Mark and headed back for the bar.

"Hold up, I'll go with you."

"You're sticking to me tonight. What's up?" I asked.

"I'm surprised you're here." He turned and shook hands with a gray-haired man as we passed.

"It is my father's retirement party; why wouldn't I be here?" I stopped to look at him. "Maybe, because I wasn't invited?"

"I didn't realize you would still be in Charlotte. Walterene's death has all of us forgetting our social graces. Forgive me for not getting you an invitation."

"Cut the sarcasm, Mark," I snapped.

His head bowed. "Sorry, I'm just feeling a little nervous with you here. I do better when we're alone. I'm sorry you're leaving tomorrow."

I smiled at him. "Leaving? No, I'm staying another week."

His face blanched. "I-I thought," he stammered, "you were flying out tomorrow."

"No, babe," I slapped his ass, "I'm staying for another week. At least."

Chapter
Fourteen

I LEFT MARK standing at the bar and made my way back to Valerie. The room had filled with people milling around, drinks in hand, bubbles of laughter rising from circles of Charlotte's elite—a sparkling spring night with me as the one little gray rain cloud invading the stars' shimmering sky. Valerie talked with a couple I didn't recognize as I approached.

"Derek," she introduced, "this is Jack and Sylvia Goldberg."

My God! I couldn't believe it. *Jews in the Harris Empire?*

"Jack works with Dad in the purchasing department."

In their late forties, Jack and Sylvia looked like brother and sister, but many long-time married couples act and look alike. "Nice to meet you both." We shook hands and took our seats. She looked like she was in better shape than he; she probably worked out regularly while he did the occasional golf outing. They both had dark hair with traces of gray and round, strong faces; they wore identical wire-rimmed eyeglasses. The glances and smiles shared between them led me to believe they deeply loved each other. *At least someone has a good marriage.* I grinned at Tim as he sat down without helping Laura with her chair.

A murmur flowed across the room, and Valerie said, "Look, there's Mom and Dad." We stood, and applause broke out as they walked to the stage to take their seats. Vernon led the way, shaking hands along the route; then came Dad with a wide grin on his face. Shorter than Vernon, he appeared friendlier. Maybe the friendly part came from his wide-set hazel eyes and the way he swung his arms when he walked. Vernon kept touching people, patting backs, shaking hands; he would make a great pickpocket. Gladys the Bitch followed Father, which surprised me; usually she made him follow her. She looked as tight and stiff as ever; I could have sworn I heard her squeak as she walked. Her eyes scanned the room without her head moving one inch; the rigid smile looked painted on.

I whispered to Valerie, "Did you tell her I would be here?"

"Yes," she admitted.

"You ruin my fun," I faked a frown.

Mark and Kathleen, Mike and Sheila, and Margaret and Gerald, Vernon and Irene's offspring and their spouses brought up the end of the line. The parade mounted the stage and took their seats. As if taking a cue from the royal family, we groundlings seated ourselves too.

Vernon stepped up to the podium to welcome everyone. He droned on and on about the company and the importance of family. Finally, he mentioned Dad and another round of applause broke out.

I watched Mark as his father talked. He kept his eyes on Vernon and nodded occasionally. He caught me watching him and grinned at me. I smiled back.

When Vernon announced dinner, a wave of excitement swirled through the room. Charlotte's society likes to honor one another, but they love to eat.

A brigade of handsome waiters served salad. Tim ordered another beer, and Laura shot him a disapproving look.

Apparently, Sylvia Goldberg noticed the tension building between my brother and his wife, so she focused on me. "Derek, do you work for Harris Construction?"

"No, ma'am. I work for a small start-up Internet company in San Francisco. I build Web sites, not buildings."

"Private or public?" Jack asked.

"Private, but we expect to IPO later in the year."

"That's exciting," Valerie said. "How many employees?"

"Some friends and I started it last year, but as of today, we've grown to fifty-four employees." Their attention amazed me; I didn't think they would be interested in my work.

"Do you enjoy the actual work of the company, or was the start-up the exciting part?" Jack asked.

I picked at a tomato and thought about it. "Honestly, I enjoyed the start-up of the company more than the day-to-day operations."

Tim joined in. "You could IPO and sell once the stock hits big, then start another company. The idea for a great business is the hard part."

"Yes, that's what is so amazing about your great-grandfather starting this company," Jack commented. "He was there for the beginning of the boom in Charlotte. He helped make this city what it is today."

The handsome waiters came back to replace our salad with prime rib. I thought about Papa Ernest working like I had to get his company started; could this have been the same man I read about in Walterene's diary? Where would he find the time to be part of the Klan, or maybe that was like being part of the Chamber of Commerce today? I looked up from my plate and caught Gladys the Bitch staring at me.

Her stiff smile had dimmed to a flat sour line.

I glanced at Dad; he smiled and winked back at me. I raised my glass to him. He laughed and raised his to me. Gladys jerked her head to look at him, but he joyfully kissed her cheek. She actually smiled at him for a second.

Valerie had seen the exchange, and squeezed my hand. "I'm so glad we're all here together."

"Me too," I admitted.

During the main course, conversation at the table lulled. Tim drank; Laura ignored us; Valerie and I talked with Mr. and Mrs. Goldberg.

"I have a question," I announced. "Back home, my friends have a dinner party game called Jung's Shadow."

Sylvia perked up. "As in Carl Jung?"

"Exactly," I said. "Carl Jung said everybody has a persona developed in childhood that projects to the world who they are, but there is also a shadow; a dark side where we put aspects of ourselves that don't fit our persona. You follow?" I looked at Tim and Laura to see if they would participate.

"Got it," Tim tapped his forehead.

I looked to Laura.

"Yes, I took psychology," she huffed.

"Okay, then, persona and shadow are complicated aspects of each person," I explained, "so, in order to make this work in a short time period, we'll each pick one face we show to the world, and admit one contradiction to that public image."

Valerie's brow furrowed.

"It's not that deep or difficult. Let me give you an example." I thought for a moment. "Say you're a priest who has taken the vow of poverty, but you love expensive cars."

"Okay," Valerie conceded, "you can start."

"My persona," I searched my mind for a good one to use, "is I'm independent and can take on the world, but," I realized this game was harder with my family present, people who had raised me, "but, I need people to be close to," I looked to Valerie, "people I know love me."

Tears came to Valerie's eyes.

"Aww," cooed Sylvia.

Even Laura smiled.

"Okay, okay, Val, your turn," I said, and took a sip of merlot. I glanced up at Mark; he and Kathleen seemed to be engaged in a lively conversation with his sister and brother-in-law. I focused back on my own sister and the game.

Valerie straightened up and said, "My persona is I'm an old maid—"

"Val," I scolded, "you're not."

"Yeah, she is," insisted Tim.

"But," she continued, "I have maternal feelings, and one day," she took a breath, "I'll be a mother."

Laura perked up. "Valerie, are you," she whispered, "pregnant?"

"Oh, no. I just want to be a mother one day." She looked at me, and I could see her eyes had welled with tears. She sniffed them back and said, "Okay, Sylvia, you go next."

Sylvia looked at Jack and smiled. "Well, I am a mother, and I guess that's the face I show the world, but I love to dance and travel, to have the freedom of a gypsy."

"Darling," Jack held her hand, "I didn't know that."

She smiled. "I'm saving it for us for when the kids leave for college. You go next."

Jack scratched his head and thought. "I'm a business man," he said with a shrug. "My shadow is I don't enjoy golf, I'd rather go camping on weekends."

Sylvia squealed, "We'll leave the kids at home next weekend and go to the mountains, sleep under the stars."

I loved how the game brought out things people didn't realize about each other. I nibbled on green beans, waiting for Laura or Tim to pick up next. Since neither volunteered, I pointed my fork at Tim.

"Okay, my persona is that," he picked up his beer, "I'm a good ol' boy, a womanizer, a dumb ass, but I'm smarter than most people think." He caught and held Laura's gaze. "I don't cheat on my wife; I never have."

All eyes turned to Laura; I knew Tim's drinking had brought out something that had been on his mind for a while, probably on Laura's mind, too.

Her stone face showed no emotion as her eyes darted back and forth. She looked like she was computing his honesty. Finally the calculation totaled, and the result was: "I believe you."

He kissed her cheek. "Now, it's your turn."

Since he had warmed up to her, Laura's iciness had melted. She thought for a moment, knitting her brow and twitching her nose. "My persona is I'm a bitch, but honestly, I'm not. That's just how to get things done in this town. When I'm nice to people, I feel like I get walked on."

"Oh, Laura," Valerie soothed, "you don't have to be that way with your family."

"Val, where do you think I learned it?"

I laughed in spite of myself. "She's got a point there."

WITH CHEESECAKE AND coffee served, Vernon took the podium again. He made a few remarks to honor Dad and mentioned the contribution of Gladys to Dad's career. Vernon also acknowledged Tim as an indispensable part of the company.

"Then, why am I not up on the stage with his boys?" Tim whispered across the table to me.

Finally, Vernon introduced Dad and presented him with a certificate and a crystal trophy to show the company's appreciation for his years of service. Vernon left him at the microphone. Dad smiled and looked across the room. "I'm so happy to see my family and friends here tonight."

I saw him glance down at a sheet of paper he had slipped out of his coat pocket.

"I want to thank my wonderful wife, Gladys, for her support and guidance. My children," he looked directly at me, "who are all here tonight. Tim, you are my legacy; Valerie, you are my joy; and Derek, you are my hope."

For the first time in my life, I felt part of the family. I wiped tears with my napkin and swallowed hard. I missed being around him.

Dad continued, "After all the years of working, now as an old man, I know that my wife and children are the most precious gifts the Harris family could ever give me. I honor the friendships I made during my years here; we have the best people in Charlotte working with us. The Harris name may be on the building, but it is the employees who make this company great. We are one big family.

"So, I leave the work to the younger men and women, knowing that they will take pride in giving our customers the best. Thank you all." With that, he turned to shake hands with Vernon and the boys. The crowd stood and applauded my father. Gladys embraced him as he returned to his seat.

Valerie pulled Tim and me to her in a hug, each of us a little misty over our father's tribute to us. He wasn't a man who verbalized his emotions, especially in public, and I was glad I had been there to hear it for myself.

AFTER THE PARTY, people lined up to congratulate Dad on his retirement. I watched as the line grew and decided to wait to talk to him in private; besides, Gladys the Bitch stayed by his side. She had shown rare emotion during the ceremony. *Could there be a crack in her wall?*

"We're leaving," Tim announced with Laura on his arm.

I hugged him and Laura good-bye; I couldn't remember if I had ever hugged Laura before. It felt like I had another sister, at least for that moment.

Valerie talked with a group of people while I nodded to the departing guests. I felt hands on my shoulders and turned to find Mark.

"The party went well, don't you think?" he asked.

"Yes, good turnout; I know he'll miss going to work each day."

Mark kept a hand on my shoulder as we talked. "Listen, it's still early; do you want to come over for a nightcap?"

"Thanks, but I need to get Valerie home. And check on Ruby." *What's up with the touching?* I thought. The man ran hot and cold; I couldn't figure him out.

"Okay," Mark rubbed my shoulder, "but we need to get together, soon. We still have some things to discuss."

"Yes," I agreed pulling away from his grip, "we need to sort things out."

Valerie joined us. "Hello Mark." She watched his eyes like a snake charmer. "Can I steal Derek away? These new shoes are killing me; I'm ready to go home and kick them off."

"Sure, Val," he said. "Derek, I'll call you tomorrow."

We waved to Dad on our way out the door.

"Mark sure takes an interest in you," Valerie commented while we waited for the elevator.

She doesn't know about our past... Or does she? "Well, you know Mark and I always hung out together. He's closest to my age of all the cousins," I rambled; the wine had made me chatty. I didn't look at her; I had a pact with Mark to keep our past relationship secret.

I dropped her off at her condo and headed down Park Road; the clear, warm night prompted me to roll down all the windows and open the sunroof. The breeze smelled of freshly cut grass. The comfortable feel of being part of a group, a family, wrapped around me in the night air—I smiled as I turned onto Poindexter, then onto Sedgefield.

Darkness covered Ruby and Walterene's house. The fact that Ruby hadn't left the porch light on surprised me, but I guessed she had turned it off out of habit when she went to bed. I remembered her "Peter Beater" and chuckled, then decided to honk the horn when I pulled in the driveway just to remind her I was coming in.

I closed the windows and sunroof, grabbed my suit jacket from the back seat, and locked the car. The oak's limbs spread over the driveway casting dark shadows around the porch. A movement in a boxwood caught my eye, probably just the neighbor's cat, or a squirrel.

I pulled out the key for the door. Something rough brushed my cheek.

I spun around and swatted near my face, making contact with...

something hanging from the tree limb? My mind snapped to the image of Mr. Sams, head slumped to one side, eyes open in an empty death stare, the limb sagging from his weight.

The rough scrape of hemp hooked under my chin, then I heard the thud of a heavy object falling to the concrete driveway. Pressure tightened around my neck. I grasped at my collar and jerked my tie loose, but I still felt the strangling sensation. The old oak's branches seemed to close down on me, blocking me from the safety of the house; I reached up and batted toward the suffocating limbs, pulled at the rope around my neck, imagined a phantom body lying limp in the driveway.

I tried to scream, but it caught in my throat, only a low *auggh* escaped. Dropping my keys, both hands fought off the thing suffocating me, holding my throat. My head drooped. A roar rose in my ears, and my knees buckled.

Chapter
Fifteen

STRUGGLING FREE, I scrambled up the porch stairs. The door knob wouldn't turn. *My keys?*

Back against the door, I struggled to see in the shadowy darkness. My elbow slid up the doorjamb, attempting to locate the doorbell to summon Ruby. Nothing moved in the yard or driveway. Finally, I felt the button with my elbow and jabbed at it.

I waited.

Leaves rustled in the oak; I scanned the limbs for a noose, something hanging from the tree—nothing. Was it a panic attack? The specter of Mr. Sams? My heart thundered in my ears, but I couldn't pick out any sound from inside the house; no lights flicked on to indicate that Ruby heard me. I hit the doorbell several more times. I surveyed the neighborhood for other signs of life; every dark house had black lifeless windows staring at me. A glint of silver caught my attention in the driveway—my keys.

Easing my way back down the four steps of the porch, I stayed alert, ready to fight. I stopped and glanced around the darkness. A shimmer of light hit the side of the house; headlights scanned the front yard as a car came to the stop sign at the corner. It turned and drove past the driveway. The encouragement of another person so close allowed me to run for my keys. As the taillights faded in the distance, I found the door key and headed back up the porch.

With a watchful eye on the dark shrubs and trees, hiding places for evil, I fumbled with the lock. I took a deep breath and steadied my hand; the door opened and I slid in, locking the deadbolt quickly behind me.

The blinds had not been closed in the den, and the television flickered with the late-night infomercials of faded celebrities. I walked into the kitchen to find a pitcher of iced tea sweating on the counter and a plate of half-eaten chicken in the sink. The brick Ruby used as a doorstop held the dining room door open. She always closed that door when it started getting dark. I eased through it and found the front door standing open. *Ruby!*

I ran back to the bedroom, "Ruby!" I yelled. "Ruby!" All the blinds hung open, no lights on, and her bed still neatly made. "Ruby!"

MY HAND TREMBLED as I dialed the police. "My aunt's missing."

"How long has she been gone, sir?" a mechanical-sounding dispatcher asked. She didn't realize the urgency of my call.

"I don't know. I just got home, and she's gone."

The dispatcher sighed. "And why do you feel this is an emergency?"

"Someone is terrorizing me, and now my aunt is missing!" I yelled.

"Sir, calm down and let me get the facts. What's your name?"

"Derek Mason. My aunt, Ruby Harris, is missing. The front door was open when I got home, and her dinner dishes are still in the sink. The lights were never turned on, the blinds weren't closed, and her bed hasn't been slept in. Someone kidnapped her."

The dispatcher answered with another question. "Is there anyplace she might have gone?"

"Oh, I don't know, it's almost one o'clock in the morning, maybe she went shopping," my sarcasm smacked back at her.

"Now, sir, there's no need to get smart—"

"Someone on this phone needs to be smart. She's in danger. I came home and there's something, probably a noose, hanging from the tree at the driveway! Someone was outside the house," a cold chill hit me, "probably inside the house, too. They got Ruby."

"Stay where you are. I'm sending a patrol car over. You're at 3003 Sedgefield Road?"

"Yes." Relief swept over me for a second, but I had to find her. "How soon will they be here?"

"Soon. Turn on your outside light and watch for them."

"Thanks." I hung up the phone, hesitated, then picked it up again and dialed. "Mark? It's Derek. Something's happened to Ruby..."

THE POLICE ARRIVED a few minutes later, no lights flashing or siren shrieking, just a tall older white man and a pretty young black woman. The man appeared to be in his fifties, heavyset and in charge. The woman, in her twenties, moved with assurance beyond her age. I let them in through the den door from the driveway. After going over the story again, Officer Gloria Blevins checked the front door while her partner, Officer Jack Hartford, inspected the oak tree for the noose.

"There are no signs of forced entry to the door," Officer Blevins reported to Hartford.

He nodded and looked at me. "There's a potted fern lying in the driveway; its macramé hanger is still on the limb. Is that your noose?"

"Could be." I rubbed my chin, embarrassed by almost being killed by a hanging planter. "Did you see anything else out there?"

"Nothing. I checked the front and back yards," Hartford said. "Could your aunt have gone to a neighbor's house?" He had his notepad out, writing.

"I don't know." I looked to the woman; hopefully, she would understand my concern. "Ruby wouldn't just leave the house open, her car here, the TV on, dirty dishes out."

Officer Blevins nodded. "Did you check the answering machine for messages?"

"Yes. Nothing there." *Should I call Valerie and let her know?* I didn't want to upset her, if there was no need.

"Do you know of family or friends who might know where she is?"

Most of the family had been at the party, and she hadn't spoken of many friends. "No," I sighed.

The doorbell rang, and Officer Hartford turned and opened the door. Mark walked in and took control.

"I'm Mark Harris. My cousin," he motioned to me, "called to tell me our aunt was missing. What's being done to find her?"

Hartford looked him straight in the eye, projecting his authority. "We're gathering information. Usually, a missing person will show up at a friend or relative's house. Since it's so late, it's probably best to wait until in the morning to start calling them." He looked at me. "You don't want to upset people in the middle of the night only to find her camped out on a neighbor's couch, do you?" The way he said this made it more a statement than a question.

Looking to Mark, then to Officer Blevins, finally back to Hartford, I said, "No, but this isn't like her. She's been gone for hours, apparently before sundown. If she were at a neighbor's, she'd be back by now. Mark?" I needed confirmation that I wasn't going crazy, that my concern was justified, that everyone should be doing more than they were doing.

Moving into the room and guiding me to sit on the couch, Mark addressed Hartford. "What more can we do? Derek is right; Aunt Ruby is in her sixties, and this isn't like her."

"Is she on any medication?" asked Officer Blevins.

Mark glanced at me for the answer.

"I don't think so." I searched my memory for images of her tak-

ing anything before meals or at bedtime. "No, no, she isn't on medication."

Hartford kept writing in his little notebook. "Any signs of
Alzheimer's in the past?" he asked. When neither Mark nor I
answered, he looked up from his scribbling. "Well? Forgetfulness,
losses of concentration, paranoia, mood changes, any of this ring a
bell?"

"No," I defended. "I was attacked a few nights ago at the
Observer Building. Tonight, a noose or something hung from that
tree outside. Ruby is missing because of that, not because of Alzheimer's!"

Officer Blevins asked, still calm, "Why do you feel someone is
after you?"

I glanced at Mark, but he kept his eyes on the police officers. "I
don't know." I tried to gather it all into a sentence that didn't sound
crazy. "There was an article in the paper this past week about me
being the gay nephew of Vernon Harris."

Hartford and Blevins exchanged a glance.

"And I received a threatening phone call." *Should I tell them my
suspicions about Mr. Sams' death? No, I'm not sure about that yet.* "The
same man assaulted me at the Observer, and now this. Ruby is in
danger—I know it."

Blevins asked, "Do you know who this man is?"

Taking control again, Mark spoke for me. "If we did, he would
be in jail right now."

The officers stood still in front of us. Hartford snapped his notebook shut. "If you hear from her, or from anyone claiming they
know where she is, contact me right away." He held out a card, and
Mark got up from the couch to take it.

He followed them out to their patrol car while I sat in a haze of
disbelief. *Why is everyone so cool about this? Do they think I'm lying?* I
heard the thud of the police car's doors slam and then Mark came
back in.

Closing and locking the door, he crossed the room to sit next to
me. His eyes looked tired; the clock on the mantel said a quarter
after two.

"Did the police say anything more?" I asked.

He leaned back and sighed. "Only that they don't think it was a
kidnapping—even with Dad running for the Senate. They think
she's staying overnight with a friend or—"

"But," I interrupted, "she wouldn't." The touch of a rope
around my throat tightened in my mind. "How do they explain the
noose hanging from the tree?"

With a gentle hand on the back of my neck, he said, "Derek,
there's no noose; it was just a hanging plant. Your imagination made

it into a noose."

My real concern clicked back to me. "I'm worried about Ruby."

"Me, too," he conceded. "There's not much we can do tonight." He got up, took my hand, and dragged me to my feet. "Come home with me."

I pulled loose from his grip. "No. Ruby might be back, or the kidnapper might call. I have to stay here."

"Okay, then I'm staying with you. I don't want you here alone." He picked up the phone and called Kathleen.

In the living room, I checked the door that had been left open; maybe he had forced his way in. I examined the front porch for any signs of a struggle, but the potted geraniums still lined the steps, not even the doormat had been disturbed. I stood on the bottom step looking out into the black night, wondering where Ruby was, and what was happening to her at that very moment.

MARK AND I locked up the house. He began turning off the lamps and kitchen lights; I insisted we leave the front and side porch lights on. "Just in case," I explained.

"We both need to get some rest." Mark pulled his shirt off and headed for the guest room, my room.

"Wait, that's where I sleep," I called after him.

"I won't bite," he teased. "There are only two beds. I wouldn't feel right sleeping in Ruby and Walt's bed. Would you?"

"No," I admitted. The thought of him in my bed didn't produce any sexual excitement, not after everything that had happened, but it did give me the security of having another human close to me. "Okay, you can stay." I kept my boxers on, and climbed into bed next to him.

Mark patted me on the shoulder, "Good night," and turned off the bedside lamp.

"'Night," I replied. I stared at the dark ceiling for a while. "Mark?"

"Yeah?"

"Do you think she's all right?"

Mark rolled over on his side to look at me. "She's okay. We'll find her in the morning."

"But, I feel like we need to do something now."

He put his hand on my chest as if to pet a dog. "There's not a thing we can do tonight except get some sleep. The whole family will search for her tomorrow. She could be anywhere. You know, I hadn't thought about it until the cop mentioned Alzheimer's, but that could be valid."

"Mark!" I sat up. "Doesn't anyone listen to me? It's the guy who threatened me. The man in the basement of the Observer, the scratchy-voiced man. He has Ruby!"

"If that's so, where do we find him?" He clicked the lamp back on, his stare intense. I wasn't sure if he believed me or not.

Rubbing my eyes with the heels of my hands, I said, "I don't know." Fatigue grabbed me and started to pull me down. "I can't think any more."

He clicked off the lamp again. "Get some rest."

I drifted into a reluctant sleep, with vivid dreams of strangers roaming the house, doors and windows open, Ruby yelling for help. I woke with a jolt. For a moment, I didn't know where I was. Mark slept peacefully beside me. His presence did help calm my nerves; he had been right, I couldn't have stayed in the house alone. He rolled over and his hand rested against my arm. I closed my eyes again feeling secure that he was there.

ABOUT TWO HOURS later, I woke again, but not from a nightmare, instead from the hardness of Mark's erection poking my leg and his arm draped across my chest. His steady breathing led me to believe he still slept, but knowing this ploy—Hell, having used this ploy before—I knew he had to be awake.

"No, Mark. Go back to sleep."

No answer from him in the form of movement or sound.

I wiggled a few inches away from him, but the weight of his arm kept me from moving too far. I closed my eyes again and let sleep pull me into its comforting haze.

Another few minutes and I woke to find him snuggled back up to me. This time his hand was resting on my stomach. I didn't care if he really was asleep; I pushed his shoulder to roll him over. "Keep your hands to yourself."

Groggy, he raised his head. "What?"

"Keep your hands and dick on your side of the bed."

"Sorry," he mumbled and fell back to sleep.

Damn, I can't sleep with him. I was glad he stayed, I certainly felt safer, but the same bed had been too much. Slipping from under the covers, I went into Ruby's room. Her bed sank as I climbed in; the sheets and quilts smelled of sweet roses, like her. I pulled them tight around me. Somewhere between sleep and consciousness, I decided I wanted a little more security. Over the side of the bed, I felt under it. Shoeboxes, picture frames, books— finally, I rolled out of the bed and got down on my hands and knees to look.

"Where the hell is it?" I muttered. Shoving boxes aside, I searched for the baseball bat. Shock and realization turned my skin icy. "It's gone! Ruby's Peter Beater is gone!"

Chapter
Sixteen

WITH RUBY AND her Peter Beater missing I knew, I absolutely knew, she hadn't gone without a fight. Searching through the house again looking for any signs of a struggle, I found nothing. I stood at the kitchen sink, looking through the window, wondering what she had seen to make her leave her dirty dinner plates out and disappear so quickly and quietly. The clock on the coffee maker said 4:28. Nothing moved outside in the darkness; no cars drove by; no people jogged along the sidewalks. The world seemed suspended, waiting for Ruby to bring it back to life.

I glanced toward the driveway. From the kitchen window, Ruby would have been able to see if anyone was there. I decided to reenact the scene, try to make sense of it. If Ruby had finished her dinner and had just started to put everything away, dishes in the sink, leftovers in the refrigerator, she would have stood right where I stood. The side porch light lit up the driveway; of course, Ruby had been standing here in the daylight. If she saw the scratchy-voiced man—and I knew it had to be him—she would go for the Peter Beater.

But why was the side door locked when I got home, with the front door open? She always kept all her doors locked, unlocking them only when she needed to. Did she lock it after he came in? Did she know him? The questions swarmed my mind as I stared into the early morning darkness through the window.

"Okay," I steadied myself, "I'll try it." She saw something that made her go for the baseball bat. I walked back to the bedroom to see how long it would take Ruby; step by step, attempting to match her pace, I returned to the kitchen.

What if he'd seen her, too?

When she returned, he would have had time to come after her. The side door was locked when I got home; hopefully, it was locked while Ruby was here.

She had the bat in her hands. Someone lurked outside. I turned to look for an escape route. "Of course, through the front door."

I walked through the dining room to the living room front door, the one left open. "Yes, this is it." Had she made it out before he caught her? Probably. I retrieved a flashlight and a pair of dirty jeans from the laundry room. I pulled on the jeans and searched around the front porch. Just as I suspected, I discovered the baseball bat under an azalea, partially hidden by ivy crushed from the impact. I held the Peter Beater in my hands, wishing I had been there to use it for her. My mind turned back to the reenactment. They must have struggled on the front porch, and then he took the bat away from her. A smug smile of satisfaction flushed over me. "That's it. That's what happened."

Then the loss of Ruby returned. I searched the dark yard again, wondering what had happened next. Where was Ruby now?

I COULDN'T SLEEP. Pacing the house didn't help make the sun rise any quicker. Mark slept on, snoring quietly. *How can he? Ruby's in danger, and he sleeps.* I decided to wake him up, then reconsidered. I needed time to think, to figure out how to rescue her from the dark clutches of the scratchy-voiced man. *I'll kill the bastard when I find him.*

Lighting a cigarette, I sat on the front porch steps. "Why Ruby? What did he hope to accomplish by taking her?"

I could see only two possibilities: someone was trying to keep me from learning whatever Ruby knew, or she was a hostage to my good behavior, to make me toe the line. In either case, it seemed connected to Vernon's campaign, his Senate race. He would be safer with me obedient, and silent. *Is that why Mark sleeps so soundly?*

Then a thought hit me. "The diaries. Maybe Ruby wasn't the only thing taken from here." I snuffed the cigarette into the geranium pot and rushed back to the hallway.

Grabbing the chain and jerking the pull-down stairs to the attic caused a loud creak, and Mark called in a raspy voice from the bedroom, "What's wrong?"

I ignored him and bounded up the rattling stairs.

When I clicked on the bare light bulb at the top of the stairs, harsh white light illuminated Ruby's motionless body tied to an overturned wooden chair.

I struggled to breathe, my lungs heavy with horror. Pushing overturned boxes of clothes and books out of my path to get to her, I reached out to touch her face, afraid of what I might find; my trembling hand felt the soft warm flesh of her neck.

Her pulse, where's her pulse? I finally found it.

"Mark," I yelled, "call an ambulance. Ruby's up here."

He rushed up the steps to join me, not bothering to get dressed.

"Ruby? She's up here?" Then he saw her. "Oh God, is she... ?"

"She has a pulse, and she's breathing, but unconscious." I turned to see him hunched under the rafters, trembling. "Go back down and call 911." Relief settled over me like a soothing, warm quilt; I knew she was safe and alive. I eased the duct tape off her mouth and untied the ropes that bound her hands and feet to the wooden chair. No sign of blood, but I found a bruise the size of a half-dollar, and a knot had swollen on the side of her forehead.

I pulled the chair away from Ruby. "Mark, did you get the ambulance?" I yelled toward the stairs.

He stuck his head up through the opening. "Yeah, they're on their way." He climbed back up to join me. This time, he had thought to pull on his khakis and running shoes. "Let's get her down to her bed."

Ruby wasn't an extremely heavy woman, just bulky. Mark and I struggled to get her down the stairs without dropping her. Delivering her to her bed, I heard the doorbell ring and Mark rushed to let the paramedics in.

As they assessed her condition and loaded her into the ambulance, I paced. *Who did this? Is Vernon's campaign that important, important enough to chance murder?* The police came back, different officers this time; two men asking all the same questions. I let Mark deal with them.

I called Valerie. "Val, meet me at Carolinas Medical Center. Ruby has a concussion."

"What?" she choked out. "She has a concussion? What happened? Will she be okay?" The questions fired out of the phone.

"Meet me at Carolinas Med. The ambulance is leaving now. I'll tell you everything I know when we get there." Then I added, "Don't tell Gladys, just meet me." I didn't want Gladys the Bitch there. She never cared for anyone but herself, and if she had something to do with this, I might just kill her as soon as she walked into the hospital.

The ambulance pulled out of the front yard; the driveway packed with Walterene's Taurus, Ruby's Oldsmobile, my rental Camry, and Mark's Mercedes hadn't allowed them access. Ruby would be pissed that they'd driven through the yard. Mark and I followed the ambulance in his car.

VALERIE WAITED AT the Emergency Room desk as we hurried in. Ruby had been taken in for examination, and Valerie filled out paperwork.

"Derek, what happened?" She shoved the clipboard of forms at Mark, then asked, "Why are you here?"

"She's my Aunt Ruby, too." He grabbed the clipboard and walked away.

She watched him plop down on a couch, then looked back at me. "Well?"

I steered her to another area of the waiting room and guided her to a chair. I told her what had happened from the time I drove into the driveway after dropping her off until the time we drove out a few minutes ago. Leaving off the more personal details between me and Mark, I told her I had called him first because he might be able to get something done faster with the police.

"You think this is the same man who's been calling?" she asked. She didn't know about the Observer building incident.

"Who else would have a reason to do something like this?" I asked, although my list of people and reasons kept growing. "But, why Ruby? Why not go after me?"

"No one has a reason, other than being mentally unbalanced, to tie up an old woman and put her in the attic." Valerie thought for a moment. "You know, he had to be a big man to get Ruby up those stairs."

The struggle we had getting her down from the attic came to mind.

"Do you think there could have been more than one man?" she asked.

Shit. I hadn't considered I might be battling more than one foe. That complicated my theories.

"Val," I felt I needed to tell her, "I found some of Walterene's diaries in the attic a few days ago."

Her face blanched.

"In those diaries, she wrote about a gardener Papa Ernest had and how he had been accused of something that made him run. From reading Walterene's account—and Ruby pointed out that they were young and didn't understand everything that happened—but from what Walterene wrote, it sounds like he was lynched because Gladys accused him of fondling her or something like that. Walterene never wrote exactly what Gladys said, but the family fired him after years of working for them."

Valerie sighed and said, "I don't remember anyone mentioning this."

"I think it happened in the late forties, before Walterene and Ruby's house was built." I shifted in the vinyl-covered chair. "You see, the oak next to their driveway was where they found him, hanged."

"Walterene and Ruby found him?"

"I don't know who found him, but Walterene suspected Papa Ernest led the hunt and the lynching. She believed that Vernon took a big part in it to help avenge the honor of his sister."

Valerie kept quiet for a moment, but her eyes darted back and forth; I almost thought I could see sparks as her mind processed this new information with things she had known or suspected for years. "I don't think it's true. Probably, like Ruby said, just young girls adding drama to their lives for the sake of the diary." She glanced over at Mark as he turned the paperwork back into the nurse at the station. "What else did she write about?"

"Just regular teenage girl stuff; she didn't like Gladys, that's for sure. A lot about the family, I didn't get to go through all of them." The realization shook me: I had been going to check for the diaries when I found Ruby; now I wasn't sure if they were still there or not.

Mark sat down in a chair next to mine. "The nurse says a doctor will be out in a few minutes. She said the initial diagnosis was a concussion, but the doctor will have to give us any more details."

Valerie's eyes searched my face as if to ask whether Mark knew about Mr. Sams and the diaries.

I answered that unasked question with, "Mark, I was just telling Valerie about Walterene's theory on Mr. Sams and the lynching that took place in the oak tree. Whoever did this knows about it; otherwise, the noose wouldn't have been there when I first arrived home." I looked to Valerie. "Can you find out how much Gladys knows?"

"I doubt she would admit remembering it, but I can ask." She glanced down at the floor. "I'd like to see what Walterene wrote exactly. I might get something different out of it, you never know."

I hated sharing Walterene's private thoughts with more people, but Valerie knew her better, and she had just as much right to see it as I did. "Okay, but Ruby didn't like me looking through them, so you better not mention it to her."

"Fine," Valerie agreed.

A young woman approached us. "I'm Doctor McConnell." Crimson lines ringed her tired emerald eyes. Her pale delicate hand reached out to shake Mark's strong hearty one. Funny, how people gravitated to him as the one in charge. Valerie and I stood to shake her hand as Mark introduced us.

"How's Ruby? Will she be all right?" I asked.

Dr. McConnell adjusted a pencil in her thick auburn hair. "She has a concussion. We're going to run a CT scan to look for any possible blood clots that could have formed near her brain."

Valerie gasped.

"It's routine at her age," the doctor assured. "We'll keep her overnight for observation. Hopefully, she'll be ready to go home tomorrow."

"Is she conscious?" Mark asked.

"Yes, but she needs rest. I'll tell her you are all here." She began to turn away.

"Wait, can she tell us what happened?" I took a step toward her, afraid she would get away.

The doctor stopped. "Oh, the police officers have already asked her a couple of questions, but she has a slight case of amnesia from the blow to her head. That's common with concussions."

Mark shook his head in disbelief. "You mean she can't tell us who did this?"

"She couldn't tell the police anything," the doctor said, "but the good news is, the memory usually comes back in time."

I looked at Mark and Valerie. "Maybe that's not so good. I'd almost prefer she didn't remember what happened."

The lack of sleep and the stress of the night began to swallow me. I sank down into the chair and held my head with both hands.

"Mark, can you stay here for a little while?" Valerie asked. "I'm going to take Derek home and let him get some sleep."

"Sure, go ahead," Mark agreed. "Derek, get some rest, and I'll catch up with you later this morning."

Valerie and I drove back to Ruby and Walterene's house in silence. The early Sunday morning sun sparkled the dew on the lawns of the neighbors. When I unlocked the door, I hesitated before going in. Would they come back looking for me? Would we be safe here? I grabbed the baseball bat from the kitchen counter where I had left it and walked through the house checking behind doors, under beds, and around corners. I asked Valerie to double-check that all the locks were secure.

"I'll stay here while you sleep," she offered.

The thought of having her in the house relieved my anxiety, somewhat. "Great. Thanks, Valerie."

"What about the diaries? Maybe I can go through them while I'm here." She headed toward the attic pull-down in the hall.

The diaries. I'd forgotten them again. We pulled down the stairs and climbed up. The remnants of the ropes and the overturned chair lay under the eaves. I found the boxes of diaries untouched where I had last seen them. Valerie and I hoisted them down to the den.

"I can barely keep my eyes open," I said.

She sat on the floor sorting out the journals. "Okay, go to bed. I'll be here."

"Thanks." I kissed her cheek and headed for bed.

I WOKE TO voices in the den. Still groggy, I checked the clock; I had only slept a few hours. I dressed, wondering who could be here and why, then opened the bedroom door slowly, trying not to make any noises, and crept to the kitchen door to listen.

Valerie explained Ruby's condition. "...and she has to stay in the hospital until tomorrow."

A male voice I couldn't identify said, "They know she's a Harris, don't they?"

Then I heard the unmistakable high-pitched voice of cousin Edwina. "Valerie, you make sure they know she isn't on Medicare and that she has insurance, otherwise those doctors will try and push her out the door as soon as possible."

I walked into the den to see Edwina, in another nylon crinkly wind suit, and Roscoe her twin agreeing with every word she said. "Edwina and Roscoe." I yawned. "Why are you here?"

Valerie answered for them, "Just a Sunday visit."

"Boy," Edwina started, "can you get me some more iced tea while you're up?"

"The name's Derek," I corrected. *Bitch, go home, I want to sleep.*

Valerie jumped up and took her glass before I could snatch it from Edwina's fat little fist.

"Your sister was just telling us about Ruby." Roscoe informed me. "We stopped for our usual Sunday visit only to find Ruby's in the hospital."

"Yes, yes, Derek." Valerie returned with Edwina's tea. She set it down on the coffee table. "I was just telling them about Ruby's terrible fall." She stared me in the eyes and nodded as if to make me agree with her.

"Yes, it was a bad fall," I agreed, unsure why I needed to hide the truth from these two. I dropped into the wingback chair next to Valerie's and glimpsed around the room for Walterene's diaries.

Valerie caught my searching glance and nodded toward the laundry room. Good, she'd put them out of sight. I didn't want the rest of the family clamoring to read them.

The clock on the mantel read 10:20; I'd only had two hours sleep. "Why aren't you two at church this morning?"

Their tired old faces blanched; maybe they thought I accused them of being heathens, since one thing in the lives of the Harris family that remained constant was regular church attendance. Roscoe piped up, "Edwina wasn't feeling well."

Edwina managed a weak cough.

So, I thought, *you decide to visit other people to make them sick.*

"Boy," Edwina started. "Derek, your father had his," she croaked another fake cough for effect, "retirement party last night, but not all of the family was invited."

My mind popped, *Yeah, so?* Instead I said, "That's right."

Edwina straightened herself up on the couch to the crackle of nylon fabric. "I thought it would have been nice if the whole family had been invited." She smiled with lipstick-stained teeth.

"You're right, but I didn't have any say in who was invited."

"Your mother did," she countered. "Gladys should have invited us. Roscoe and I are on the Board; we're shareholders just like Gladys and Vernon."

Valerie tried to soothe her hurt feelings. "The party was very small. You know how Dad doesn't like a lot of fuss. Just us kids and a few of the people who worked directly with him were invited."

I hadn't been invited; I had to push my way in. If I hadn't, maybe Ruby wouldn't be in the hospital. No one had expected me to be there. Is that why the scratchy-voiced man came here? Expecting to find me me? I spoiled his plan by going to the retirement party when I hadn't been invited. The party sure gave the family a tidy alibi.

Roscoe fidgeted with the zipper on his jacket. "Ed, you ready to go? We still got a couple more stops to make before lunch at the Rodale's."

"Rodale's steakhouse?" Valerie asked.

"Yeah." Edwina hoisted herself off the couch. "They have an all-you-can-eat buffet."

"Good food," Roscoe added.

Valerie stood to walk them out. I waved good-bye and ducked into the laundry room to retrieve the diaries. I had some reading to do.

Chapter
Seventeen

VALERIA HAD KEPT the diaries sorted chronologically as I had left them a few days before. I couldn't figure out why, but something was wrong, maybe the way she had stacked them back in the box. I pulled out the journals from the forties and reread some of the entries. Valerie joined me at the dining room table and flipped through some of the later books.

"I never realized Walterene kept these." Valerie stacked several more on her side of the table.

The cardboard box and the table held twenty or thirty books. Some of them, especially the earliest, were actual diaries with the little locks and keys, but the majority were spiral-bound notebooks or hard-bound blank books given to her as Christmas presents from Ruby. As I read an account of Uncle Earl visiting from New York City, the phone's ring jarred me back to the present.

"I'll get it." I left Valerie in the dining room and grabbed the phone in the den.

"How'd the retirement party go?" Daniel's voice boomed through the phone with enthusiasm.

The events of the past night rewound in my mind until I realized it had started with the party. "Fine, but that's just the beginning of my adventure." Taking a deep breath, I said, "You know I can't go anywhere without a catastrophe." *How much should I tell him? He's a reporter, and news like this is hard to ignore.* "Have you been to work today? Heard anything from your friends at the paper?" I wondered if he had seen the police reports.

"No, I'm off today, remember?" His voice softened. "Are you okay?"

I settled into the wingback chair and lit a cigarette. "I'm tired, but all right. This is strictly off the record, right?"

"Of course, I hope you feel like you can trust me."

Did I? The sting of the newspaper article from our first meeting still ached, but the more time spent with Daniel, the more trust I developed. I hadn't shared anything about Mr. Sams or the diaries with him. *Is it time?*

"I came home from the party and found..." I had intended to tell him the same story Valerie had told Edwina and Roscoe, but realized Daniel would have access to the police reports and might catch me in the lie. "I found Ruby missing. I called the police, and then, later in the night, I discovered her bound and gagged in the attic."

"What? Is she okay?" His surprise reassured me that he didn't know about it, from the newspaper or from any involvement in the actual act. Did I really believe he could be connected? I wasn't sure of anyone or anything, but craved someone I could trust with my confidence, with my emotions, with my heart; I hoped it could be him.

"She has a concussion and is being held at the hospital for observation."

"Any idea who did it? Or why? What did the police say?"

"You know about the phone calls I've received and what happened at the Observer building." I tapped the cigarette ash off into the glass ashtray and took a sip of iced tea. "I believe it's the same guy—or guys."

"You mean more than one?" he asked.

"Sure. Mark and I had a hard time carrying Ruby down from the attic; there had to be more than one person to get her up there."

Silence settled heavy on his end of the line.

"You still there?"

Daniel cleared his throat. "Uh, who's Mark?"

Shit, I hadn't said anything to him about Mark. "My cousin, Mark Harris."

"He was there?" He clipped his words.

"Yeah, I called him after I got home and couldn't find her."

Silence again.

His reaction puzzled me. "Do you know Mark?" I asked, meaning more personally than professionally.

"Yes. I've had dealings with him in the past. What does the hospital say about Ruby?"

Good dodge. But I didn't let it go. "Dealings? Like what?"

"Well," he sighed, "his father is running for Senate; he's helping manage the campaign; he's the young, handsome poster boy employed to appeal to the younger voters. That's my job, to know and talk to these people."

His defensiveness worried me. Could he and Mark be more than casual acquaintances? There was Mark's secret to be guarded. I had always assumed I was the only man in his sexual past, but was that naïve? I decided to let it go, for now.

Valerie walked into the den and waved her hand in quick jerks as if she had something to tell me.

"Hold on a minute," I said into the phone, then placed my hand over the receiver.

Valerie held her oversized pocketbook on her shoulder and dangled her car keys. "I'm going back to the hospital to sit with Ruby. Why don't you stay here and rest?" Her watery eyes drooped, and her black hair fell over her cheek. She looked older than the sixteen years she had on me; of course, the events of the past week could've worn the strongest person down.

"Okay, but I'll be there in a little while." I winked at her. "Val, thanks for always being here for me. I love you."

"I love you, too." She kissed the top of my head as she left.

Taking my hand off the receiver, I said to Daniel, "Sorry, Valerie was leaving for the hospital."

"That's okay. So, you think the same guy who went after you in the morgue did this to your aunt?"

"I hope it's the same person; I don't want to think there are that many different people in Charlotte after me." I snuffed out the cigarette. "Listen, I need to get back to the hospital to see Ruby. Can I call you tomorrow?" I wanted to see him face to face and bring up Mark again to get his reaction.

"Sure," Daniel replied. "In fact, come by the office around six, and we'll grab dinner."

I processed the new information after I hung up the phone. *Daniel knows Mark, but how well?* Mark knew I had seen Daniel; actually, as I thought back on the day after the Observer basement incident, he'd known Daniel's name before I said it. *Damn, how'd he know?*

The walls of the house crowded me; the oak looming above the roof held the spirit of a struggling, dying Mr. Sams. Wind rustling the leaves produced a cry for help, a cry for vengeance. Why had Walterene and Ruby wanted to live with that tree? Maybe it was the California coming out in me, but the energy in the house seemed to have cursed the people living here. Why now, after all these years? In less than two weeks, Walterene had died, I had been attacked, and now Ruby was in the hospital; I needed to get out of there, so I grabbed my car keys and headed for Carolinas Med to join Valerie at the vigil by Ruby's bed.

RUBY'S ALERTNESS REINFORCED our hope for a speedy recovery. She still could not remember what had happened to her, from the time she sat down for supper Saturday night until waking up in the hospital Sunday morning. The doctor decided she needed to stay in the hospital until Monday for a full range of tests to be performed. Valerie and I sat with her until late, and then I spent the night at Valerie's condo.

Monday morning, Valerie went to work with word to call her as soon as the tests came back. I hung out at the hospital until they took Ruby. Finding no cute interns to entertain myself with, I decided to go see Grandma again. Gladys the Bitch attended her book club on Monday afternoons, so I knew I could avoid her.

The azaleas appeared brighter and heartier than the last week when I had stopped by Grandma's house on Dilworth Road. Maybe it was knowing that Ruby would be okay, or maybe it was knowing that I wouldn't run into Gladys the Ice Bitch of All Time. She knew about Ruby, but hadn't come by the hospital, or even called Valerie to find out how she was.

Grandma Eleanor's house, dappled in spring sunlight through the oaks and maples, wore the veil of the most peaceful place on earth. The warm afternoon allowed me to drive with the car windows down, and when I drove up the driveway, I could smell the sweet scent of the flowering hyacinths by the steps of the front porch. I rang the doorbell and waited for Martha to answer.

"Mister Derek, come on in." Martha smiled and stepped back for me to enter.

"How's Grandma doing?" I asked.

She closed the door, and said, "The poor old girl has her good days and bad days, like most of us, I guess."

"What's today?"

"Today, she's pretty good, but she been talking about her mama and daddy. After breakfast, she asked me if her daddy was coming to take her home." Martha shook her head as if she saw the same fate coming for herself. "Miss Eleanor will be glad to see you."

She led me through the entrance hall and past the curving staircase back to the sunroom where Grandma sat on the rattan couch reading her mail.

Grandma Eleanor's simple A-line buttercup-yellow dress complimented her emerald rings and necklace. Her thin gray hair framed the soft and composed features of an elegant woman in her nineties. "Derek." Grandma looked up and smiled. "Come sit by me." She patted the cushioned couch next to her. "Gladys and Thomas aren't here, just me and Martha."

"I know, Grandma. I wanted to see you. You feeling okay today?"

"Yes, I feel fine. How about you?" she asked as she held tight to my hand.

"Great. I thought I'd come visit, since I knew Mother would be at her book club. Where's Dad?"

"He's playing golf. He's starting out his retirement like most men." She shook her head in mock disapproval.

Martha brought out a glass of iced tea for me and placed it on the coffee table. I always liked the warm clean smell of Martha, a cross between mocha and Windex. She gathered up Grandma's mail. "Miss Eleanor," she leaned in and raised her voice, "I'm going to put this mail on the desk for you."

Grandma grinned at her and nodded. I wasn't sure if she had heard everything Martha had said, but she seemed to understand.

Unlike my last visit, neither Ruby nor Gladys was there to change the subject when Grandma started talking about the past, and since Martha had mentioned Grandma's reminiscing, I seized my opportunity. "Grandma? Do you remember a black man who used to work for Papa Ernest called Mr. Sams?"

Her smile wilted, and Martha stopped mid-step.

"Is that a yes?" I asked looking from one to the other.

"Where in the world did you hear that name?" Grandma asked. Martha turned to watch us.

"I heard he was killed in that oak next to Walterene and Ruby's house." I watched their stern expressions.

Grandma glanced up at Martha. "Go on and put that mail away." Martha left us alone, and Grandma regained her composure; patting my hand, she said, "Mr. Sams did a bad thing. Papa fired him, then they found him in that tree. That's all there is to that story."

"But," I felt like she still thought of me as a six-year-old, "someone hung him from the tree. What did he do that Papa Ernest fired him?" I wanted to compare her story against what I'd read.

She fidgeted with a linen handkerchief she'd pulled from her pocket. "A Negro can only get so close to a white family; why, Martha has been with me for over forty years, but she still knows to keep her distance."

"Distance?" I asked.

"Getting too familiar, friendly, acting like part of the family." Her moist hazel eyes held me for a moment, then she said, "Derek, you've grown so much. If you had a daughter who told you an old friend had touched her in her private places, wouldn't you do something?"

"Grandma," I held her shaking hands, "sometimes little girls make up stories to get attention."

"Oh, I know that, but Papa wouldn't hear of keeping Mr. Sampson on—"

"Wait," I interrupted, "his name was Sampson?"

"Yes, Caleb Sampson, the children called him Mr. Sams; it was easier for the young ones to say." She let her eyes drift to the floor.

I wanted to get as much of the story as I could while she was willing. "Go on. You said Papa Ernest wouldn't hear of keeping Mr. Sampson on as the gardener."

"Well, Vernon was always Papa's favorite. He saw him as his rightful heir. My brothers never satisfied Papa, so Vernon was his last chance.

"Gladys, being my second child and a girl, always took a back-seat to what Vernon got, and she knew it. I tried to make her feel special, and her father doted on her like she was a princess, but it never seemed to be enough." A tear slipped down her wrinkled cheek, and she dabbed at it with her handkerchief. "I think that's why she said what she did."

I thought back to Walterene's account. "Could it have been an accident? I mean, Mr. Sampson playing with the kids as he had always done, and Gladys taking it as something more?"

"Oh, yes, that's what we all thought, but she wouldn't back down. Papa finally decided, in order to make peace, he would get rid of poor old Mr. Sams. I think it devastated that man." She took a deep breath and sat up a little straighter. "He worked here for years, started when I was young, and he so loved Gladys, watching her grow from a baby to a young woman, but that ended the day Papa fired him. Then they found him dead."

She didn't continue, so I prompted her, "Did you know that some people thought Mr. Sampson had been lynched by a group of white men?"

The statement didn't seem to surprise her; she sat for a moment thinking, then said, "No, Papa wouldn't do that. He cared for Mr. Sams, but again, he wasn't family. We always were most important to Papa. He watched over us—and still does."

"How does he do that?" I asked, wondering if she might be getting confused in her thinking.

"He's in our blood. He made sure we married the right people, had the right children." She laughed a short chuckle. "We're like race horses. The bloodline stays pure. Do you know that Theodore is my third cousin?"

Damn, my grandfather was my grandmother's third cousin. "Isn't that illegal?"

"No, no," she laughed. "Papa Ernest put us together, and within a year Vernon was born..." She drifted off into her own thoughts.

"That kept the Harris name and bloodline for Vernon and Gladys," I said.

"Vernon more than Gladys," she added off-handedly.

Confusion needled me. *Vernon more than Gladys?* "How so?"

"Oh, never you mind." She patted my hand again. "When a man touches a girl in the wrong way, he must pay for it."

"But you just said that no one really thought Mr. Sams—"

"Not Mr. Sams. Papa." Her gaze was far off.

Confusion prompted me to keep asking questions. "Papa Ernest? He touched someone?"

Her eyes returned to me, and I hoped her mind had clicked back to our conversation.

"This has been on my mind lately." She shifted on the couch and straightened her dress along her thin thighs. "I haven't thought about it in years, but it keeps coming back, especially as the end gets nearer." She rubbed her hand over her mouth as if trying to keep the words in. "Derek, you should never tell this to anyone." She stared hard into my eyes.

Nodding, I said, "Okay, Grandma, I promise."

"Papa Ernest... He..." She struggled for the words.

"Go on, Grandma," I said.

"Vernon is... Vernon's daddy is Papa Ernest."

I couldn't catch my breath.

"He would come to me during the night after Mama had gone to bed. It started when I was sixteen." More tears spilled down her cheek, and she brushed them away as if they stung.

Chills tingled my hands, and my head ached. *Papa Ernest molested Grandma, and Vernon was the result.* Did anyone else know this? Gladys? Vernon?

She leaned in closer to share her secret. "You see, I was afraid for Ernestine. She's two years younger than me, and I thought he might try the same thing with her. So I never complained, never gave him a reason to stop with me and go to her."

Thoughts rumbled in my mind, but I concentrated on her words; I wanted to hear everything she had to say. I could tell her mind was clear; she didn't seem to be confusing timeframes or searching for words as I'd heard her do before. She had something to tell and needed to clear her soul to someone. I felt honored she'd chosen me.

The tears returned and flowed quickly down her face. She didn't try to wipe them away this time. "He only stopped when I realized Vernon was on the way. Theodore and I married within a month. Papa said that the baby would have his blood and Theodore would give it the Harris name, making it the rightful leader of the family."

My confused thoughts bounced in my mind, but shock paralyzed me. I couldn't ask questions; I could only nod.

She continued, "Theodore was good to me, and we loved each other, but Vernon had the birthright, and as he grew up, he knew he was chosen."

I recovered enough to ask, "Does Vernon know who his father is?"

"Yes," she sighed. "Papa told him before he left for college, and

I admitted it when he confronted me."

"But, why are you telling me?"

"You never know everything about your family, and as families go, we have a lot of secrets hiding in dark corners. I know you aren't close to us, and I don't know why, but maybe a little truth about why we are the way we are might help you understand us—especially Gladys. I know she loves you and wants only the best for you."

Yeah, that's why she does things like sending me away, banishing me from my family.

"She has the best intentions," Grandma said. "But, like with Mr. Sams, sometimes she doesn't realize the full consequences."

I took the handkerchief from her and wiped away her remaining tears. "Grandma, thanks for telling me. I'll keep it to myself." Inbreeding, that explained a lot about Vernon. We sat on the couch holding hands, her head on my shoulder. Silence settled over us as my mind tried to absorb all my grandmother had revealed. I felt a little guilty about having pushed her for details, but I'd wanted the truth, and she seemed like the only one who knew the full story. Footsteps and rattling pans told me that Martha was in the kitchen.

Grandma lifted her head. "I think I'd like to lie down for a while."

"Okay, Grandma. Let me help you upstairs." We walked slowly up to her bedroom. I hugged her good-bye and promised to come back soon.

Before leaving, I found Martha in the kitchen preparing a roast for dinner. "Can I ask you a question?" I asked.

"You can ask, but I might not be able to tell you the answer," she stated and turned from the oven to face me.

"What do you know about Mr. Sampson's death?"

She took a breath, then turned back to the oven. "Nothing. Way before my time here."

"You never heard the name before?" I moved next to her so I could see her face.

She walked away from me, fiddling with a timer. "I heard the name, but not much else."

"But," I started.

"Mister Derek, you best let the dead lie in peace. Don't go bringing up ghosts that nobody wants to see." Martha crossed her arms over her chest, and stared at me.

Smiling, I conceded, "Okay, I understand." Although I knew she would be a dead-end, her attitude only intrigued me more.

Papa Ernest, Grandma, Vernon, Martha, and Mr. Sams; I drove away from the house on Dilworth Road wondering what else my family hid from me and hid among themselves, and how these secrets stirred the fog we viewed each other through.

Chapter
Eighteen

VERNON IS PAPA Ernest's son. The fact coiled in my head as I drove back to Carolinas Med. The shock of being a product of incest must have devastated him and influenced his relationships with the family. Did Vernon ignore the truth, or did he despise his grandfather for what he did to his mother? I pulled off Scott Avenue and into the parking garage.

"What a fucked-up family," I muttered.

I sat in the car for a while, my mind numb, before I could muster the courage to face Ruby. Did she know? Did any of the cousins know? Vernon was the oldest of their generation, but that doesn't mean he was the only one sired by their grandfather. Papa Ernest's only other daughter was Ernestine, Walterene's mother; could Walterene be another of his offspring? I reached Ruby's room and took a deep breath before entering.

She lay in her bed watching *Oprah*. "Derek," she clicked off the television and slapped the remote on the blanket, "that young woman doctor told me I'd have to stay another night."

"Why? What did she say was wrong?" I hated that I hadn't been there when she'd been brought back from the tests.

Ruby rumpled the covers up under her ample chest. "Says I have to wait for a technician that won't be here until tomorrow morning. I bet this is going to cost a fortune. Me laid up in bed for three days like some old woman."

I opened my mouth to remark that she was an old woman, but she must have read my mind; she held up her index finger to stop me from making the mistake of stating fact. "I," she protested, "am just as strong as you young folks, and I don't need all these expensive tests."

"Does your head still hurt?" I wanted to remind her why she needed to obey the doctor's orders. "Dr. McConnell only wants what's best for you, and if that means waiting for one more test, then you'll do it."

She smiled and held her hand out for me. When I came within reach, she grabbed my hand and jerked me to her. "See, I have plenty of strength." She grinned.

I laughed at her display. "It's that bump on your head we're worried about, not your biceps."

Doctor McConnell opened the door and pulled up a chair. I sat beside Ruby on the bed. The doctor opened her folder and explained the tests in detail as we listened.

"So, she will be okay?" I summarized.

"Yes, the test tomorrow is procedural, but I don't think anything surprising will come from it." Dr. McConnell closed the folder and stood. "Ms. Harris, get some rest, and we'll have you out of here by noon tomorrow."

"Thanks, Doctor." I walked her to the door. Once outside Ruby's room, I asked in a quiet voice, "Is everything really okay?"

"Oh, yes," she said, "Ms. Harris is extremely healthy for her age. She could stand to lose some weight and cut back on her cholesterol, but overall she's fine."

I thanked her again and returned to Ruby. She had opened a box of chocolate truffles Valerie had brought her and stuffed one in her mouth.

"You know," I began, "the doctor said it wouldn't be a bad idea for you to lose a little weight."

"My girlish figure is my trademark," she managed to say between licking her fingers.

I let that opening slide since she was in the hospital. "Call Valerie and let her know about the tests. I need to get back and shower. I have a dinner date with Daniel."

"Bring him by." She smiled, then changed her mind. "No, don't. I can't have him seeing me in this sexy nightgown. I might steal him away from you."

I rubbed the flannel sleeve of her gown. "You're right, I better not let him see you in this." The thought of nightgowns led to bedrooms and late nights; my mind clicked to Papa Ernest. "Oh, how long had Great-Aunt Ernestine and Uncle Walter been married when Walterene was born?"

"I don't know; Walterene was older than me, but I think about three years. Why?"

"Just trying to get family history right in my mind."

She squeezed my hand. "I'm glad to see you're interested in us. For the longest time we were afraid you had disowned the Harris family."

If only I could.

THE OBSERVER BUILDING loomed before me as I pulled into the parking deck. The last time I had been there, I'd barely escaped with my life. The spring sun, still high in the sky, allowed plenty of light into the parking deck. I glanced around at the other cars, checking to see if anyone lurked nearby. Maybe I was overly cautious, but I eyed the entrance to the lobby and bolted toward it. A stocky black woman manned the reception desk. I asked for Daniel and she called him down.

"Hello," Daniel greeted. "I'm glad you could make it. How's your aunt doing?" His brown eyes held me for a moment; a smile extended below his mustache, framed by those irresistible dimples.

"She's doing much better, but they still have one more test tomorrow morning."

He motioned me toward the elevator. "I still have a few more things to do. Come on up." He pushed the button for his floor, then he turned and pinned me against the back of the elevator. "We've got twenty seconds before that door opens again."

Half of my thoughts involved alarm, panic, terror; the other half melted into lust, desire, and craving. *Should I be afraid or excited? Why does he elicit both from me?*

His strong hands grasped my waist and pulled me to him; I closed my eyes, flinching and pursing my lips at the same time— ready for either outcome. His lips brushed mine; a tingle sparked through my spine, sizzling into a bolt that squeezed my arms around him. I pulled his body closer to me, not wanting to let him go. The fear of a second before shifted to embarrassment at suspecting him of anything sinister. Our kiss became more urgent as the elevator slowed. I felt him pull away, but I held him tighter.

"Whoa, man." He laughed and straightened his shirt. "Put that thought on hold. I can finish up my work in five minutes."

"Sorry. I'm just glad to see you. I'll behave." I grinned at him as the doors opened to a group of workers heading home for the night.

Settling into the side chair as Daniel finished typing on his computer, I searched his cube for pictures of old boyfriends, but saw none.

"There," he pronounced, "I just need to submit this to the editor." With a few more keystrokes, he turned off the monitor and grabbed his jacket. "All done. Want to grab a beer?"

"That's what's been missing today—a beer." I winked at him. "I knew something still needed to be done."

SEATED AT A sidewalk table in downtown's Rock Bottom Café, we sipped our beer and watched people wander between restaurants and bars. Daniel's choice of drinking locations intrigued me; the café shared the block with Mark's Church Street penthouse. Coincidence? Maybe.

The waitress scooted between the packed tables and chairs to reach us. Over the chatter and laughter of the crowd, she asked, "Can I get you two more?"

Daniel flashed his dimples and ordered another round of beer. "This is a great place," he commented. "There are pool tables inside, if you want to play."

"Do you come here a lot?" I asked, tearing off a small corner of the beer-soaked napkin and rolling it into a little ball. The warm breeze mingled with the spicy aroma of sizzling steaks and garlic-seasoned potatoes.

"Not really," he said.

I searched my mind for a way to bring up Mark; I wanted to get his honest reaction.

"I was thinking," Daniel continued, "people in Charlotte aren't that homophobic. I mean, the threatening phone calls and this incident can't be because of my article. Not that I'm trying to excuse my mistake," he added quickly. "I believe there has to be another reason. You haven't been in town long enough to make any personal enemies."

Fascinated that he had thought so much about it, I asked, "If I left town, do you think it would stop? Everything seems directed toward me..." My words trailed off into a hazy white space in my mind; the fog parted with an image of Mark and me smiling and laughing like we did years ago, here in this town with Daniel, Walterene, Ruby, Valerie, Tim, Grandma, Dad, and even Gladys the Bitch. San Francisco, my job, Emma, and my other West Coast friends dissolved into the mist; all that remained were my family and Daniel. *Could this be where I belong?* In spite of the bizarre events that seemed to pop up around my existence in Charlotte, I felt anchored, like I had a stake in the actions surrounding me.

A familiar voice snapped me out of my trance. "What a surprise to see you here." Mark stood over the table smiling at Daniel and me.

I almost shit.

Daniel stood and offered his handshake. "Daniel Kaperonis."

"Dan," Mark shook his hand, "no need for introductions. We've met before, several times." He pulled up a chair and signaled for the waitress; she dropped off our beers and retrieved another one for Mark.

"Mark, I didn't know you knew Daniel," I said, checking Daniel's expression, which stayed cool and unreadable.

"Oh, yeah," Mark confirmed. "We've met before." He didn't

look at Daniel, but kept his eyes on me.

I studied one man, then the other, waiting for either to continue. Finally, I asked, "Where?"

Mark glanced at Daniel as it to confirm a prior pledge. Daniel didn't return his gaze. Mark shifted in his chair. "Dan has interviewed me a couple of times. So, how's Aunt Ruby doing? I called her this morning, and she said she still has another test to go through." He turned to Daniel to clarify, "Ruby's our parents' cousin, a first cousin once removed. We call her 'aunt' for simplicity."

"She's doing well. I just left her before I met up with Daniel." I checked Daniel's expression, which remained calm and detached. *Does he not like Mark, or does he want to hide something from me?* I had the distinct impression I could be the third wheel at this table, and that feeling began to piss me off. "Daniel, you're being awfully quiet."

"No, I was just thinking about where we might go for dinner. This place seems a little crowded." He sipped his beer and grinned at me.

Mark, not missing a dig like that, responded, "Sorry, I didn't realize you two wanted to be alone."

Daniel kept quiet.

Now I felt a little sorry for Mark; Daniel could have been more civil to my cousin. "No, Mark, that's not it. I'm glad you stopped by, but we are on our way to dinner. Why don't you stay with us and finish your beer?"

He turned up the glass and chugged the last half of his beer. "Done," he said. "Derek, Dan, good to see you both again." He stood and dropped a twenty on the table, then hurried through the crowd.

"I'll be right back," I said to Daniel, then rushed after Mark. An older man in a navy business suit had blocked Mark's retreat and patted him on the back as they talked. I stood back until he had escaped the man's grip and continued toward the back door of the restaurant. "Mark, wait up."

He stopped at the courtyard patio door. "Sorry, I didn't mean to intrude. Anyway, I need to get home."

"You weren't intruding. Daniel's a bit uneasy around you, and I'd like to know why."

He shifted his eyes back and forth, as if that helped his mind work up an answer. "You should ask him that."

"I'm asking you."

He sighed and let his gaze settle on me. "I think he knows about Allen Harding."

"Who?"

"The ex-employee I told you about who's threatening to sue."

I couldn't remember. "Why?"

"He said we fired him because he claimed we were slack on the building codes and paid off inspectors. He's threatening to inform the city inspectors, if we don't settle." Mark ran his fingers through his hair, then paused. "Of course," he thought for a moment, "Harding's basically blackmailing us, so why would he trust a reporter?"

Mark's take on the story started to make sense to me. "You think Daniel is gathering information from Harding about the company? And about Vernon?"

"Of course. Your *friend* Daniel Kaperonis is trying to defeat Dad's campaign anyway he knows how, and a story about a business scandal involving Dad would suit his purposes." He shifted his weight and leaned against the wall glancing back in the direction of the restaurant. "I just don't get the connection—if Dan publishes the story, Harding's threat is gone."

"You didn't sleep with him?" I asked, my mind more interested in the personal aspect than the political.

Horror contorted his face. "Harding?"

"No, Daniel."

"Sleep with Daniel?" He laughed and shook his head. "No, no. Do you think I'm that stupid, to have sex with a reporter if I didn't want all of Charlotte knowing?" He stopped laughing when he noticed my expression. "Oh, sorry."

"Well then, why is Daniel so against you?"

"Politics, or it could be you," Mark said. "Maybe he's jealous. You didn't tell him about us, did you?" His forward stance and hardness of his eyes, almost threatening, created compassion in me because he was scared, really terrified someone might know about our relationship.

"No. I wouldn't do that."

"Well, then, unless he thinks I know he's talked to Harding, and I get the company to confront the allegations before his big story breaks," he shrugged his shoulders, "who the fuck knows?" Mark turned to leave, then stopped. "He's your boyfriend, ask him."

I rejoined Daniel at our table. He sipped his beer and took a drag from a cigarette. "Is everything all right with your cousin?" he asked.

"I thought you were a little rude to him."

"You mean the comment about it being crowded here? Sorry, but I have never really trusted Mark Harris, and I didn't want to end up spending a lot of time with him." He reached across the table and touched my hand. "You're the one I want to be with—alone."

Pulling away from his touch, I asked, "So, what do you have against Mark?"

He sighed and ground his cigarette into the ashtray. "Mark is a closet case, if you didn't already know, and I think you do. That skinny wife of his is just a cover."

"Why do you say that?" I felt sweat break out on my upper lip. This was Mark's big secret; something he would kill to keep buried. Then my mind took a different direction: *I thought I was the only one.* "Did you sleep with him?"

Daniel smiled. "No, but I probably could have."

"Do you know anyone who has?"

"No," he admitted.

"Then how can you say Mark is gay if he never said it and you don't have first-hand proof?" I sat back in the chair. "Gay men are so petty sometimes; if a good-looking man is nice to them or not talking about pussy every minute, he's labeled gay. Is that wishful thinking, or just trying to burn a brand on people?"

"Whoa, why the defensiveness? Being gay isn't bad, but lying is." He watched me for a second, then continued, "I'm sorry I started this, and I'm sorry I was rude to Mark. I don't want to fight with you."

"Thanks," I said. "He's family; no matter how distant we get, we're still family and tend to take up for each other. Mark is the closest cousin in age to me, and we've been like brothers." I finished my beer and pushed it toward the end of the table. "What about grabbing some take-out and going back to your place?"

WE SNUGGLED ON Daniel's couch in front of a warm fireplace; the lights off except for the fire and a few candles, and the fragrance of garlic and butter from the shrimp scampi we'd devoured a few minutes earlier. With my stomach full, sleep threatened to take me at any moment. Safe and warm in his arms, I didn't want to get up and drive back to Ruby's empty house. "Would you mind if I stayed over?"

"You don't have to ask," he murmured in my ear. I closed my eyes, with a fleeting thought of Mark, Daniel, the scratchy-voiced man, and what they all really had in common.

Chapter
Nineteen

I SLEPT DEEP and warm beside Daniel, but I dreamed of Mark holding me tight and close, our bodies sweating from the mountain's summer heat, youthful exploration beside a dying campfire. Waking beside Daniel brought security and contentment to my weary body. Physically trying to erase Mark from my mind, I shook my head, then watched Daniel sleep for a few minutes, his chest rising and falling with each breath. I edged over to him and traced the line of hair down his stomach with the tips of my fingers, waiting for him to stir. So innocently, he arched his hips as my hand traveled lower; I knew he had to be awake, so I slid my fingertips back up to his chest. He stretched his arms over his head and yawned; a smile played across his lips. I straddled his chest and pinned his arms to the head-board. "So, Mister Kaperonis, have you any last words?"

"Please be gentle. I'm new to this, and I worry that I might like it." He almost got it out without laughing.

I slid down lower so that we pressed face to face, chest to chest, stomach to stomach, crotch to crotch. "You seem to be wide awake," I said.

He swiveled his hips. "You, too."

I licked his lower lip, still holding his arms against the head-board, then whispered in his ear, "Don't move." The sensation of my body pressed against his, skin touching skin, the heat, the rhythm of our breath, the pulsing of our hearts, bound us as one person. The silence of the night folded around the bed, so that all I knew at that moment was Daniel. Nothing else mattered, no time or place existed outside of us, no history, no threats, no deaths, no secrets, no family. "I wish we could stay like this forever."

He pulled his arms loose from my grip and wrapped them around me. His lips found mine in the dark, and the world dissolved in his kiss.

DANIEL LEFT FOR work while I stayed to clean up after the royal breakfast I had cooked for him. With the last pan and plate stored away, I glanced around the kitchen, the place where he lived day after day. The sun glimmered through the window over the sink, catching a hanging crystal that showered the small kitchen with prism rainbows. I wrote a quick "Thank You" note for the evening and stuck it on the refrigerator door.

Entering the den, I looked around at the room. The ashes from last night's fire lay flaky and gray under the grate; the wool blanket we had shared was still slung over the back of the couch, until I folded and placed it in the leather trunk Daniel used as a coffee table. The wall behind the couch was lined with bookshelves; I ran my hands over the spines and read a few of the titles: mythology, classic and contemporary fiction, current events, biographies of Robert Kennedy, Randolph Hearst, and the Binghams of Louisville.

The self-help books caught my eye. *What would a man like Daniel need to improve on?* One book on maintaining long-term gay relation-ships almost jumped into my hands. "Well," I reasoned to myself, "he's bound to have had a few relationships in the past, maybe even a couple of long-lasting ones..." I turned to look at the photographs on the mantel. Some pictures, I assumed, of his family, since the older couple and the two guys and girl with him all had the same dark handsome appearance; in fact, in a picture from the beach, the three buffed brothers stood side by side in front of the breaking waves in nothing but their swim trunks. *That could be the makings of some great fantasies,* I thought. "Brothers doing it," I mocked an ad I'd seen for a porn video. "The closer the kin, the deeper it goes in." Obviously, the other two brothers were straight, because no gay man would wear those big loose-fitting trunks; Daniel stood in the middle wearing Speedo briefs. As I replaced the beach picture, I saw another it had hidden. A younger Daniel sat on a mountaintop pic-nic table with a cute blond guy, both in mid-nineties grunge flannel shirts and ripped jeans. I took the photograph down for a better view. The blond looked familiar, but I couldn't place the face. "All blonds look alike," I snipped, and put the picture back.

Some newspapers scattered on the floor next to the bookcases asked to be straightened. I stacked them next to his desk in the cor-ner. A file folder on the desktop got my attention. The label read: Vernon Harris.

Daniel's private file. I wanted to read it, but the betrayal of his privacy weighed me down with the mass of unspoken suspicion. Trust him? Most of the time I trusted him, but how well did I really know him? He wasn't family—*yeah, like that would lead to trust.*

I glanced around the room, then sat down and carefully opened the folder, trying not to disturb the order of the pages. Several articles, some written by Daniel, filled the file, along with hand-written notes. Descriptions of political positions and past deeds that supported them covered most of the note pages, but one page had my name on it. I read it quickly, not believing he had written the words. My head spun as I finished. Placing the file back in its original position, I pushed the chair back under the desk. I crumpled up the note from the refrigerator, shoved it in my pocket, and pulled the locked door closed behind me.

I fought tears driving back to Ruby's house, then pulled into the driveway and hurried up the steps. Wanting to talk to someone, but with Ruby still in the hospital, and Valerie and Mark both at work, I picked up the phone and dialed San Francisco.

"Emma, it's me." I knew she would be at home, probably still asleep. "Did I wake you?"

"What time is it?" her groggy voice asked.

I checked the clock. "Ten, then it's seven there. Sorry, I didn't realize it was quite so early."

She coughed, and I heard the click of her lighter. "Are you okay? I haven't heard from you in over a week." I could visualize her sitting up in her bed, smoking her first cigarette of the day, surrounded by piles of discarded clothes and fashion magazines.

"I told you about Daniel, the guy I met," I said trying to jog her memory and giving her time to wake up.

"Yeah, the stud reporter. Excuse me, I need to pee."

I waited, thinking she would put down the phone, but she didn't.

"Go ahead. I can listen and pee at the same time."

"You have the phone in the bathroom with you?"

"Yes, I do my best talking in here."

The intimate visual was too much now. I sighed and tried to decide where to begin my story of emotional trauma; finally, I just blurted it out. "I found a folder in Daniel's house about my uncle Vernon."

"The idiot Republican?" She flushed the toilet.

"Yeah, but the file also had information about other members of my family, and a couple of pages on me."

"You? Like what?" Now, apparently in the kitchen, she clanged the coffeemaker's pot under running water.

"Stuff I had told him in confidence. Like some phone calls I had received after his article came out and Ruby's assault."

"Her what?"

"It's a long story," I said. "But, he also had my sister and brother's names written down, plus my parents." Shock and betrayal shrouded my logic; I needed Emma to help me think, to take an unemotional view, to console me.

Emma stayed quiet for a while. "Okay, maybe he just wants to remember things you told him. You know, to keep things about you straight... No, shit, that sounded lame even as I said it. What are you thinking?"

"I want to believe he's not up to anything, but I can't understand why he's keeping notes on me." I kicked off my shoes and grabbed my cigarettes. "He has notes on everywhere I told him I've been."

"What can he do with that information?" she asked, then answered her own question, "Nothing." Cabinet doors slammed in the background, and her muffled voice came through from the phone wedged between her shoulder and chin. "I need more sugar, damn. Sorry, now the notes on you were in the file on your uncle. Why?"

I thought for a moment, my mind making and breaking connections. "Could be that the file really is about Vernon's campaign, and my notes are just to get more information about his family, which just happens to include me." Not sure if that fit, but glad to have something, I relaxed my clenched jaw and lit a cigarette. "But, I don't want to be used for politics. He can get his information from other places. The file must be political. You think?"

"Could be. The file didn't have your name. God damn it! That fucking cat shit on the side of the litter box again. Lola," she screamed, "you whore!"

Just like being there, I thought. "Hey, Emma, you leave that cat alone. At least it wasn't in your shoe."

"My shoes!" Footsteps and the phone ran back to her bedroom. "Good thing for her ass she didn't get near my shoes." Emma's voice calmed. "When you coming back? We miss you."

"Sounds like you and Lola are getting along better since I left." They had been mortal enemies since Emma moved in.

"Yeah, we're bonding."

"Two divas in the same house will always cause friction," I said.

"Darling," she purred, "three divas usually occupy this place. When are you coming home?"

Home. A moment passed before I realized she meant San Francisco. Charlotte had slipped into my soul as the place of family, the place that needed me, that I needed. The idea of leaving didn't appeal; it didn't even seem possible, I had so much to do. Mark and I had to resolve our relationship; Valerie needed encouragement to marry and start her own family; Ruby deserved someone to watch over her; Tim had to have someone on his side, someone to trust; Dad wasn't getting any younger, nor Grandma. Gladys and Vernon could rot in hell. But overall, the pluses outweighed the minuses of life in Charlotte.

"Hello? You still there?" she asked.

"Yeah, I don't know yet. I'll call you in a couple of days." We said our good-byes, and I hung up the phone. Ruby would be released from the hospital soon, so I decided to straighten up the house, then get to Carolinas Med to bring her home.

RUBY HAD HER clothes on and bag packed when I walked in her room. Her cardinal-crested hair had been coiffed for the short ride home. I noticed the style partially covered the bump on her forehead.

"Look at you," I smiled. "I feel lucky to have such a beautiful woman to escort out of here."

"Sally came by this morning and set my hair." She patted the side of her head with care.

"Sally?" I asked.

"She's the girl that fixes my hair. Valerie called her." Perched on the side of the bed, she beamed.

"That was very nice of Val to think of it."

"I just feel a hundred percent better with my hair done."

Another diva in my life, I thought. "I know what you mean. Nothing feels better than looking good."

"I taught you well," she smiled. "So when can we go?"

"The nurse wanted Dr. McConnell to stop by to release you. She should be here any minute." I glanced at the door as if I had just given the cue for the doctor to walk in, but she must have missed it. "Got any of those chocolates left?"

Ruby just grinned, cocked her head and raised an eyebrow. "They're all gone. Those nurses must get hungry during the night."

"Nurses, my ass. Ruby Harris, you ate that entire pound of chocolate." I tried to act stern, crossing my arms and frowning.

Late on her cue, but finally showing, Dr. McConnell walked in the room. "Ms. Harris, you passed all your tests." She took a seat across from Ruby and glanced at her clipboard. "I want you to lose some weight."

I tried to catch Ruby's attention to give her an I-told-you-so look, but she kept her eyes on the doctor.

"And, I've talked with your family doctor and set an appointment for a week from tomorrow for you. Call him right away if you have blurred vision or headaches, but I think you should be fine." The doctor scribbled something on her clipboard. "Okay, you can check out at the nurse's station." She got up to leave, then turned back to Ruby. "And I don't want to see you in here again. Stop wrestling burglars."

Ruby giggled, "I bet he got the worst of it." We checked out, and once in the car, Ruby asked, "Can we drive by the cemetery? I want to see if the grave stone has been placed for Walterene."

"Are you sure you're up for it?" I asked, pulling the car out of the parking deck into the bright sun.

"I haven't done anything but rest for the past three days. I want to go. Turn right."

"Okay, maybe we can stop for lunch—if you aren't full on chocolates," I kidded. "Where's your favorite lunch place?"

She stared out the window for a while, not responding.

"Ruby? You okay?" I worried she might still be experiencing lapses from her head injury.

She turned to me with a sad smile. "I miss Walterene. We would go to lunch on sunny spring days like this, or maybe do a little browsing at Park Road Shopping Center. But here I am, old and alone."

"You have me," I offered.

Her smile widened a bit. "You have your own life back in California."

"Valerie and the rest of the family are here. I know they come to visit."

Her gaze returned to the passing houses and small shops as we drove down Seventh Street. "Do you know I have never lived by myself? Walterene and I moved into that house straight from our parents' houses." She rubbed her eyes. "I don't know what to do with myself without her."

"We're only a phone call away. Valerie is just a few minutes' drive from you." As I said it, I realized that hadn't been the case Saturday when she'd been attacked. No one was there to help her; she had been alone and vulnerable. I wanted to say I would stay with her, but knew that was impossible, even if I lived in Charlotte. My hand found hers. "Ruby, you'll be fine. We all go through changes, losses, but we keep going. Wouldn't that be what Walterene would tell you?"

She turned toward me. "Yes, Walterene would say, 'Ruby, toughen up.'" She began to cry again.

I pulled off the road into a gas station. "I miss her, too."

We hugged and cried until neither of us could catch our breath. "Okay," I sniffed, "let's not let Walterene see us bawling like two old women."

She laughed a short snort. "Right. She wouldn't like that."

At the cemetery, the day glowed warmer and brighter than the last time. Of course, the lack of hundreds of mourners dressed like black crows crying over the open grave made this visit easier to manage. Only Ruby and I stood over the dirt patch that outlined Walterene's plot. The mourning crows had been replaced by cardinal-crested Ruby and me, the scruffy robin confused about where to nest.

I wandered away from the grave to allow Ruby some time alone with her thoughts and Walterene. I found myself under the same low-branched willow oak where Mark and I had talked after the burial, sat on the cool grass, and looked up through the branches at the deep blue sky. "Walterene," I called. "Please look out for Ruby. I failed." But she probably already knew that. "I don't know how to help her, but I will do whatever it takes. You or someone up there—you know, maybe someone with a high rank and experience, like maybe Mary or Joseph, maybe even Jesus—could help me find the way to do it right, to make her feel safe and loved the way you did." I didn't pray very well in words, but I cleared my mind and pictured Ruby happy and strong, living on her own. "Thank you."

I sat quiet for a moment feeling the breeze and sunlight on my face, letting my thoughts go where my mind wandered. Daniel drifted into my meditation, not speaking, not moving, just a calm image of him. His dark eyes glistened as the wind caught his hair. I didn't allow my mind to jump into the state of why, who, or how; this wasn't the place for analysis, just reflection and observation. A slight sigh woke me from my contemplation, and I couldn't remember how long I had been there.

Still by the grave, Ruby kept her head down, lips moving. I got up, brushed off my pants, and strolled from one grave to the next, idly reading markers to give Ruby time to finish up. Walterene had the same kind of mind as me: logical, a little emotional, sometimes too judgmental, a lust for pleasure, but she had the wisdom to handle it. I did miss her. *What would she do in my situation?*

I smiled as the answer came to me.

Chapter
Twenty

FUCK 'EM. THAT was the spiritual message I'd received from my prayer to Walterene, the woman who taught me how to get along with people I didn't like, to take the polite, Southern approach to conflict. Of course, that had been fifteen years earlier; maybe as she aged, she'd decided being genteel wasn't all it was cracked up to be. Certainly, Vernon and Gladys had never employed the tactic. *Are these words to live by?* I sat on the front porch of Walterene and Ruby's house smoking a cigarette and contemplating the meaning of "Fuck 'em."

"Ruby," I called. "Want to go see Grandma?"

She pushed the storm door open and asked, "You going over to the Dilworth house?"

"Thinking about it," I said.

Ruby wiped her hands on a dishtowel she seemed to always have nearby. "You go ahead. I might take a nap in a few minutes." She started to turn away, then stopped. "You know, Gladys will probably be home."

"I know."

MARTHA ANSWERED THE doorbell; the dark skin surrounding her eyes sagged with wrinkles and time. On my previous visits, I hadn't taken a good look at how she had aged like the rest of the family. "Good afternoon, Mister Derek. I'm sorry, but your grandmother is sleeping and your mother and father aren't home."

"That's okay." I walked in the door she had opened only a crack. "I had a few things I wanted to ask you."

She scurried after me as I headed for the kitchen. "What do you want to talk to me about? You should be talking to your parents if you got questions, not me. I don't get involved in the matters of this family, never have, never will. Mister Derek, you stop walking away from me." Her frantic monologue pulled out my smile.

"Martha, relax." I sat down at the small kitchen table in the breakfast nook. "Come sit down." As she fidgeted and settled down on the chair across from me, I jumped up. "Let me get us some tea."

"I'll get it." She almost rocketed out of her seat.

I smiled and returned to my chair. "Is it okay to smoke in here?" I placed my Marlboro Lights on the table.

The iced tea swirled in her hands as she checked the door. "Okay." Her reluctance evaporated. "In fact, I might just join you." She handed me two glasses and placed the pitcher of tea on the table, then, with the slow movements of someone not wanting to make any noise, she pushed the sash of the window up to let the anticipated smoke drift out of the room.

I poured our drinks while Martha slid into her chair and produced a pack of Camels from her dress pocket. She touched the end of her cigarette to my flickering lighter and inhaled.

"Whew," she exhaled stormcloud-gray smoke, "I needed this."

Lighting one for myself, I asked, "Hard day?"

"Almost over. I don't like to smoke in the house, but if anybody asks, I'll blame it on you." She grinned, and I knew we had a common vice that bound us. "Now, I told you yesterday that I don't know anything about that old man."

"Mr. Sams?" I asked.

"Don't get coy with old Martha. I reckon that's why you're here, talking to me." She gulped her tea.

"Martha," I soothed, "when I was little, I'd come in here and watch you cook and talk for hours. You used to call me your daisy."

"Daisy." She laughed, then opened her mouth to say something, but she must have thought better of it.

"Daisy," I repeated. "Pansy is what you meant, wasn't it?"

"No, oh, no, Mister Derek. I never thought that." Her eyes pleaded for forgiveness as she held my hand across the table.

"Martha, this isn't the fifties. I'm gay. It's not a secret; it's not something to be ashamed of; I love men, always have. That's why I liked being in here with you. I knew you were a strong woman who loved men. I remember seeing you and your husband together and wishing that my parents acted as in love as you two did. I always thought you knew a secret to make men love you that the women of my family didn't have."

She blushed a little. "Mister Derek, you flatter me."

"And you can stop calling me Mister Derek. We're both too old for that."

"You know," she began, "since Oscar died, this job and this family have been my life. We never had kids of our own."

"I'm sorry to hear that." I ground out my cigarette in a cereal bowl she had placed between us.

"Oh, don't be. I have a bunch of nieces and nephews just like Ms. Ruby and Ms. Walterene do, although it does get lonely going home to an empty house. I used to watch all of you playing around here and wished me and Oscar had a big place for the whole family to gather." She wriggled the bowl back and forth. "My niece, Gloria, is a vice president at Bank of America downtown. She does some kind of computer work. Janeen, another niece, is a nurse over at Presbyterian Hospital."

"I'm sure you're proud of them." I watched as the memories played across her face.

"They were all such good children. Reminded me a lot of you and your brother and sister. That Tim sure would get into trouble from time to time." Tim's reputation as a rascal never wavered in the eyes of those who knew him. "And Valerie was such a sweet girl."

"Since I came back for Walterene's funeral," I decided to get to the point, "stories and denials about Mr. Sams seem to be everywhere. I'm curious about that. I know Walterene loved him like one of the family, and now that she's gone, I can't find anyone who wants to talk about him or his memory."

Martha lit another cigarette and took two quick drags. "Like I told you yesterday, that was before my time here."

"But you must have heard something."

"Mister Derek, let the dead stay dead."

"That's not the way to honor their memory. I won't do that for Walterene, and I know you won't do that for your husband Oscar. I want the same respect for Mr. Sams; he meant a lot to Walterene."

She stared at the bowl of ashes for a second, then took another drag from the cigarette.

I waited.

"I see what you mean. I never mentioned this to anyone in your family, not that it matters, but Mr. Sampson lived across the street from my mother. He loved working here, just like I do." Her tired eyes held me for a moment. "I remember him always talking about what a good family Mr. Ernest Harris had. Mr. Sampson didn't have any family of his own, just this one."

"Wait." Words from Walterene's diary came back to me; she had seen his daughter in town. "Didn't he have children?"

"Oh yeah," she said. "His wife died in childbirth, but the grandparents, Mrs. Sampson's folks, raised the baby girl. He didn't know how to deal with a baby."

"Is his daughter still alive?"

"No," she sighed. "Back in the seventies, she was killed by drugs. That family was doomed. His wife died, then him, and finally, the only daughter shoots poison up her arm. When his wife died, and with the baby growing up across town without him, he worked all the time; kept his mind off things, I guess. I think that's why he stayed on so long with Mr. Harris, and why it hurt him so much when he was fired. Mama said he killed himself, but us kids thought the men in sheets got him."

"The Klan?"

"Yeah." She nodded. "Those were some bad times. You didn't hear that much activity in Charlotte, usually only out in the country. But, time to time, they'd come through Brooklyn."

"Brooklyn?" I asked, not aware of any area in Charlotte called that.

"Downtown, used to be a black place called Brooklyn. It's where the government buildings are today. Also, Wilmore was a beautiful place, just over the railroad tracks past South Boulevard. That's where Mama's house was, and Mr. Sampson's. Wilmore and its neat clean old mill houses was the place where all the colored people lived who worked for the white families in Dilworth and Myers Park. Now, all that is rundown, almost as bad as the projects. Anyway, the Klan didn't have much need to be here."

"Is there ever a need?"

A sad smile graced her black somber face. "You and me know there ain't ever a need for that, but some folks do. That's why it's still around."

"So, you think the Klan killed Mr. Sams?"

She considered her stance. "Mr. Sams killed Mr. Sams. Although Mama said nobody who knew him thought he had done anything wrong, he ran like a guilty man. Why else would he be in those woods alone at night?"

"But wasn't he chased? Do you remember anyone around his house that night?"

"I couldn't have been more than ten or twelve, and probably fast asleep when it all happened. Mama didn't tell us anything about it except that he was found hanging in a tree." She took a long sip of her tea.

"The tree outside Walterene's house," I added.

Hands still on her glass of tea, her brown eyes widened. "What?"

"Yes, ma'am. Walterene knew exactly which tree he had died in, and when that area was developed after the war, she and Ruby bought the house built on that plot of land."

Martha stood and leaned against the sink, hands supporting her weight. "Ms. Walterene always had a sentimental spot in her heart for old Mr. Sampson."

I took over rotating the bowl as I talked. "Yeah, she has a collection of elephants, apparently started by an old stuffed toy Mr. Sams had given her." I counted the number of bowl rotations from a good spin: two and a half. A few ashes flew out onto the table, and I wiped them up with my hand.

"That was Mr. Sampson, I remember he claimed his ancestors rode elephants across Africa. He always talked about elephants." Martha returned to her chair at the table. "Mama said he was full of baloney and sawdust. 'That old man ain't no African prince any more than I am Cleopatra's wash woman.' Mama was a good Christian, but she didn't like to hear people putting on airs."

I smiled at the thought of Mr. Sams telling African fairytales to little-girl versions of Walterene and Ruby. "Does the elephant have any special significance in," I wasn't sure how to phrase it, "in African folklore, uh, culture, life?"

"Ask an African," she shot back with a smirk. "I'm American." To my relief, she winked at me as if to say, *stop trying to be so politically correct*. Then I remembered Walterene's message from the grave: *Fuck 'em*. Fuck 'em if they take themselves too serious; fuck 'em if they ignore you; fuck 'em if they lie to you; fuck 'em if they try to fuck you. I smiled back at Martha as she tapped her cigarette pack on the table. "So, what does an elephant symbolize?"

She lit another Camel and exhaled. "Strength and dignity, that's the elephant."

"He must have seen that in Walterene," I said more to myself than to Martha.

"Yes, sir. Ms. Walterene had strength and dignity."

The kitchen door burst open. "Martha," Gladys barked. "Is that cigarette smoke I smell?" She stood in the doorway glaring at me. Martha snuffed out her cigarette and jumped to her feet. The jerky, stick figure of Gladys the Bitch made me think of Nancy Reagan on crack, her fists placed on her thin hips in an expression of power like an emaciated Wonder Woman, meant to put terror into the hearts of Martha and me. It only made me laugh.

I leaned back in my chair and lit another Marlboro. "Gladys," I blew smoke in her direction, "I've been waiting for you."

Gladys didn't move.

Martha looked from me to Gladys and then back to me. "I should go check on Ms. Eleanor." She excused herself and hurried past Gladys without a second look.

I stared back at the Bitch, waiting for her to twitch—a standoff worthy of a John Wayne Western. She dropped her hands and walked to the cabinet opposite me, not letting her eyes stray from mine. I smiled at her crumbling to make the first move, and then I took a drag from my cigarette.

"I don't allow smoking in this house," she pronounced.

"This house belongs to Grandma, not you."

"Nevertheless," she leaned against the counter, thin arms folded across her bony body, "you'll do as I ask. Please put out that cigarette and leave."

"Please?" I laughed. "Aren't you polite? But I came here to see you."

"Why?"

I straightened up in the chair, ready for my time in the ring with her. "I want to know why you treat me like a bastard son."

"What?" she huffed. "I do no such thing."

The Bitch had the audacity to deny it. "Cut the crap, Gladys. Ever since you found out I'm gay, you've hated me. You tried to ignore me, and when I wouldn't let you, you banished me to that Lynchburg brainwashing college. You told me never to come home, but here I am. I'm grown, and I accept who I am, what I am. I know myself better than any of your country club friends will ever know themselves if they live to be a hundred." I pushed the chair back and took a step toward her. "You see, I haven't played the role you set up for me. I made my own decisions and paid for the wrong ones. Living on my own, in a place far from the strangling grip of the Harris family, I succeeded by my hard work and knowing my true self."

She pushed herself from the counter, away from me, to a neutral corner by the stove. "You think you know yourself," she spit the words toward me. "I raised you; I've been on this earth longer than you will ever be. Don't come in here, twenty-five years old, and tell me you have all the answers. That arrogance shows you don't know anything."

I walked toward her again, and she glared at me. Grinning at her, I said, "I admit I don't know all the answers. That's why I'm here." My cigarette smoldered in the cereal bowl. "Tell me, Mother." I turned my back to her and took my seat again. "Why do you hate me? Is it the gay thing? That little secret is out."

"Published in the *Observer*," she slammed her tight little fist against the marble countertop, "like some cheap trailer park trash on one of those horrible talk shows. You bringing Vernon's campaign into it."

"Vernon's political aspirations come before your own son?" The second I said it, I knew it wasn't worth asking.

She stalked across the floor as she talked. "Our reputation in this city, this state, is spotless, or it was until you decided to tell the world you like boys."

"Correction, I like men. I like big strapping men, the kind who work in construction. Isn't that perfect, how my family owns a construction business?" Horror contorted her face. "Gee, Mom, do you think Vernon would give me a job in personnel? I could test-drive the workers before they go on site."

"You vulgar, vulgar boy." She started toward me, but I stopped her with a blast of cigarette smoke in her face.

"What, Mother dear? Were you going to hit me?"

Rage burned her thin translucent cheeks. Gladys the Bitch trembled with anger. "Get out!"

I took a deep breath; better to let her lose her temper without me joining. "So, that's it. You hate me because I'm gay. I thought you were more complex than that."

A measure of calm had settled over her; she seemed embarrassed by her outburst. "If you have learned anything at that job of yours, you should know sometimes the greater good of a group is worth the sacrifice of a few."

So, I was the sacrifice. Banished because I didn't fit the mold. Her statement hit me harder than she knew; I wouldn't give her the satisfaction, so I steadied my hands on the table and watched her lean over the counter and push the window up higher to either let out the cigarette smoke or to cool herself down.

"This family is all we have." She turned back to me.

"We?" I asked.

"Yes. Vernon plans for us; the Senate seat is just the beginning. His sons can go even further."

"What does that do for your own children? Tim? Valerie? What does Ruby get from Vernon's success? Edwina and Roscoe don't see it that way."

She shook her head side to side. "Edwina and Roscoe are imbeciles. They only want what benefits them; they give no thought to the rest of the family."

"But, isn't that what Vernon is doing for his sons? Again, what does it do for the rest of the family?"

Her gaze slapped me like I was missing the entire point. "Status, influence, control, standing, power. Don't you see that as Vernon's position increases, ours does too? Our family will be regarded in the ranks of the Kennedys, the Bushes; forget the Charlotte families, we've surpassed them, John Belk, Harvey Gantt."

I didn't get it. "What more could you want? All the cousins are rich. None of them, or their children, could spend the money they have. If it's power and influence, isn't it dangerous to push someone like Vernon into that position?"

"Vernon is wiser than you think."

"I hope so." I replayed the meeting I'd had with him in his campaign office. "He strikes me as a bigot, a chauvinist, and a racist. But besides Vernon taking this family to national prominence, how does all of this factor into you sending me away? That's what I want to know. Forget fame and fortune, let's talk about you and me."

Her sharp eyes focused on the chair opposite me. I motioned for her to take the seat. She settled on the cushion like a skinny hawk perching on her nest. "If you want to talk to me, please put out that vile cigarette." Apparently, smoke riled her feathers.

"The fact that I'm gay was published in the newspaper," I stated. "Your biggest fear has seen the light of day—welcome to the world out of the closet."

She glared at me.

I ground out my cigarette. "Vernon did not burst into flames on his soapbox; you are still accepted at the country club; people may whisper behind your back for a few days, but before long, something more sensational will come along." I looked her in her cold gray eyes; I wanted her to admit it, that I'd been sacrificed. "This is why you sent me away at seventeen?"

"You can't begin to understand. The simple fact that you are a homosexual means very little to me."

"What? That's all you've dwelt on for the past eight years."

"No," she interrupted. "That's all you have dwelt on for the past eight years. I have moved on to other things."

"Other things to hate about me?"

"Things you rebel against." Her voice composed, she added, "Things you represent."

We circled back. "Not living the life you set for me?" I asked.

"One day, you'll see I knew what was best for you." She actually seemed to believe what she had just said.

My head ached as if each word she uttered tightened a vise. "You will never know what's best for me, because you don't have a fucking clue as to who I am."

"Don't use that tone with me," she warned. "Remember you are in my house."

"I've been in your house too damn long." I stood. "Vernon will not get elected. Your dreams of being Rose Kennedy will not come true. I know secrets about this family that will make a scandal over a gay son pale by comparison."

She flew from her perch. "Go home, Derek! You shouldn't be here! Go back to San Francisco!"

Chapter
Twenty-one

I STORMED INTO Ruby's house and found her and Valerie fussing around the kitchen, putting away groceries Valerie had brought. I realized I should have gone to the grocery store during Ruby's hospital stay, but had forgotten. "Sorry, I didn't know we were out of so much." I helped put the food away.

"That's okay," Valerie said. "I dropped by the store on the way home." She stopped and stared at me for a moment. "You look like you just had a run-in with a mad dog."

"I did."

"Gladys was home?" Ruby asked.

"You went to see Mother?" Valerie sat a bag of Dixie Crystal Sugar on the counter, but didn't move her hands from it.

"Yeah, I guess I should have been ready for a fight." I sighed and leaned against the counter. "Any time I'm around her, she gets me so unnerved. I end up yelling; she ends up yelling. Do you know she thinks Vernon is going to pave the way for a big political family in Washington? She actually believes that Mark or Mike will one day follow him into national politics."

Valerie released the sugar and brushed her hair away from her face. "I didn't know his boys wanted a career in public service."

"Public service?" I quipped. "There's nothing service-oriented about running for office. It's all money, power, and influence, getting your way, helping out your contributors. Policy-making is just another way to grant, or repay, favors."

"Vernon won't get elected," Ruby pronounced. "He's too dumb for that. People will see through him."

"George W. Bush got elected," I pointed out. "All you have to do is say what the people want to hear."

"I don't want to talk about Vernon." Valerie shut the cabinet doors and scrunched up the plastic grocery bags.

The rustling crinkle of the bags reminded me of Edwina's wind suits. "If Vernon leaves the company to go to Washington, who takes over?"

"The Board will decide." Valerie stuffed the bags in the recycle box. "Why?"

My mind tried to link the possibilities. "Mark or Mike? What about Tim?"

"Tim? My brother?" Valerie laughed.

Ruby didn't smile but sternly said, "Edwina and Roscoe think Tim could do a good job. They talked to Walterene about getting him moved up once Vernon was gone. In fact, I may vote for him myself."

Valerie and I stared at her as if someone else possessed her body, talking of company business and strategic moves.

"Well," Ruby began to sound like herself again, "Tim isn't that bad. And if Vernon leaves, it would be good to have someone to represent us."

"Us?" I asked.

"Me, Walterene, Edwina, Roscoe, Sam, Odell. Vernon and Gladys have always run that Board, the other cousins need some say in what goes on." Ruby crossed her plump arms over her ample chest.

"Edwina been talking to you?" Valerie asked.

"Walterene talked about it. Edwina says Tim needs to be on the Board to look out for our interests. It's not Vernon Construction; it's Harris Construction. We all own it."

"But what if Vernon doesn't get elected? The Board continues as it does today," I said.

Ruby thought about it. "I suppose Vernon will get elected, even though I hate to see it. Edwina and Roscoe said he will."

I laughed. "Edwina and Roscoe aren't astute political analysts."

"Let's talk about something else," Valerie pleaded. "Politics and Vernon are not my favorite subjects." She turned to me and smiled. "So, you spent the night at Daniel's?"

Daniel. I had some questions for him. The thought of the folder on the family and me, plus his attitude toward Mark, propelled me to go directly to his house, but because I had spent so little time with Ruby since she left the hospital, I squelched the urge to call him. "Yes, I saw him," I answered in a slate-cold tone.

"Sounds like Mom wasn't the only one you had a fight with."

"Just some things I need to get settled." Now it was my turn to change the subject. "What time's supper?"

"Seven o'clock," grinned Ruby. She loved having people around at mealtime. "Valerie, stay for supper."

"I need to get home and feed the cat," Valerie said, "but I'll be back."

"Yeah, I want to go for a run." I kissed Ruby's soft powdery cheek. "All this energy needs to be burned off."

RUNNING DOWN POINDEXTER, I took a left onto Park Road and headed north. The spring sun warmed me as I passed blooming white dogwoods and pastel tulips. Traffic and exhaust fumes were heavy as rush hour picked up and uptown Charlotte emptied. I hit a tempo in my run, exhaling on the fourth step, feeling like a chugging train. I hooked left to follow Park Road into Dilworth, or Lower Dilworth, where the houses were more mill houses than the mansions surrounding Dilworth Road and Latta Park. Lower Dilworth, where Daniel lived. Maybe I had this in mind when I decided to go running, but now, as I ran along the shaded sidewalks, the thought of talking to him seemed like fate, something I had to do. Turning the corner, I saw Daniel sweeping off his front porch; *how domestic, how serene*. He must have noticed me, because he leaned the broom against the railing and waved.

"Hey, Derek," he greeted. "I can't believe you jogged here."

"It's..." I panted, finally stopping and realizing how far I'd come, "It's not..." I tried to catch my breath. "It's not that far."

"Come on in and get some water." Daniel led me inside, and I glanced at his desk and the folder as we walked through the den. "I'm glad you came. I've been thinking about you all day."

Sweat streamed down my face, but I felt strong and energized. He handed me a glass of ice water, and I drank it down with greed. I gave him back the empty glass to refill. "Thanks." I pulled off my wet shirt and walked out to the back patio.

Daniel came up behind me and trailed the cold glass of water down my back. I drew back. He kissed the back of my neck, and I flinched again. "You okay?" he asked.

I decided to get right to the point. "I saw that folder on your desk."

Confusion clouded his face. "What folder? My desk?"

"The one labeled 'Vernon Harris.' This morning, I started to straighten up the house after you left for work... I just saw it." I hated to admit I snooped. "There on your desk, with Vernon's name on it." Walking a few steps away from him, I ran my hand along the rough bark of a silver maple hovering over the patio. I had thought confronting him would be so much easier; his deep brown eyes bored into me, his smile fading. "I thought you said everything between us was off the record..." My voice trailed off.

"You went through my files?" Hurt and anger cracked his voice.

"No, not files, just one. But it was out and had Vernon's name on it," I explained in a weak, small voice—the tone of a boy begging for forgiveness. That sound sickened me.

Fuck 'em blasted through my head.

"Never mind how I saw it. I did." I took the offensive. "Why are things I said to you in confidence written down in a file on Vernon's campaign?" I took a few steps toward him, and he backed up. "I trusted you. I thought you cared for me."

"Hold on." He reached out to touch my shoulder, but I dodged his grasp. "Derek, I didn't have anything in there concerning you."

"No?" I asked. "Let's just see about that." I brushed past him and retrieved the file from his desk. Coming back to the patio, I grabbed the glass of water and gulped it down. "Here." The folder slapped the table as I sat down and rooted through it. "This hand-written page with my name at the top. Who could that be about? You know another Derek Mason?"

He sat down across the table and reached for the page, but I jerked it away. "Says here: 'Derek Mason is the gay nephew. Living in San Francisco. Works at a computer software firm. Here for his mother's cousin Walterene's funeral. Staying with Ruby Harris on Sedgefield Road. Brother to Valerie and Tim. Estranged from Mother and Father.'"

"But, that was stuff from the article." Daniel interrupted.

That statement pissed me off. *How dumb did he think I was?* "How do you explain the rest?" I continued reading. "'Doesn't understand the dynamics of the family. Visited Vernon Harris, Mark Harris, and Bill Robertson. Received harassing phone calls after article. Investigating something from the 1940s—find out what. Attacked in the morgue of the Observer, claims he heard the same voice as the phone calls. Ruby Harris hospitalized after a home invasion—could be connected to the phone calls. Research family's history especially related to views on gays/lesbians. Likely a family dispute—research police records for past incidents. What happened between Derek and his parents?'"

Staring into his eyes, I said, "You are shit. You used me. I want to know why." A sick feeling wallowed in the bottom of my stomach; maybe it was from drinking the water so fast after running, maybe it was the stress of confronting Daniel, maybe it was knowing he was ready to tell a hell of a lie.

Strong hands ran along the edge of the table as he stared at the paper I held across from him, obviously churning up a performance so believable an Oscar would be awarded. He took a deep breath, frowned, eyes darting to the right. "I always take notes." His eyes met mine. "Derek, believe me, I'm not using you for any political reasons, no professional reasons. What has happened to you in the past two weeks mystifies me; I just wanted to get the facts, see what I could find out to help you."

I sat stone-faced, allowing him to go deeper.

"I know you haven't told me everything that's going on. Things don't fit," he said clasping his hands together on the table. "Your uncle's campaign doesn't warrant the things that happened to you or

Ruby, there isn't that much risk to justify the means. No opponent or activist opposed to him, and there are plenty, would go to such extremes." He rubbed his mustached lip. "Besides, anyone wanting to defeat Vernon Harris would welcome you."

"Politics. That's where you took this discussion." I stood and grabbed my wet shirt from the back of the chair. "I should have known. Your first interest in me was because of Vernon, now I guess that was all there was."

"No!" He bounded from his seat and held my wrists with his hands to keep me facing him. "That's not true. You attracted me, physically, mentally. Being Vernon Harris' nephew had nothing to do with it—it only complicated things."

"Sorry." I pulled loose from his grip and headed around the side of the house toward the street.

"Derek!" Daniel called, but he didn't follow.

VALERIE, RUBY, AND I fixed an incredible supper of vegetarian lasagna, crusty-garlic rolls, and drank a couple of bottles of smooth Merlot. By the end of the meal, giggling dominated any attempted conversation. I dismissed Daniel as a wrong turn on the road of life; in fact, the mention of his name never surfaced after I returned to Ruby's. The women probably sensed he wasn't a subject to be discussed, like a pimple on the end of a nose. We all knew it was there, but we also knew it would be impolite to call attention to it. Daniel, a pimple, seemed appropriate to me.

Ruby sipped her wine, but as she raised the glass to her mouth, the burgundy liquid wanted to slide to the side. She titled her head to maneuver it toward her lips, almost spilling on the table. Valerie glanced at me to see if I had witnessed our aunt's drunken stunt. I winked at her, and we both burst into laughter.

"What's funny?" Ruby slurred.

"That vino is getting slippery in the glass, isn't it?" I asked.

A crooked smile slid across her lips. "You making fun of your old aunt?"

"No, no, never," I lied.

Valerie kicked me under the table. She grabbed the glass as Ruby tried to sit it on the rim of her plate. "Let me help you, Aunt Ruby."

The thought of Ruby letting loose a little delighted me, especially after all she had been through. Then it hit me. "Val, do you feel okay?"

"Yes, why?"

"Me, too. Why is the wine walloping Ruby?"

Our aunt giggled at my choice of words. "Wine wawa ping

Wuby," she repeated.

I retrieved her medication from the kitchen counter. "Avoid mixing with alcohol," I read. "Shit, what should we do?" I circled the table, ready for action: rush her to the hospital, call the ambulance, perform CPR.

Valerie tried to calm me. "We'll just let her lie down."

We led her back to her bedroom, and she stretched out, yawning. "Time for bed already?"

"Yes," Valerie soothed, "Just relax while we put away the dinner dishes."

"Oh, I can help." She tried to lift herself off the bed, but soon gave up. "Come get me if you need something." Ruby's heavy eyelids won their fight, and she drifted off to sleep.

As Valerie loaded the dishwasher, I called the pharmacy to confirm we hadn't killed her. "Val," I yelled into the kitchen, "the pharmacist said wine will just make her sleepy."

"Good, she needs her rest." Val finished up in the kitchen and joined me in the den with more wine. "So, what about you?"

"Me?" I lit a cigarette and offered the pack to Val.

She declined. "You. As in what's going on with Daniel?"

Leave it to Valerie to want to pop the pimple. "Daniel was a mistake. I thought I was more than a news story to him, but today I found out otherwise."

She didn't push it. "We all misjudge people from time to time."

We sat in silence for a moment as if in memory of the relationship.

Val hooked her hair behind her ears and cleared her throat. "So, you saw Mother today?"

From one problem to the next. The memory of Gladys and her ranting sent my head back into a vise. "Let's talk about something else. Her agenda is self-serving, just like Daniel's."

"Mother thinks of us more than you know." She raised her glass to her lips, but stopped when she saw my face. "Really, she does."

"Can't prove it by me. Everything she said to me was meant to run me off. I can't believe a mother could hate her son so much." I knew what Val would say to that.

"She doesn't."

"Val." The defense of Gladys began to wear thin. "I know what she said. I know how she treats me. The Bitch wants me to leave." I couldn't understand this blind devotion to Gladys, and why Val cared so much that I join her in it. Valerie had always been more of a mother to me than Gladys ever dared. Born so late in Gladys' life, I must have been a burden, and she never let me forget it. I glanced back at Val. "She told me to get out, that I wasn't needed here."

Her eyes searched the stem of her glass for an answer, all she came up with was, "She loves you."

"If that's love, I don't need it."

Valerie sighed and sipped her wine.

THE NEXT MORNING, Ruby and I slept until almost ten. After a light breakfast of cereal, we drove to the Farmers Market to get four flats of impatiens for her front flowerbed. I planted the flowers while she supervised. The wine from the night before had given her a good night's rest, and she bounced around the yard like a young girl.

During our lunch break, the phone rang. Daniel came to mind with the first ring, so I convinced Ruby to tell him I wasn't home; he wasn't worth arguing with.

"It's Mark," she handed the phone to me.

Taking the receiver, I said, "Hey Mark, what's up?"

"Kathleen left this morning for Asheville. Going to spend a few days with her girlfriends at the Grove Park." His voice held a tinge of excitement as if he was a teenager again and his parents were on their way out of town. "Meet me at the office, and we'll go down to the Y for a workout and then dinner."

"Is that a command or a request?" I kidded him because I knew there was no chance of me saying no. Kathleen out of town, Mark and me together again; how could I refuse?

Mark laughed, "Sorry, that was a request. Are you available? Or does Daniel Kaperonis have dibs?"

"I'm available." I smiled into the receiver. *Am I ever.*

"Listen, I want to apologize about the other night at the restaurant when I saw you and Daniel together. I was rude; I admit it."

"Daniel wasn't what I thought he was." I hated to own up to it.

"What do you mean?"

"We'll talk about it over dinner." I knew I would need a couple of drinks to explain it all. "So where are you taking me?"

"Taking you?" he asked. "I'm cooking," he added with pride.

Dinner at his place, alone, my mind jumped to many scenarios until I physically knocked the ideas out of my skull with a whack of the phone receiver to my forehead.

"What was that noise?"

"Nothing. What time?"

"Come by about five, and be ready to work up a sweat."

Damn. The images flooded back into my mind in a tsunami of anticipation. How could I think of anything else for the rest of the afternoon?

Chapter
Twenty-two

MY HANDS SHOOK as I unbuttoned my jeans and pulled them off. All around me, men in various stages of undress joked and laughed among the orange metal lockers. Mark seemed to know everyone. He greeted a tall dark man in his late thirties, probably of mixed-race descent, with tan skin, loose close-cropped black curls, wide-set emerald eyes, and a strong roman nose. They discussed the man's medical practice. I checked his left hand for a wedding ring— married. The cute married guy slapped Mark on the shoulder and took a locker a few rows over.

Mark changed out of his suit. I stole a few peeks. Eight years had passed since I had seen him naked, felt his body against mine, tasted his skin, breathed his scent. He pulled loose his tie and slung it over the locker door. The first time we made love, camping in the mountains, filled my mind with memories: the scrunchy, fragrant pine needles; the tight, hard muscles of Mark's chest and stomach; the silky smooth caress of his exploring tongue. I quickly pulled on my shorts and sat on the bench to help hide the erection my thoughts had produced. Mark emptied his pockets onto the top shelf with a metallic clank of car keys, coins, and wallet. I remembered how much I'd loved to carry his keys around before I could drive. I'd acted like they were my car keys, not his; I was the football star, grown up, driving a copper-colored Chevy Camaro. The rush of falling fabric caught my attention as he dropped his suit pants and stepped out of them. A quick glance told me he folded his clothes carefully on a hanger before he completed undressing. His starched shirt came off next and joined his pants on the hanger. Mark stood before me in his black boxer-briefs. That, I had seen before at Ruby's. But then I'd had no interest in him; I had my own man. Now, I was available, and his wife was out of town.

He hooked his thumbs around the waistband of his underwear and pulled them down to his ankles. I had to look, but I didn't want to get caught staring; not like I was fifteen, never touched another boy, wanting to compare. I'd compared and touched a lot since then, but here was my first lover, my older cousin reaching into his locker for shorts. Opportunity began to slip away.

I tied my shoes as if they were the most interesting strings I had ever seen. I shifted my eyes to Mark. He had improved with age; his body thicker than at twenty-two, sturdier and more solid; the distinct definition of muscles under his tanned skin was softened by his thick dark body hair. His cock won the award for most improved member. It snaked to the left as if an erection promised to develop the longer it was exposed to view. *Does he know I'm checking him out? Probably.* He took his time pulling on his T-shirt, so that I would have a chance to look without getting caught. I took the opening.

He straightened his t-shirt and winked at me. "You doing okay?"

A grin I couldn't control turned into a laugh at the sight of Mark in nothing but a Georgia-Pacific T-shirt with his dick beginning to arch up. "Whoa, baby. I'm great, but put that monster away and let's go lift."

He smiled and scratched his balls, then pulled on his shorts.

AFTER FORTY-FIVE minutes in the weight room, my muscles burned, but I kept up with Mark on every lift. I proved, in a gym-kinda-way, that I was an equal man to him. We returned to the locker room, the dread of showering with him and keeping down an erection in a public place clouding my mind. Old techniques from high school gym class came back: think of math problems, name the state capitals, imagine the cheerleaders in their underwear. To my relief, Mark suggested, "Let's go back to my place and get cleaned up. I don't want to have to put this suit back on after working out."

We grabbed our stuff from the lockers and headed back to his Church Street penthouse. As I followed in my car, my mind kept inventing possible scenarios for the night. *Should we start something up again?* A few days ago, Mark assured me that he was happily married and didn't consider himself bisexual, let alone gay. What plans did he have for the night? What did I really want from him? Would I be doing this if Daniel hadn't turned out to be such an asshole?

Mark pulled into the parking garage underneath his building, and we parked in the two spaces assigned to his penthouse. Sweat still poured down my face from the workout, or was it in anticipation?

"I'll fire up the grill while you get showered and changed." He pushed the elevator button for his floor. My mind flashed back to the elevator ride with Daniel in the Observer building and how I couldn't stay away from him. I held onto the brass railing until the elevator stopped at the top floor. Our running shoes squeaked across the marble tile to his front door. I had forgotten how grandiose his place was: columned foyer, two-story living room, leather, mahogany, and a skyline view from huge windows. Mark showed me to his bedroom, opening a door to a walk-through closet where he hung his suit, then on to a gray-marbled bathroom with a double-headed shower, whirlpool, and floor-to-ceiling mirrors.

"You can use my bathroom," Mark offered. "Kathleen's is on the other side. I get a little dizzy when I go in there, with all that pink tile. I'll start the grill in the kitchen."

"Thanks." My awe from the surroundings made me blurt out, "This bathroom and dressing area are almost as big as my entire apartment." What did I expect him to say to that? He smiled and pulled the door shut as he left. I could see what the Harris money and name could buy. Was this what Gladys wanted for her family, wealth, security, prestige? I thought of the tiny, cramped Castro apartment I shared with Emma and Lola the cat, how different it was from this. Did Gladys think I could cause the family to lose this style of living?

I stripped and jumped in the shower, turning on both showerheads. The shampoo and soap smelled of juniper, sandalwood, and Mark; closing my eyes, I let the steaming water run over me. Dried with a large, fluffy terrycloth towel, I sprayed some of Mark's light, cool-smelling Hugo cologne on my neck, wrists, and stomach. I dressed in khaki shorts and a turquoise Polo shirt.

Pots and pans rattled in the kitchen as I entered and found Mark setting things out for dinner, still in his workout clothes. "You look like you're going to do some major cooking. Want some help?"

He smiled and handed me a bowl with Italian-marinated chicken. "You can grill this while I shower." He pointed toward the stovetop that included a full gas grill. "We're having spinach tortellini and chicken with a pepper and garlic tomato sauce."

My sweet-smelling Hugo-sprayed stomach growled. "Great. What else can I do?"

"Open a bottle of the Chardonnay in the refrigerator. I'll be right back." He left to shower, and I found the wine, popped the cork, poured myself a glass, then placed the chicken on the grill. Since there was no stool nearby, I hopped up on the countertop across from the chicken and watched it sizzle. The workout had left me thirsty for something besides wine, so I drank a couple of glasses of water. I pulled out my cigarettes, but didn't see an ashtray, so I flicked the ashes in the sink. "Two cigarettes," I calculated, "then turn the chicken. That should be enough time." Switching back to the wine, I sipped it and strolled to the stereo. I found a Chris Spheeris CD and turned it down low.

As I finished grilling the chicken, I put a pot of water on for the pasta, and Mark appeared, with wet, combed hair from his shower and dressed in jeans and a half-buttoned crimson silk shirt. He smelled of Hugo cologne too.

"How's dinner coming?" he asked.

"Great," I said as he walked by, and I felt his hand grasp the back of my neck in a firm rub.

He poured himself a glass of wine and leaned against the counter. "So, I want to apologize again about the other night. I shouldn't have been rude to Daniel. He's a friend of yours, and I had no right bringing politics into it."

"Daniel is no friend," I said. "Turns out he was using me to get information about the family." I hated admitting my misjudgment, but it was history now. "Anyway, that's over."

Mark walked over to me and put both his hands on my shoulders in a brotherly grip. "Sorry. Are you doing okay?"

"Mark," I put my hands on his waist so that we were in a semi-embrace, "we only dated for a week. I've had colds that lasted longer."

He smiled and pulled me closer to an official hug; my nose against the nape of his neck, I inhaled his scent, my cheek against his. He pulled away before I did and turned to the stove to work on dinner.

"Well, I'm glad it wasn't serious." He buttered a long loaf of sourdough bread and placed it in the oven. "How's Ruby?"

Not sure if I was ready to change the subject, but following his lead, I answered, "Good. We planted her front flowerbed today. Valerie picked her up for supper at Mantis, then they were going to stay at Val's condo tonight. Kind of a girls' night out."

"Valerie is such an attractive woman," Mark commented, stirring the pasta, "wonder why she never married? Of course, Walterene and Ruby never married either."

"Finding the right man is difficult." I winked at him. "Look at me, twenty-five, single, can't keep a relationship over a week."

"You were just spoiled with your first," he said matter-of-factly, still stirring the pot—and me.

My mind numbed. *What do I say to that?* "I," stammered out of me, "I believe you're right." *Why not take the opening?* "Not many men can compare to Mark Harris."

A chuckle escaped him as he turned to me. "And don't you forget that."

"But, you're married, and the shining son of a soon-to-be US Senator," I teased.

He only smiled in response. Pouring more wine, he asked, "Do you think Valerie might be a lesbian?"

"What?" I was a little shocked, not that being a lesbian wouldn't be an improvement to a woman's life, but I really had never thought of my sister's sexuality. "I don't think so. No, she would have told me. She likes men, I guess she has sex with them, but she's happy on her own. Probably from growing up during the Women's Lib thing in the seventies, she knows she doesn't need a man to make her complete. I often wonder if Gladys would have married Dad if Grandpa Ernest hadn't pushed it."

Mark rubbed his chin. "Ruby and Walterene didn't follow Grandpa Ernest's edicts."

"No, they were rebels."

"Okay, dinner is almost ready," he announced and began draining the pasta. I set the large mahogany table so that we sat at one corner and could see the setting sun's last shimmer. One candle flickered above the rose flower arrangement, and I left the lights low.

We ate as if starved and opened another bottle of Chardonnay. The talk, laughter, food, and wine lasted for well over an hour, "an orgy of the senses" to use one of Emma's phrases. We left the pots, pans, and dishes in the sink and settled on the leather couch facing the lights of Charlotte's skyline.

"This reminds me of when your parents would leave town," I said, our feet on the coffee table, sitting close, shoulder resting against shoulder.

"Yeah," Mark agreed, "Margaret married, Mike moved out, hot summer nights on the patio, smoking pot, drinking beer while Mom and Dad vacationed in Europe." He sat up and looked at me. "God, that was great: the freedom, no responsibility, no job, no wife." Settling back into position, he sighed, "Will I ever have that again?"

"Retirement, maybe, in thirty-five years," I suggested.

"But your life isn't like this."

"No," I said, "like I mentioned, my apartment is the size of your dressing area and bathroom, and I share that with an anorexic model and a neurotic cat. It's all in what's important to you."

He sighed again and repositioned himself facing me. His right hand stroked my hair. "You staying the night?"

"If that's what you want." I tried to play it cool as I wiped my sweaty palms on my shorts.

Leaning over, he brushed my lips with his, letting his tongue slide over my bottom lip to my chin, where he nibbled gently. My heart raced, my breath held without realizing it. His hands pulled me down on the sofa with him on top; strong hands caressing my shoulders, arms, and chest. Exploring hands pulling at my shirt and fumbling with my zipper.

Searing heat ignited a wash of hormones that buckled my body.

My brain checked out, leaving my desire in control of my actions. Shirts with buttons flying, jeans and khakis kicked across the floor freed us for sensory overload. I couldn't get my hands to all the places I wanted. I couldn't press my body against his hard enough, wanting to melt into him, to become part of him, to ride his waves. No words were exchanged, only grunts and groans of pleasure.

He pulled away from our twisting tangle to lead me to the bedroom, where we explored, moaned, kissed, laughed, wrestled, and spent ourselves. I drifted off against his warm chest, rising and falling in the rhythm of deep sleep.

I WOKE WITHOUT Mark at my side, but stretching in a cat yawn, I replayed the night in my mind. Excitement rose again under the linen sheets, then it occurred to me that these were Kathleen's sheets, her book left on the nightstand, her and Mark's wedding picture on the wall. *Fuck her, I don't want to think.*

I found Mark in his shower and slipped in with him. The water streamed down his taut body. I took the soap and glided it over his chest.

"You'll make me late for work," he warned.

"Don't go." The soap rounded his waist and traveled up his back.

"I have to go. People are depending on me."

I pushed him back under the showerhead to rinse off the lather; the water cascaded over his face.

He sputtered, "Drowning me won't help."

The steam rose as I turned up the hot water and leaned against the cool tile, pulling him to me.

He was late for work.

Chapter
Twenty-three

AS I PULLED into Ruby's driveway, I saw the black Lincoln Towncar warning that Edwina and Roscoe were visiting. *Great, can't I just bask in afterglow for a little while longer?* I parked next to them and went inside. No one was in the den, but I saw Edwina's pink wind suit through the window. She and Roscoe sat in the backyard talking as Ruby snipped at her rose bush. *Good, let them sit outside.* My bed called for me to come take a nap after a night of pure passion.

Just as I kicked off my shoes and stretched out on the bed, their voices drifted in through the window screen.

"You have to," insisted Edwina.

"But I hate those things," Ruby's voice whined.

Roscoe cleared his throat as only old men can; it sounded like his lung was coming up. "Walterene wanted it. We discussed it with her; now that she's gone, we have to have you. You have her shares."

Edwina overlapped him. "The board meeting is Monday at nine o'clock. We are going as a united front. We have to have someone to look out for our interests."

"The boys will do that." Ruby sounded uninterested in their pleading arguments. "Mike and Mark will take care of the company."

"Vernon will still control them," Edwina implored. "He and Gladys will push us out. Tim's our only chance."

Tim as an executive? I couldn't imagine my overgrown frat-boy brother in a board meeting.

I remembered going to Chapel Hill for a football game one weekend with Dad, when I was about six. At Tim's frat house, the other guys kidded Tim that I was his son, not his brother. "He's not my squirt," Tim shot back. At the game, I begged Dad to let me sit with Tim and his fraternity brothers. They drank out of a flask the entire game, yelled at girls walking by, punched and hugged each other based on the team's success or failure of a play. They smelled of sweat, Jack Daniels, stale beer, and Polo cologne. He called his friends fuck-heads. On the way home, I decided to use that term with my dad; we pulled off the highway, and I learned that wasn't a word to be uttered. But Tim still used fuck-head as a term of endearment. I could see Tim at the board meetings calling Vernon's sons fuck-heads.

"And Derek needs to go home." Edwina's comment forced my attention back to the yard conversation.

"That's not for you to say." Anger tinged Ruby's voice. "He's staying for as long as he wants; in fact, I want him to move back here."

"What?" Edwina screeched.

"I like having him around. He needs to be with his family, not out there in California with a bunch of strangers."

Roscoe spoke up. "He's in the way of getting Vernon out of the company. Because of him, Vernon might not get elected. That leaves us where we are today. He needs to keep his mouth shut about all that California queer stuff."

"Right," seconded Edwina. "That *Observer* article hurt Vernon's campaign. Derek needs to get married, to a girl, or go away."

"Edwina, that's the stupidest thing I ever heard come out of your mouth, and over the years," Ruby got louder, "you have let loose some doozies."

"We aren't against Derek," she tried to soothe Ruby.

"Or his kind," Roscoe added.

"But, the fact is, when Vernon goes to the Senate, we can get Tim added to the Board to take care of our interests. If that doesn't happen, get ready to be booted out."

"Well," Ruby's voice was quick and short, "consider yourselves booted out of my house. Go. Get. Now."

I heard the gate slam shut with their retreat. Staring at the ceiling, I wondered if they were right. *Could I keep Vernon from being elected?*

I rolled over the possibility in my mind like a silver ball shot in an old-fashioned pinball machine; it struck a button that repeated in a raspy voice: "Get out, faggot." A flag popped up: Danger! *Could the scratchy-voiced man, the man who tried to kill me at the Observer building, the man who hurt Ruby, be part of this Board takeover?* But a place on the board of directors wasn't worth murder; at least, I didn't think it was.

The storm door slammed shut as Ruby entered the house. I yelled from the bed, "Ruby."

"Oh, shit!" she shrieked, and her footsteps hurried back to the bedroom. "You scared the piss out of me. When did you get home?"

"A few minutes ago." I sat up on the bed. "I heard Edwina and Roscoe in the yard. What's going on?"

She leaned against the doorjamb, arms folded, lifting up her generous bosom. "Those two need a hobby. They want me to go to the Board meeting to get Tim positioned."

"Positioned?"

"Yep, so when Vernon goes to Washington, Tim will be added to the Board."

"Why is that important?" I knew Edwina and Roscoe's reasoning, but wasn't sure Ruby subscribed to it.

"The company has always been divided. Gladys and Vernon on one side, the rest of us on the other." She sighed like she hated talking about the business. "Since Vernon's boys have moved up in the company, their side always gets the votes on major decisions. Tim will help even the odds."

"You don't think Tim will have a loyalty to our mother?"

She smiled. "That's the first time, in a long time, that I heard you call Gladys 'mother.' That's nice to hear."

A little shaken by my slip-up, I corrected myself, "I meant Gladys."

A chuckle tumbled from Ruby's smiling lips. "Tim never got a lot of support from your mother—"

"Big surprise there," I interrupted.

"Lord," she looked up at the ceiling, "let me get this out so we can stop talking about it."

"Sorry, go on. Tim wasn't supported by Gladys..." I led her.

"Our side knew we needed a young executive, and Tim was the most logical choice in the company."

"The only choice?" I asked, sounding bitchier than I meant.

"Unless you want to start working there?" She grinned and turned to go back to the kitchen, but stopped. "You and Mark have a good time last night?"

"The best," I replied. I began to slip into the memory when the phone rang.

Ruby padded down the hall to answer it. "Derek, it's for you."

I joined her in the den, and she handed me the phone.

"Yes?" I said into the receiver and sat down in the wingback chair.

"Derek. It's Daniel." He added quickly, "Don't hang up."

Ruby took her clippers and returned to the backyard.

"What do you want?" I asked.

"I want to explain."

"You've got one minute." That was all I thought I could stomach.

"When I first met you and found out you were part of the Harris family, I wanted to get information—"

"I know." I interrupted, not wanting to hear this.

"But," Daniel continued, "as I got to know you—as you, not as part of this political family—my motives became personal. Complications sprang up as I struggled between getting a story and being attracted to you. I met with my editor, and told her I couldn't write another article on you or Vernon. I was too personally involved."

"What did she say?" I couldn't believe he gave up following the Senate campaign for me.

"I'm assigned to the county commission and city council meetings." He sighed, then added, "It's not as boring as it sounds, really."

I had to laugh. "Sorry you got reassigned."

"It's for the best. Besides, I want to help you."

"Help me? How?" I grabbed my cigarettes, tapped one out, and lit it.

"The attack here in the morgue, at first I thought that was about my article and you getting in the way of Vernon's campaign, but you must be onto something serious considering the harassing phone calls and the attack on your aunt Ruby."

"Yeah, maybe." I still didn't trust him, even if he wasn't writing articles on Vernon's campaign.

"I've been researching the archives for information on your family from the late thirties through the fifties, you know, the time you had looked up that night in the morgue." He waited for my reaction.

I kept silent.

"I found some information on Caleb Sampson."

"What?" I almost jumped out of my seat. "What did it say?"

"So you were looking for that?" he asked.

"Yes. Walterene wrote about it in her diary. What did you find?"

"Caleb Sampson worked as a gardener for Ernest Harris. He was found hanged in a tree and the Klan was blamed. No official investigation took place, which I thought was odd for the employee of a prominent citizen."

I was disappointed; I knew that much. "Anything else?"

"That's not the kicker," Daniel explained. "I researched backward and forward. That was the only instance of Klan activity within Charlotte for thirty years, before or after. Sure, there were reports in surrounding counties, but nothing within the city."

"Are you saying you think it was staged to look like the Klan?"

"That's more likely than what was reported in the paper."

Ernest and Vernon did it, and made it look like a Klan killing. I knew this wasn't something I should say to Daniel. "That's the mystery," I said, "who did it?"

"That's why someone is trying to scare you away. I think you have an idea."

"Not really, Daniel. I just know he died. I wasn't sure if it was suicide or murder. Now I know. Thanks."

"But, Derek—"

I hung up the phone.

THAT AFTERNOON, I dropped in on Mark. His assistant, Becky, told me he was in a meeting and would be back soon, so I wandered the streets of downtown Charlotte, enjoying the warmth of the sun and the endless parade of people scurrying from building to building. Mr. Sams' death kept coming to mind; I tried to imagine that the Klan had done it, and that it wasn't significant that no other activity preceded or followed it. There hadn't been any investigation back then, and the police had known much more then than I knew now.

I found a sidewalk café to sip a cappuccino and smoke a couple of cigarettes. From my table, I could see the Observer building to the south and the Harris Tower to the north; I sat between the two, thinking about the men in each, wondering what they were thinking at that very moment.

Thoughts of Daniel choked my mind with guilt. *A reporter can never be off the clock; he's always thinking about a story and how to dig deeper; of course, that's a drawback.* Was his phone call meant to work another angle with me? Trust, respect, and openness was what I wanted, not deception. My family seemed to thrive on deception: plots to take control of the board, schemes to get elected to the Senate, lies to cover up a lynching... Cheating on your wife with your cousin.

A secret held for more than eight years. How could Mark do it? Physical urges had to overcome him. *No one knows, so maybe he never acted on those impulses. That's impossible!* The thought shook me. Out-of-town business trips would have allowed Mark the cover of anonymity to meet other men who didn't recognize his name or associate it with the family. What a prison to be locked in, no one to talk to, no community, no support, no love, no life. But, what if that wasn't true? I knew other closeted men whose secret lives forced them into an underground society where one betrayal could end a life built on lies—"discreet" was the personal-ad synonym for closeted. I imagined covert meetings in a dark sports bar where the code words "My wife is out of town" signaled the promise of a new brother into the fraternity of silence.

I ground out my cigarette and headed back toward the Harris Tower, wondering how to unlock the prisoner trapped in the plush cell at the top. As I ambled up the street, a chill sensation of someone watching me crept up the back of my neck. Few retail shops lined the streets, so I stopped at a bank window as if I was absorbed in the posted interest rates. I watched the reflections of people passing behind me and especially of anyone who had stopped too. A dark-haired man in his thirties checked a map on a bus shelter about fifteen paces behind me; I waited to see if he moved on. He didn't.

The corner-crossing signal had just changed; I watched for the red flash to warn pedestrians not to leave the curb, then bolted across the intersection just before the traffic light turned green, and the man was cut off from following me. Looking back, I saw him cross to the other side of the street. Paranoia left me in a cold sweat; I pushed through the revolving doors of the Harris Tower lobby and checked for the man; he was across the street, staring at the doors I had just entered.

As the elevator stopped on Mark's floor, Becky greeted me, saying that Mark was out of his meeting and that she would let him know I was back. I waited for a few seconds until he opened his office door and invited me in.

"Sorry," he said, "but we're still meeting about Allen Harding's threats. Our attorneys want us to pay him off, but Dad says that implies we did something wrong."

I felt like I should say something about it, but that was company business and my business seemed more urgent and important. "I think someone tried to follow me."

"Where?" Mark asked, setting down a file folder on his desk.

"On the street."

He smiled. "Could they just be walking in the same direction?"

"Never mind." I plopped down on the sofa.

"If you really think someone is following you, I can send security out to check."

"No, don't bother," I was pissed that he would find it something to smile about. "So let's hear about your problem with this Harding guy."

"Sorry," he replied, "I didn't mean to make you mad."

I got up, wrapped my arms around his waist, and kissed him. "That's okay."

Pulling away, Mark took a seat behind his desk. "We need to talk about last night..."

"And this morning." I added.

"Yes," he smiled. "Derek, I'm married, and not in a position to have a relationship."

I waited to see where he wanted to take this. I wasn't sure what I had expected to develop between us, but I wanted something more than what we had.

"Like I've said before," he continued, "I need to keep parts of my life separate—"

"Me separate from your respectable life." I finished for him.

"No, it's just, a wife is what's expected of me, and I want to be up front with you, not lead you on." He arranged some papers on his desk, not looking at me.

"How important is keeping your secret?" I asked, wondering if the scratchy-voiced man and attacks had less to do with Mr. Sams and more to do with Mark's sexual cravings. The creeping possibility that he could be involved wrapped around my heart and pulled it into my throat.

Mark froze, papers in hand. "You wouldn't," his voice grew stern, "you wouldn't try to blackmail me."

My heart dropped. "Mark, I love you. No, I would never hurt you." *Could he say the same to me?*

He stood and placed both hands on my shoulders, holding me firm, staring into my eyes. "I love you too. I wish the world was different, where we didn't have to hide."

"It is different," I said. "The world you have to hide from is only in your mind."

"No, reality is I would lose everything." He pulled me into an embrace and whispered in my ear, "I want it all."

The warmth of his arms, and the safety I felt there, melted away doubts about his involvement in trying to scare me away. "Your secret is safe with me."

We settled on the couch and made plans for after work; he had dinner arrangements with Vernon to discuss the upcoming board meeting, but after that we would have a repeat of the previous night. The backyard conversation of Ruby, Edwina, and Roscoe came to mind. "What do you think of Tim?" I asked.

"Your brother?" He leaned back and sighed.

"Yeah, is he moving up in the company?"

Shaking his head from side to side, he said, "Tim is here as a favor to Aunt Gladys. He's a good guy, but his potential is limited."

"Not ambitious enough?"

"Well, yes, but also, he doesn't have a knack for strategic thinking." He chuckled a short staccato laugh. "In fact, Tim seems to take for granted that we owe him something for being part of the family. He just doesn't want to work for it."

I felt a need to defend my brother. "Mark, you are a senior vice-president at thirty; could you have achieved that in a company not run by your father?"

Offended, he shot back, "Derek, you don't know all I do here—"

"Mark, you don't know the real world. I've ridden out the ups and downs of Silicon Valley—"

"That's not real world."

"What the hell is it, then?" I jumped up from the sofa.

"Hold on," he grabbed my hand, "I admit I've moved up fast, but I don't think I would have if I didn't prove I could do the job. Dad isn't going to let the company flounder just to have his sons in high positions." He let go of my hand, and leaned back on the couch again. "Anyway, is Tim complaining about us?"

"No, I just wonder, if Vernon wins his Senate race, will there be room for other family members to help run the company?"

"Hell, no." Vernon burst through the door.

Jumping to his feet, face flushing from almost being caught too close to a known fag, Mark said, "Dad, Derek was just asking about Tim."

Vernon paced to the window, then turned to me. "I thought you were leaving town."

"Guess you thought wrong," I said, walking toward him, but stopping within five feet. "I wanted to wish you well on your campaign."

"The best wish for my campaign is to have you back in California." He walked to a chair in front of Mark's desk and sat down, leaving his back to me.

I glanced at Mark, who rolled his eyes, then sat down behind his desk, ready for business. "One thing before I leave," I said. "Vernon, do you remember Mr. Sams?" I wished I had asked the question when I could see his face, but Mark's horrified expression reflected his father's well enough.

After a moment of thick silence, Vernon spoke without facing me. "Never heard of him."

Mark looked down at some papers.

Dropping into the chair next to Vernon, I propped my feet on the desk. "Well, that's odd, since Grandma remembers him, and Ruby and Walterene remember him."

A slow smile spread across Vernon's assumed political mask. "Oh, you mean old Mr. Sams. Yes, he worked for Papa Ernest."

Papa, exactly, I thought. "He was lynched, do you recall that?"

The smile faded and his face took a hard turn. "That old man was killed by the Klan."

"Yeah, that's what the newspaper said. Odd, though there hadn't been any Klan activity around Charlotte in years. Why did they choose Mr. Sams?"

Vernon's patience evaporated. "What are you implying? If you think you can associate any member of this family with the Klan, you are stepping into slander."

"Derek," Mark spoke up, "there is no way anyone from our family could have been involved in that murder. You know that."

"Do I? From what I've found out, Mr. Sams was lynched the

night Papa Ernest fired him. How did the Klan find out so soon? Who pointed him out? Who tied the rope? Who tightened it around his throat? Was it you, Vernon?"

"Shut up!" he yelled.

"Was it Papa Ernest showing you how to do business?"

"Enough." Vernon stood, knocking over his chair.

Mark tried to grab his father's balled fists from across the desk.

I braced myself for the first hit, ready to knock the old bastard on his ass as soon as he gave me reason.

Mark righted the chair and directed Vernon back to his seat. Vernon calmed himself. "Don't imply that Papa Ernest or I were ever part of that group." His voice quivered. "Mr. Sams was one of the few men I respected growing up. He worked hard and never complained. I disagreed when Papa Ernest fired him, but I didn't have much say in it. We had no association with the Klan."

I believed that, but had they killed him and let the Klan take the blame? "Do you know who killed him?"

Turning to me again with anger clouding his eyes, Vernon said, "No. The police said it was a Klan lynching. If I knew who they were, I'd drag each one of their old carcasses out and throw them to the wolves. You don't know this family, so don't ever accuse us of something so horrible." He straightened his necktie. "Your queer friends are just trying to dig up dirt to stop me from being elected, but let me tell you one thing, mister: I won't dick around with my good name, or that of this family. Anyone bringing up some lie about us will find their ass in court."

Mark leaned on the edge of his desk. "I'm glad to hear you say that, Dad. Let's talk about Allen Harding's lies. I think we need to confront him, not settle out of court."

With that as my chance to get out, I signaled to Mark to call me and slipped out the door, still not sure if Vernon had been involved with the lynching.

Chapter
Twenty-four

"I CAN'T BELIEVE you accused Dad of being part of Mr. Sams' death." Mark sipped his wine. The city lights sparkled through the window of his penthouse; soft, smooth jazz played low in the background. His tone implied he wasn't offended but knew his father couldn't have been part of the appalling act. Vernon had cemented his innocence in Mark's mind, at least that's the way I read Mark's reaction.

"I'm still not sure who really killed him." I pushed my body away from leaning against him on the couch, so I could see his eyes as we talked. "Walterene's diary said she believed Papa Ernest and Vernon were involved; the newspaper report said the Klan did it; Vernon says they were never part of the Klan and never had any association with them, but what if they did it, and let the Klan take the blame?"

Mark sighed hard. "Derek, I believe," he paused, "I know Dad would never do that. Do you honestly think any member of this family would be involved in murder?"

"Someone tried to kill me in the Observer building; someone hurt Ruby; someone made threatening phone calls to me at Ruby's house. Who else, besides family, knows I'm staying there?"

Mark thought for a second. "Your boyfriend Daniel."

"Why? Why would he? What does he have to gain?" I had tossed those questions around before and never come up with a logical answer.

"Maybe," Mark drew out the word as he thought. "Maybe he would do it to make it look like someone in the family so you would blame us, maybe cause problems for Dad's campaign."

"Damn it," I said, "I'm sick of hearing about that stupid campaign. The world doesn't revolve around Vernon's Senate race."

"Hey, you asked." Mark massaged the back of my neck. "Let's go back to the bedroom."

"Is that it? No foreplay?" I kidded him. "I bet Kathleen gets at least some cuddling, some romantic words."

"She needs to be warmed up," he admitted. "But, you," his hand rubbed the crotch of my jeans, "you are always ready."

MARK LEFT ME sleeping the next morning. I woke and called Ruby.

"You boys stay up all night drinking, then sleep half the day away," Ruby scolded.

"Mark's at work, and I've been up for hours." I fluffed the pillow and scratched my bad case of bed-head. "Did Valerie stay with you last night?"

"No, I sent her home."

"What?" I sat up. "I wouldn't have stayed here if I thought you were going to be alone."

"I have to learn to be alone sometime," she said. "Besides, I feel safe. I keep the doors locked and my Peter Beater within reach."

"That may be, but you shouldn't have sent Valerie home."

"Hogwash. I'm a grown woman; I can take care of myself."

I didn't believe her for a minute. "I'll be home in a little while—and don't use that Peter Beater on me when I come through the door."

I hung up the phone and headed for the shower. The water steamed as my mind drifted toward what Mark had said the night before. Was it possible that Papa Ernest and Vernon hadn't had anything to do with Mr. Sams' lynching? Could a young Walterene have made up the connection because she didn't like Ernest and Vernon?

I rinsed the shampoo out of my hair and soaped up my tired body. I hated to admit it, but Mark's sexual appetite wore me out. After a few more minutes of the hot water running over me, I turned off the shower and dried with a large soft towel. Clean and wide-awake, I draped the towel on the rack and walked into the bedroom. *Where did I leave my clothes?*

I glanced around the room, then a movement in the corner of my eye caught my attention. Kathleen stood in the doorway, my boxers hanging from the tip of her index finger. "You looking for these?"

Panic struck me immobile. The secret revealed—Mark's worst fear, now mine. Naked before her, I didn't know what to say or do. She tossed the boxers to me, and I snatched them in mid-flight, quickly pulling them on.

"I was just leaving," I stammered.

"How long?" she asked.

How long? What a question to ask a man you've just seen naked. "What? What do you mean?"

It seemed ice cloaked her stance; her pale emerald eyes bore into me. "How long have you and Mark been sleeping together?"

By reflex, I glanced at the rumpled bed. Screw her; I had him first. "Since I was fourteen."

She recoiled from the fact. "Fourteen? That son of a bitch." She turned and stormed out of the room, returned with the rest of my clothes and slung them at me. "Get out." Tears flooded her frantic eyes as she left me there at the scene of the crime.

HAS SHE CALLED Mark yet? I waited for the traffic light to change, wondering if I should go to his office to warn him, or just get back to Ruby's. The gleaming buildings of downtown Charlotte seemed to mock me and the mess I had made for Mark; neat and tidy, the sidewalks hosted bankers, lawyers, professionals moving in their uncomplicated, clean, respectable lives. I steered the car toward South Tryon, driving past Harris Tower, bank headquarters, and finally the Observer building. Within a few minutes, I pulled onto Sedgefield Road, then Ruby and Walterene's driveway.

"Ruby, I'm home," I yelled as I walked in the door.

She came into the den wiping her eyes; she had been crying, so I hugged her hard. The emotions of the morning plagued me: hurting Kathleen, the one innocent in the whole tangle I had brought Mark into; outing Mark, by accident, but still as I considered it, maybe I had wanted to expose our relationship. I was the one who said I wouldn't hide, but he was the one hurt. My arms wrapped around Ruby's soft, plump body, and my mind came back to her feelings. "What's wrong?"

"Just thinking about Walterene. I get so wrapped up in thoughts, I don't know what to do without her." She sniffed back more tears.

Rubbing her arms, I looked into her eyes. "It's okay to think about her. Remember how she loved working in the garden?"

"Yeah," she sniffed, "the tulips she planted last fall are gone; other flowers have taken their place. She loved planning what to add to the yard."

"She kept a beautiful garden," I agreed.

"Once," Ruby managed a small smile, "we planted daisies next to the birdbath; she said I put them too close together, and I said they were just right. We got into an argument right there in the backyard. She starting pulling them up, and I tried to stop her." Ruby chuckled between sobs. "I pushed her while she kneeled pulling up my daisies. I didn't expect her to fall over, so I lost my balance and fell on top of her." She looked at me and smiled. "Imagine what the neighbors thought. Two old women wrestling in the backyard, crushing daisies as we fought."

"Who won?" I asked.

"I did. I grabbed a daisy and hit her on the head with the root end of it. Dirt flew everywhere. She had just had her hair set. She stormed back into the house, yelling that I'd just cost her ten dollars."

I had never thought of them fighting, but all couples do. I said, "Lucky for her, it wasn't a rock garden."

"That's right," she smiled. "Let me fix you something to eat." She pulled away from me and headed for the refrigerator.

"No thanks, I have no appetite."

"Good Lord, are you feeling okay?"

The encounter with Kathleen left my stomach in knots; I wondered how Mark was reacting. "I'm okay," I lied. "I need to call Mark." Leaving Ruby in the kitchen, I went to her bedroom to use the phone in private.

Becky, Mark's assistant, said that Mark had left the office, but she would be glad to put me through to his voice mail.

"Mark, it's Derek. I guess you've heard from Kathleen." The scene replayed in my head of Kathleen standing in the doorway of her and Mark's bedroom; I couldn't express the terror I still held from that moment. "Mark, if you need anything, or if I can help, I know I can't do much at this point, but please call and let me know how you're doing." I hung up the phone and rubbed my aching forehead.

Confusion, guilt, and grief banged my thoughts like Ruby thumping Walterene with pulled-up daisies. I needed to get out. I needed to leave town, leave the mess behind. I wanted to go back to San Francisco, to never think of Mark, Daniel, Vernon, Mr. Sams, Gladys, or any of them again. I wanted my old life back. Grabbing my running shorts from the dirty clothes pile, I yelled to Ruby, "I'm going for a run."

Without another word to her, I left the house and started running as hard and fast as I could, keeping my mind on each step. Sweat formed and dripped down my face as the heavy blanket of humidity kept the sweat from evaporating and cooling me. A car came up behind me, and as I glanced back, it signaled to turn on the street I was about to cross; I jogged in place at the corner waiting for the driver to turn, but he didn't drive by. I looked back and the car was gone. "Bitch," I muttered and crossed the road.

I kept running faster and faster. As I approached Park Road, the light changed, so I ran across the four lanes and toward Freedom Park. The sun's rays filtered through the thick leaves of the overhead oak and elm limbs leaving me running in cool shadows. Freedom Park was the place we'd gone for summer concerts by the duck pond, to festivals and on field trips when we were kids in school. It was a popular, beloved gathering place, away from the concrete and cars of downtown; Freedom Park was the outdoor heart of Charlotte, nestled in the old neighborhoods, protected from mindless development, and open to everyone like a plump, happy mother opening her arms and offering a cookie and hug to a hurt child. I needed that hug. Rounding a corner to a new baseball field built on the edge of the park, I spied a water fountain, and headed straight for it. Energy drained by my sweat, I drank and drank, then splashed the water on my sweltering head, face, and chest. For a Friday lunchtime, the place was almost deserted. A sidewalk wound through the park, so I walked it to cool down and catch my breath, focusing on what I would say to Mark. He would be upset, of course, about Kathleen knowing, but would he convince her nothing happened? Would he try to deny it? How could he? Kathleen acted like she suspected; it hadn't been like "Oh my God," it was more "How long has it been going on?" I added another name to the list of people wanting me out of Charlotte.

The sun beamed hot on my back. Cranking back up to a jog on the concrete walkway bordering the pond, I discovered slick piles of goose shit posed slippery hazards to my run. I veered to the right on a dirt trail that headed into the woods. The cooler, shaded trail let me concentrate on Mark, not on goose droppings or the scorching sun. *What is he thinking right at this moment?* He had left the office, probably after Kathleen had called. Maybe he was trying to call me. Two young women jogged past me, they said "Hello" as they ran, but all I could do was nod an out-of-breath "Hey."

A thought broke through: Mark might be calling right now. I decided to turn back. As I followed the trail to what I believed would take me back to the pond, a dark-haired man stepped out from behind a tree and grabbed my arm. Luckily, sweat made me slippery, and he lost his grip.

I sprinted away, but heard his footsteps fast behind me. Not having the breath to keep running at a getaway speed, I knew I would have to fight. No branch or rock was within reach; his hand grabbed my shoulder and jerked me back.

I fell, rolling across the damp dirt and soggy leaves.

Struggling to get out from under his weight, I saw his face. He wasn't familiar; he could have been the man who followed me the day before in town, but I wasn't sure. His identity didn't mean much to me at the moment; I just wanted to get away.

A hit to the stomach knocked what little breath I had out of my body. I couldn't breathe in. I gasped for air, but continued to struggle with the stranger. He didn't seem to have a weapon, no knife, no gun, no blunt object. I hadn't felt anything but the strike of his fists to my stomach, jaw, and side of my head. I got a good hit to his nose, and he rolled off for a second. Pulling in a lungful of air, I felt I was breathing again for the first time in hours. By my second breath, he was back, pounding on my body.

Is this it? Death? In the woods?

Blood smeared my hand. I wasn't sure if it was his or mine. A hard left hook to the chin caught him by surprise, and I saw the bewildered look in his eyes and his bloody nose.

"Didn't think a fag could fight, did you?" I pushed him off me. I was on my feet first, and when he started to get up, I kicked his knee out from under him. He fell with a thud. "Remember the Observer building?" I yelled.

He pulled himself up to his good knee. "Fuck you, faggot." His scratchy voice froze me for a moment, a moment I didn't have. With my next kick, intended for his balls, he grabbed my foot and tripped me to the ground. "You bastard," he hissed. His hands tried to pin me to the damp decaying leaves. The dank smell of his body, or maybe it came from the forest floor, sickened me. I struggled to keep my hands free and fighting.

With a swift tug on my arm, he flipped me over, and twisted my hands behind my back. The fiend jerked down my running shorts. "Now," he growled, "you get what all faggots want."

Tremors shook my body. *Rape.* The word couldn't convey the brutality, hate, and viciousness of the act. He forced my face into the raw dirt with his shoulder as he held my wrists tight. I felt him struggling to unzip his pants with his free hand. This was my last chance to get away. With all the strength I could gather, I bucked my hips up to knock him off my back. He fell to the side and lost his grip on my wrists. Kicks to his head forced him back further.

My shorts around my knees tripped me as I scrambled to get up. I pulled them back up, and on hands and knees, struggled to get away from his snatching hands.

"There! There!" a woman screamed.

I turned to see the two female joggers with a man from the park patrol. The scratchy-voiced man, stunned by the presence of others, stopped to look, too.

"Hey, asshole," I yelled to get his attention. He turned his blood-and-sweat-smeared face toward me, and I did my best Emma-style kickboxing strike to his nose.

He yelped in pain as blood gushed from his flattened nostrils.

AGAIN, THE POLICE recorded a statement from me, and when I refused to be taken to the hospital, drove me back to Ruby's. The asshole, identified as Bert Carter, was taken to Presbyterian Hospital with a broken nose.

Ruby fussed over me. I tried to calm her down, so I could talk to the police more: Who is Bert Carter? What does he have to do with me? Why? Why? Mainly, what I wanted to know was why.

The police told me nothing.

After a hot shower and a few too many cigarettes, the phone rang. Ruby said, "It's Daniel. He heard about the..." She didn't have words for it, neither did I. "Do you want to talk to him?"

"Yeah." I took the phone from her. "Hey, guess good news travels fast."

"Are you okay?" His low, soft voice soothed my frayed nerves.

"I think so. A little shaken, but I'll be all right."

"I saw the police report," he began.

"How'd you do that?"

"I have my sources," he said. "Can I come over? I want to see that you're okay."

His presence would comfort me. No one else knew, except Ruby, and she still fluttered around me like an edgy mother hen. "Yeah, come on. I have some things to talk to you about."

Daniel rang the doorbell less than five minutes later. Ruby let him in. He introduced himself, and she busied herself with making coffee and baking a lemon cake. "I just handle things better when I'm doing something with my hands," she explained. Her activity in the kitchen left privacy for Daniel and me.

"What do you know about this Carter asshole?" I asked.

"He has a police record." Daniel sat on the couch across from me. I did feel calmer with him around. "A couple of drug possession arrests. Employed at a family steakhouse as a cook. He didn't do this for political reasons; not his, anyway. I think he's just a hired gun."

"A thug," I mumbled.

"Right. The police are still talking to him. As soon as I find out more—"

"I want to go down there," I insisted.

"To the jail?"

"Yes, I want to know what else they've found out. They have to tell me, don't they?"

Daniel considered it for a moment. "No, not necessarily."

"But you can make them."

"I'm a reporter; they'll talk to you before me."

I thought of Mark, using his influence to get some answers, but then the mess he had with Kathleen came back to mind. "I don't care, I can't sit here waiting. Go with me?"

"Let's go." Daniel got up and headed for the door. "Nice to meet you, Ms. Harris," he said to Ruby as I kissed her good-bye.

At the Charlotte-Mecklenburg Police Department, we waited in a small, bland room, only big enough for a table. I glanced up at the fluorescent light in the ceiling. "How do they shine that in a suspect's eyes to make him talk?"

Daniel looked up and smiled. "They wheel in the big lamp with the electric shock equipment."

Officer Gloria Blevins, the young black cop who had been at the house the night Ruby was missing, came in. "Guys, he's confessed to the attack on Ruby Harris and to the one on you," she nodded toward me, "and Harold Grouse at the Observer offices."

I asked the obvious next question, "Why?"

"Says," she looked at some papers in front of her, "he was hired to scare you. Doesn't know, or won't tell us, who hired him."

"Scare me?" I jumped up from the metal chair making it scratch across the concrete floor. "Scare me? He put Ruby in the hospital." I stared at Daniel, then back at Officer Blevins.

Sitting on the corner of the table, she leaned in as if she intended on sharing a secret with us. "Carter said that Ms. Harris saw him outside; he went to the door, and she came at him with a baseball bat."

"How'd she end up with a concussion in the attic?" I asked.

She scanned her notes. "Carter says he left her there, tied to a chair so he could get away before she called the police. He swears he never hurt her."

When I found Ruby, she was tied in an overturned chair. *Could she have knocked it over and hit her head in the fall?* "Did he say who helped him?"

"Helped him?" Officer Blevins asked.

"Yeah, he couldn't have carried Ruby up those attic steps."

"I assumed she climbed them herself." Blevins looked over Carter's confession again. "He said he was there alone, and she was conscious when he left her."

Daniel rubbed his chin. "Did he say what he did after he left Ruby's house?"

"No," Blevins answered. "Why do you ask?"

I looked at Daniel, wondering where he was going with the question.

"If you're hired to scare someone, and that person isn't where you thought he was," he constructed the scenario, "and you tied up an old woman in an attic, I would say you botched your job. Wouldn't he have told whoever hired him?"

"Why?" I asked. "Why would he bother?"

"If something had happened to Ruby... say no one came to check on her for several days, she could have died. He would have committed murder. He's not a murderer."

"You weren't the one he attacked this afternoon. I think he's capable of murder."

"Maybe," Daniel said, "but he didn't come at you with a weapon. He didn't have a weapon that night with Ruby. He left her hidden, and I think he told whoever hired him where she was."

Officer Blevins jotted down something. "We'll get his phone records to see what numbers he called that night. Is there anything else you can give me?"

"Won't his lawyer stop him from answering questions?" I knew the police were getting too much information for any attorney to be involved.

"Read him his Miranda, and he declined counsel." Blevins grinned. "I'll be right back." She left the room, closing the door behind her.

"Damn," I looked at Daniel, "I forgot to ask about the noose."

"What noose?"

I hadn't told him about the noose hanging from the oak. "When I got home that night, there was a noose hanging from the oak; the police tried to say it was just a hanging basket, but I think he strung a noose from the oak to frighten me. The same oak Mr. Sams was hanged from."

"Mr. Sams?"

"Sorry, Caleb Sampson. Walterene and Ruby called him Mr. Sams. That was part of the scare, because I knew about Mr. Sams."

Daniel stood and opened the door; he looked down the hall for Officer Blevins. "Let's go find her."

Just as we started out the door, she stepped around a corner. I ran up to her. "Did he say anything about using a noose to scare me? Can I talk to him?"

"No and no. We found no sign of a noose Saturday night, just a macramé flowerpot holder," she said while steering me back to the little room. "You need to stay here. We're still getting information from him."

"But..." I started as she closed the door. Daniel sighed and leaned against the cinderblock wall. "If he put the noose there..." I trailed off as thoughts took over. The phone calls, the attacks, never mentioned Mr. Sams. I had linked them together. Could I have interwoven what I read from the diaries with what happened to me? Clearing my mind of Mr. Sams' death, I tried to piece together what the capture of Bert Carter and his mission to scare me out of town meant.

"You okay?" Daniel asked as he walked over and touched my shoulder.

"Yeah, I think I am." I smiled, glad that he was with me. "In fact, I have a few questions for some family members."

Chapter
Twenty-Five

THE ATTACKS DIDN'T occur because of what I knew about Mr. Sams, I had concluded that much, but Carter was hired to scare me out of town. Why? I sat on the front porch chain-smoking, flicking ashes into Ruby's geranium pot. Vernon would become a senator no matter what I did. So why would the family, his supporters, or whoever, want me out of the way? I wish I did have the power to derail his campaign. His small-mindedness, his bigotry, his intolerance should not be added to what already inhabited the Senate.

Ruby opened the door. "Mark's on the phone."

I jumped up and almost ran to pick up the receiver. "You okay?" I asked.

"Can you come over?" He sounded defeated.

Fifteen minutes later, I entered his penthouse. The sun had set, and few lights illuminated the grandeur of the place; the darkness and shadows fit his mood. Mark, still in his navy business suit, led me into the living area and plopped down on the leather couch.

"Kathleen's gone," he mumbled.

"What happened?" I asked in a low voice.

He pulled his tie off and popped loose the collar button of his shirt; his weary eyes held tinges of red around the edges, and an empty bottle of beer sat on the coffee table in front of him. "She knows. Fuck, she knew all along."

"What happens now?" I was almost afraid to ask. He didn't seem to be in a mood to discuss the future since the recent past had hurt him so badly.

"I'll give her some time." He looked up at me as if the plan was set in his mind. "Then I'll bring her back home."

A sentence for life, time to serve as the dutiful husband and son; he was going to deny who he was and what he desired to be the man everyone expected. The stranglehold tied him to the life planned for him since the day he was born, and he was too fucking weak to break it. Sickened by the sight of him, I stood to leave.

"Where are you going?" he asked, not moving from the couch.

"The air in here is choking me." I started for the door but decided he needed a few words. "You are pathetic. Your wife found me here this morning; she knew about us. It was no surprise; in fact, the only shock was the confirmation. You are out. You're free. Someone knowing didn't kill you. Now, you tell me you're going to crawl back into that closet. Beg Kathleen to come back. If she does, she's a bigger fool than you."

He didn't look me in the eyes. A mumbled "Get out" slipped from his lips.

"All I wonder about is if Bert Carter was hired by you or Kathleen." I waited for his reaction.

No flinch or sign of recognition came from him.

"Did you hear me?" Walking toward him, I raised my voice to make sure he heard me clearly. "I was attacked again today, but this time he didn't get away. The asshole is in jail, and it's just a matter of time before he spills everything." I turned back to the door, then thought better of it. I sat down across from him. "Where's Kathleen?"

"Richmond. At her mother's," he added. He lifted his head to look at me. "You mean they caught the guy threatening you?"

"Bert Carter," I repeated, hating to say the name again, the memory of my face being forced into the vile, rotting leaves and dirt as he tried to rape me, his grunting as he struggled to unzip his pants. I wanted to go back to the police station and kill him. Slowly. Wrap a rope around his neck until he could barely breathe, take Ruby's Peter Beater and crack his ribs one at a time, take a razor and slice thin lines across his back, then bury him to his neck in the woods and let the flies, mosquitoes, worms, slugs, and rats finish him.

"Who?" Mark's tired voice brought me back to reality.

My sadistic thoughts scared me a little; hate was something I fought, something I denied, a sign of a lower consciousness, too primitive for an enlightened person. A deep breath settled my mind. "He confessed to the phone calls, the Observer building, and to tying up Ruby in the attic. All we're waiting on now is for him to tell who hired him."

"You think Kathleen?" Mark seemed to be coming out of his stupor, gaining his wits again.

"She knew about us; she wanted me out of here before I ended up in your bed." I watched his eyes dart back and forth as he processed the information. The devil of hate crept back into my mind as I started integrating the wild facts of the past two weeks.

"No, she wouldn't do that," he said. "Not Kathleen, she would never stoop to that."

I didn't think she would either, but I wanted him to squirm.

Mark sighed. "I have to admit, I didn't believe there was ever anyone after you."

I pushed myself out of the chair, then decided not to backhand his stupid mug, but went to the refrigerator for a beer instead. The curse of southern politeness prompted me to bring a beer for Mark, too. I did feel pity for him; my cousin, my lover, the one I had always looked up to was now no more than a weak, confused stranger. "You don't know Bert Carter, do you?"

"No," he shook his head, "and before you jump to another suspect, I'm sure Dad doesn't know him either."

I had a list of suspects, but Vernon wasn't one of them. Gladys wouldn't associate with someone like Bert Carter. Mark, although strong in business, had shown his complete inability to deal with anything personal, to understand emotions: his own or other people's. My thoughts scrambled within my mind, trying to match names with motives and opportunities. I decided to share my suspicions to get his reaction. "I've been thinking about who might have hired him, and the top contenders are Edwina and Roscoe."

"Those idiots?" Mark's shock brought his mind to full speed. "Why would they hire someone to attack you?"

"Vernon's campaign," speaking my logic out loud, fitting it together as I spoke, "getting him out of the daily business of Harris Construction. If he goes to Washington, a seat opens on the Board, and they have a candidate for it."

"You mean Tim?"

"Right," I said. "The only thing that would stop their plan was Vernon's defeat. I'm the only negative he has."

He sat forward and took a swig of his beer, thinking. "But you couldn't hurt his image."

"No, but they don't believe that." I sat my beer bottle on a *Southern Living* magazine and lit a cigarette. Thoughts kept churning in my brain, then what Emma called "a brilliant flash of the obvious" hit me. "They gave themselves away when they came by Sunday." My voice grew louder with excitement. "They knew Ruby had been left in the attic. They came to find her. Instead of going to church on Sunday morning as usual, they were at Ruby's."

"Just playing devil's advocate for a minute," Mark said, "maybe they had a good reason for not being in church. You can't go to the police with just that."

"Okay, but why would they stop by Ruby's," I stressed her name, "before noon on a Sunday?"

"You're right," he admitted.

We both knew Ruby Harris would only miss church if she physically couldn't make it. The hate-devil prompted me to find the two old farts and take my revenge, but I knew it would be much worse for them to be questioned and arrested by the police. The shame would hurt more than any physical pain. I fished Officer Blevins' card out of my wallet and dialed the phone.

I LEFT MARK to his self-loathing, and drove to the Observer building to see Daniel. The dark parking garage held no fear for me. The knowledge that the scratchy-voiced man paced behind a cell door allowed me to see the building in a new light, no more shadowy, lurking danger. Daniel met me in the lobby and escorted me up to his desk. Stacks of files, press releases, commission reports, and newspaper clippings overflowed his desk. He pushed a pile off his side chair so I could sit down.

"I think I know who hired him," I said without honoring Carter as a person with a name.

Daniel asked, "Who?" And I explained my theory about the campaign, the Board, the timing of the Sunday visit. Officer Blevins had thought the information was good enough to bring Edwina and Roscoe in for questioning. "Sounds like they paid him to scare you, and he got carried away."

"Honestly," I said, resting my feet on the corner of his desk, "I don't think they thought he would hurt anyone. Edwina and Roscoe are not very smart. I just think they found someone that turned out to be a little psycho."

"Are you really okay?"

I nodded.

"You want to have dinner with me tonight?" he asked. "I'm not pushing you. I just want to make up for keeping those notes."

I kept a straight face, not letting him read my emotion. His dark brown eyes scanned my expression, until I couldn't help but break into a grin. "If you weren't so damned handsome, I'd never give you another chance." I gave his knee a playful knock with my foot, ignoring the soreness my body used to remind me of Carter's attack and all I had been through. I asked, "Do you still have that file?"

"In my briefcase." He picked up a black leather case, pulled out and handed the file to me.

As he worked and made phone calls, I read the file. He didn't have much I didn't know about the family, until I came across some of his handwritten notes. Daniel had information about Valerie and Tim from when they were teenagers and Daniel, his brothers, and sister had attended the same schools. His brother, David, had been a year behind Valerie and a year ahead of Tim during school; Emily, his sister, was two years younger than Tim. Daniel had interviewed his own brother and sister about my brother and sister. I scanned the pages on how Tim was the class clown, but good in sports. Apparently, Emily had dated him for a couple of weeks until she didn't put out, and he dumped her. Valerie had been studious and popular, plus a cheerleader, which, in the South, automatically made her the favorite for Homecoming Queen and Prom Queen. The one odd note was that Valerie had left school in October of her sophomore year and then returned the next September to start her junior year. Daniel had written the rumor: abortion.

I looked up at him as he talked on the phone. Did his brother really think Valerie had an abortion at sixteen? The math ran through my head, making the room spin. "Daniel." I shook his shoulder to get his attention.

He put his hand over the receiver and asked, "What?"

"I have to go." I stumbled, almost knocking over a pile of papers. "I'll call you tomorrow."

"But..." he started as I ran for the stairs.

I DROVE TO Valerie's condo off Park Road. Her parking space was empty. "She's home every night of the week, except when I have to talk to her." I gritted my teeth. Betrayal gnawed at my soul. *Valerie.* Ruby must have known, too; Walterene surely knew; probably the whole family kept the secret from me. I sat in the parking lot, staring at her brick townhouse, willing her to drive up. After about thirty minutes of waiting and turning over reasons in my mind, I pulled out and drove back to Ruby's house.

I turned the corner at Sedgefield Road and saw Valerie's white Honda Accord next to Ruby and Walterene's American-made cars. Sweat broke out on my lip. I wasn't prepared to see her. I had thought so, but now I knew I couldn't face her, couldn't face my fear. I didn't really want to hear why. A thousand encounters with Bert Carter, or with Gladys the Bitch, seemed better than what truths Valerie held for me.

Chapter
Twenty-six

THE TRUTH, A bitch who pulled no punches, needed to be confronted. The Truth would never let me back into the world I knew before, although that's exactly where I wanted to be. Calming my breathing, I got out of the car and went into the house. Valerie and Ruby stirred pots and cut vegetables in the kitchen. The sight of them chilled my body; the Truth slid her icy fingers up my spine. I shivered. "Hey, I'm back," I announced.

Valerie came into the den and hugged me. "Are you okay? Ruby told me what happened."

My cold clammy hands shook as I pulled away from her embrace. "Yeah, it's been a bitch of a day." I reached behind me to find the chair and lowered myself into it. The sum of Kathleen finding me in Mark's bedroom, being attacked by Bert Carter in the park, realizing Edwina and Roscoe were behind the harassment, and now this, didn't add up to a red-letter day. My mind and body ached as if one more life-changing event would turn me inside out—and what I knew was inside, the betrayal and anger, would not please anyone.

"Are you sure you're okay? You're pale as a ghost." Valerie wiped her hands on a dishtowel she had tucked in the waist of her jeans, then felt my forehead.

I jerked away from her touch. *How could she have lied to me all these years?*

"Maybe you need to lie down for a little while," Ruby offered from the kitchen. "Have you eaten?"

"No," I mumbled.

Valerie still stood in front of me, staring as if she didn't recognize the person who sat before her. "Derek, what's wrong?"

"Well, everything." I said, the tension in me ready to explode. My head throbbed; my heartbeat felt like it rattled the walls of the house; what little food I had digested during the day tried to creep up my throat. I couldn't play the game, now that I knew. "Valerie, why did you leave high school your sophomore year?"

The blood drained from her face as she cast her eyes toward the window, then stared at the floor. She didn't seem to know what to do with herself; frozen in time, maybe memories flooding back, her body didn't move. Finally, the trance broke, and she reached for the remote control and clicked off the television, then, with trembling hands, sank into the chair next to mine.

In the kitchen, Ruby turned off the stove and covered a pot, then sneaked back toward her bedroom. Valerie and I settled into the silence and solitude of the den.

I watched Valerie wipe her eyes with the dishtowel. My breathing shuddered my whole body. Trying to calm myself again, I focused on the vase of roses on the coffee table and how the breeze from the ceiling fan fluttered their jagged leaves against the unforgiving thorns jutting from their stems.

A deep sigh signaled Valerie's intent to say something to break the silence. Her reasons deserved to be heard; hopefully, they could make up for the hurt I felt. I wiped the sweat from my upper lip and dried my hands on my jeans, braced for what she had to say.

"Mother and I went to New York to stay with Uncle Earl," she began. "You never met him, but he was the youngest of Grandma's brothers. Our intent was to take care of my pregnancy."

The word hit me hard. I fished my pack of cigarettes out of my jeans, tapped out two, lit both, and handed one to Valerie. I inhaled deep, letting the smoke fill my lungs and the nicotine absorb into my system.

After a quick hit on her cigarette, she continued, "Uncle Earl took us to a doctor he knew, but in the waiting room, knowing what I was about to do, I couldn't. Mother and I cried all night." Valerie glanced up at me, tears spilling down her cheek. "We all knew adoption was out of the question, but a family member could raise the child. Walterene and Ruby popped into our minds first, but the questions from the neighbors and other family members would be too intrusive. Uncle Earl offered to help me with the baby; he always wanted children. The prospect of raising a family in the Village seemed appealing to me at the time. I imagined staying on with Uncle Earl, and together, teaching this child about art, music, life, but Earl was almost sixty and not in good health, and I knew I couldn't manage the city and raise a child alone. That night, Mom decided she would take the baby and raise him as her own son."

I noticed the long drooping ash at the end of my cigarette and tapped it into the ashtray between us. Avoiding direct eye contact, I nodded to keep her going.

"Afraid of the stigma, we decided to stay in New York until you were born."

The finality of hearing her saying "you" brought tears to my eyes that I swiped away with my hand.

"And," she continued, "tell everyone Mom was pregnant, not me." She didn't look up at me, but I saw the tears trickle down her face.

"Mother did come back to Charlotte for weeks at a time during my stay. She wore maternity clothes and had Dad prepare a nursery. Tim never knew what was going on. I came home for Christmas, starting to show, but covered my secret with bulky sweaters. I told my classmates I attended a private school focused on art, which I did. I can't begin to tell you how scared and happy I was during that time, walking the city streets with Uncle Earl, the gallery visits, the lectures at NYU, the occasional dinner party, and the theatre every Saturday afternoon."

I stole a glance at her faint smile of the memory.

She puffed on her cigarette in thought; the tears had stopped. "You were the most popular baby in the Village. Uncle Earl knew everyone, and they were so accepting of a pregnant teenager." She slipped out of her chair and kneeled next to me, holding my hands in hers. "Derek," her pleading eyes searched mine, "I'm sorry I never told you. A secret so covered with lies soon becomes the truth to everyone involved."

Sorrow for the life I never knew, the life I didn't have with my real mother, the possibility of how things might have been, teemed within me as if the grief would churn my heart into pieces. We held each other and cried. I wanted to say how proud I was that she kept me, how thankful I was for having her in my life, how I didn't hold anything against her for her decisions. Tears streamed down my face. "I love you, Val." I couldn't say any more; sobs of pain for me and for her took over my body.

She stroked my hair. "I meant to tell you when you were old enough to understand, but the timing never seemed right. You left us before I had a chance."

"Gladys sent me away. No evidence, no crime," I said; resentment for the Bitch still harbored in my soul.

The words seemed to hit Valerie hard; she pulled back to her chair and wiped her eyes. "I think Mother was afraid you would find out and misunderstand. She wanted to shelter you from the truth. Send you out into the world to be your own person, not someone shaped by the secrets and lies of this family."

That statement didn't hold reality for the person I knew as Gladys. "Who else knows?" I asked, wondering how many people kept the undisclosed truth.

"Walterene, Ruby, and Father," she answered. "Ruby and Walterene confronted Mother with their suspicions, but held the secret safe. That's why I worried when you found Walterene's diaries. She mentions it and says how much she and Ruby wanted you as theirs; in fact, over the years, they helped raise you as much as I did, as much as Mother did."

"I didn't see anything about me in the diaries," I said.

"I took them last Sunday before Edwina and Roscoe came over." She rubbed her eyes, weary from the conversation.

"Edwina and Roscoe are talking to the police about the man who hurt Ruby and threatened me." I briefly explained how the phone calls and attacks focused on getting me out of town to avoid hurting Vernon's campaign. I wanted to get back to us, not allowing the stupid antics of family business politics to swerve the discussion away from the words we had avoided for twenty-five years.

"I hate them," Valerie stated with a flat tone. She looked back to me. "If you didn't see the diaries, how did you find out?"

I tried to explain as simply as possible. "I read about Mr. Sams. Walterene thought Papa Ernest and Vernon had been part of the lynching."

Valerie rubbed her forehead and stared at the floor as I talked.

"Daniel didn't know what I wanted to research at the Observer archives, but thought it had something to do with the family. He did some digging, talked to a few people—specifically, to his brother who was a year behind you in school. I saw Daniel's notes saying you left school the year I was born." The pain I saw in her face almost kept me from venturing the next question. "I wasn't a child of a high school sweetheart, was I?"

"No," she mumbled.

Fear seized my mind. The truth and shock of who my mother was led to the dread of discovering the identity of my father, and from the secrecy and pain of Valerie's pregnancy, I could only assume I was a product of rape. Brutality, cruelty, violence, and aggression resulted in my creation. My eyes watched her, posing the question of who the fiend had been.

"No." She shook her head. "Derek, you know enough."

Anger stirred in me again. "Val, we got this far; there's no going back. You owe me the truth. Was it rape?"

She bowed her head letting her dark hair hide her face; her thin body slumped in the chair. For the first time I considered how much we resembled each other; as brother and sister, the fact seemed natural, but as mother and son, I wanted to know why my genes coded me so much a Harris. Papa Ernest had raped his daughter, producing Vernon; could Dad have done the same to his daughter? The thought struck me as ridiculous as soon as it snapped within my brain; the gentleness and kindness of the man I called my father, and Valerie's devotion to him, cleared him in my mind. But Dad wasn't my father, he was my grandfather; the question of my biological father persisted. "Val, who?" I couldn't call the man "my father." The phrase evoked love, tenderness; this man was a rapist, a child molester; he had raped a fifteen-year-old girl. "Who did it?"

Sobs shook her shoulders. She mumbled something.

I kneeled at her feet, holding her hands in mine as she had done to me a few minutes before. "It's all right. He can't hurt you now. Who was it?"

She said the name again.

I couldn't believe it. "No!"

"Yes," she cried, "Vernon, Uncle Vernon raped me!"

Hate boiled in me. "Why is he not in jail? Did the Bitch cover for him? I can't believe she can even look him in the eyes."

Valerie cried, "No one knows. I never told anyone. Mother never knew." She gasped for air between sobs and words. "She thought it was some boy from school. I couldn't tell her the truth. I was too ashamed."

"You never confronted him?" Anger tore at my soul, but I tried to be compassionate, to consider her feelings. Surprised she had kept me and not gone through with the abortion, I couldn't imagine the fear and loathing she must have for the entire family. Gladys supported Vernon's every decision, in the company and for the whole Harris clan. The star and head of the family, he commanded everyone. How could she have pointed to him? No one would have believed her.

"Derek, please! I want this to stay buried," she pleaded. "It's history. Nothing can be done now."

I glanced at the clock: eight fifteen. "Let's go." I pulled her hand to help her out of the chair. A movement from the corner of my eye caught my attention; Ruby stood in the doorway crying. She had heard it all. "We're going to see Gladys," I told Ruby.

I PULLED UP to the door of the Dilworth house; Valerie sat unmoving beside me. The front porch lights were on, and Dad, Gladys, and Grandma sat in rockers under the breeze of ceiling fans sipping their after-dinner coffee. Gladys stood when she saw me.

Opening the car door for Valerie, I helped her out. The worried look on Gladys' face as she watched Valerie's stumbling steps told me she knew the secret was gone. "Gladys, we need to talk," I said as I climbed the stairs with Valerie.

She didn't say a word, but rushed to Valerie's side to help her into the house. Dad and Grandma began to follow, but she said something to make them stay outside. She led Valerie into the back sunroom, away from the presence of Grandma and Dad. "What have you done?" Her accusing eyes slashed into me.

Valerie between us on the couch, I shot back, "Found the truth. The truth you hid. Lies you made up to save yourself embarrassment. You're a bigger bitch than I ever thought possible."

"Don't talk to me like that," Gladys seethed. "Leave Valerie here and go."

"Stop it!" Valerie woke from her daze. "Stop it, both of you." She got up and grabbed onto a chair from the table to support her weight, then dropped into it. "We're all we have. I'm sick of the snide remarks and digs you take at each other." She focused on Gladys. "Mom, Derek knows."

"What?" She jerked to attention so fast I thought her thin body would snap like a twig. "Knows what?"

Valerie took a deep breath and braced her hands on the table. "And he knows who his father is."

Gladys looked to me, then back to Valerie; her body still stiff and alert. "Some no-account boy from Myers Park," she turned to me, "that your sister couldn't say 'no' to."

I watched Valerie as she shook her head from side to side.

"What do you mean?" Gladys asked. "I thought it was that Watkins boy who played football with Tim. That's what you told me."

"I never said who it was. You assumed." Valerie's arm trembled from the stress of pressing her hands on the table. She released her grip on the tabletop and crossed her arms in front of her as if to help protect herself from what she was about to say. "One night, when I stayed over at Margaret's, Uncle Vernon told us we were making too much noise, so he made us sleep in separate bedrooms."

"Mike?" Gladys jumped to the conclusion it was Margaret and Mark's brother.

Valerie ignored her and continued, "It happened only once. At first, I hoped and prayed it had been a nightmare." She watched Gladys perched on the edge of the cushion. "Vernon," she began, but Gladys jumped to her feet.

I thought she was going to smack Valerie, so I lunged forward to grab her arm, but Gladys slipped away from me and wrapped herself around Valerie. She held her daughter and rocked back and forth as if Valerie were still a little girl. They both cried. Never having seen this kind of emotion from Gladys, I held my seat, stunned, wondering what they had gone through together: mother and daughter guarding a secret, Gladys not knowing the whole truth, and Valerie too afraid to confide in anyone.

For several minutes, I stayed quiet while they held each other and cried, then I noticed Gladys' body straighten and return to her normal stiff posture. She guided Valerie back into the chair and then turned to me. "He won't get away with this."

My spine tingled at the sight of a woman I'd thought I knew. I had expected her to deny it, to cover scandal, to blame me, but her eyes flashed with blue fire, and I knew her anger wasn't directed at me. Gladys turned back to Valerie and touched her face as if she stroked fine silk. "Stay here," she commanded with such gentleness it sounded like a question.

I jumped up. "I'm going with you."

Her eyes flashed at me, then the fire receded. "Take care of your mother. I'll take care of Vernon."

"But, I want to be there," I almost pleaded. "I'm not a child any-more. This is about Valerie and me. I have a right—"

"Okay," she conceded before I could finish. "But you must con-trol your temper. I know how to deal with him." She thought for a moment. "Yes, you should be there. He will face what he did to my daughter and me, and to my grandson."

I smiled at her, glad that she was on my side. We walked out to my car, and I waited while Gladys said a few words to Dad, then I opened the passenger side door. She smiled at my newfound man-ners for her. The short drive to Vernon's home on Queens Road allowed Gladys time to remind me to let her do the talking and to stay calm no matter what he said. Along the way, I thought about the arguments and tension between us; she had wanted to protect me from this secret, to keep Valerie safe from the rumors and accusing stares of the self-righteous in Charlotte's society. Maybe telling her I was gay years ago had given her the opportunity to force me to leave, have my own life without the shadow of being the bastard child of the Harris family. I glanced at her, hoping she would spill the reasons for our years of discontent, but her own silent thoughts stilled her as we neared Vernon's house.

This woman wasn't my mother, but my grandmother. The fact was hard to keep in my mind. All the family relationships I had known for twenty-fives years were false. Panic gripped my gut as I thought about Mark; I hadn't considered any one else besides Valerie and me since I heard the truth, now the revelation that Mark and I were brothers slapped me into reality. *I had sex with my brother.* All my abomination of incest within the family—Papa Ernest with his daughter, Vernon with Valerie—I had to add Mark and me to the list. Of course, as I turned the car onto Queens Road, I rationalized that two men can't be considered incest; laws against it are there to pro-tect offspring of those relationships. Me, I'm the offspring of incest; twice over—Papa Ernest fathered Vernon, who fathered me. I felt acid bubble up my throat, the bitter bile pushing its way out. I calmed my breathing and dismissed my lineage from my thoughts.

As I pulled the car into Vernon's driveway, Gladys warned me again, "Let me do the talking."

Aunt Irene opened the door of their sprawling house along the oak-lined street of Charlotte's elite. Her eyes widened behind her half moon reading glasses. "Gladys, I didn't expect you this time of night."

"I need to talk to Vernon," she said as she pushed her way past her bewildered sister-in-law. I followed, only nodding to my aunt.

We found Vernon in his study, puffing on a cigar, reading through a folder of newspaper clippings. "What the hell are you two doing here? It's almost nine o'clock."

"We know what time it is," I started, but a quick hawk-like look from Gladys stopped me.

"Vernon, I," she glanced at me, "we need to talk to you. Derek, please shut the door; I don't think this is something the rest of the house needs to hear."

I closed the door as Gladys took a seat across from Vernon's desk. A couch against the wall where I could see them both seemed like a good vantage point for me. Vernon's jaw muscles twitched as he chomped on his cigar. He looked at Gladys then at me. Gladys poised in her chair, expressionless as a raptor ready to swoop down on her prey. The hate I felt for Vernon had to be contained; Gladys knew how to handle him. I would only end up in jail if I acted on my instincts.

"My daughter had a child at sixteen," she began as if reciting facts from a history book. "I had always believed the father was a high school boy—"

"Now wait one minute." Vernon sat forward. "What kind of lies has Valerie told you?"

"The guilty always deny before the accusation." She stood and placed her hands on his desk, staring into his eyes. "You bastard," she spit the words, "you stole my daughter's innocence and ruined her childhood. I have spent twenty-five years covering up what I thought was her mistake."

I tried not to take the word "mistake" personally.

"But you took what you wanted without thinking who you hurt. I should string you up by the balls." Her face flushed with emotion.

"You listen to me." The cold bastard didn't take his eyes off her. "I didn't do anything she didn't want."

I couldn't stop myself. "You fucking—"

Gladys glared at me, her index finger extended to shut me down. Her head and finger turned to point at him. "Vernon," her voice calm and calculated, "she was a girl of fifteen when you did this. She's your niece. You robbed my family. Your own son," she pointed to me, and my gut ached, "would love to make you pay for this by exposing you to the public."

His face paled, and he laid the cigar in the ashtray.

"But I know what family means to us," she continued, "even

though you don't. I don't want this to go public. I don't want to hurt Valerie or Derek anymore." She picked up his folder of newspaper clippings and thumbed through them. "You will resign from the Senate race tomorrow."

"Are you out of your mind?" He came out of his chair and jerked the folder from her hands. "Who the hell are you to come in here and tell me what to do with my life?"

"I'm the mother of the girl you raped." Her controlled voice rumbled through the room.

"I'm not giving up this election," he yelled, "for something that happened twenty-five years ago. It's just her word against mine."

Gladys pushed him back toward the desk with her pointing finger. "You don't have a choice. If I don't attend a press conference tomorrow before noon, I'll hold my own. I have put up with your bullying for too long." Her predator side took over. "You will resign from the campaign, and you will resign from the board of Harris Construction."

He leaned on the edge of his desk, his face white and frozen. The wrath of Gladys had apparently surprised him.

She pushed the folder across his desk. "Something for your scrapbook. Derek," she motioned to me, "let's go. I'm sick of the sight of him."

I opened the study door for her, but she stopped to address Vernon one last time. "I have you by the balls, and I won't let go until they're mine."

A LARGE GROUP of reporters assembled for Vernon's press conference: television and newspapers from Charlotte, Raleigh, Greensboro, Wilmington, and Asheville. I saw Daniel across the room, and he winked at me.

I stood with Gladys. "So, what should I call you now? Grandma Gladys?"

She shot me a look I had seen too many times before; I had crossed the line. "Mother will do. I don't want this getting out; I bluffed Vernon with taking it public. Valerie doesn't need everyone in this city knowing what happened."

"You're right. Thank you for what you did for her," I hesitated, trying to get the rest of the words out, "and for me."

She only nodded, staring at the lectern as Vernon came to the microphone. He explained that the stress of his campaign for political office and the toll that stress took on his family was more than he was willing to give. He would sacrifice his ambitions for the good of his wife, children, and grandchildren. I spotted Mark behind his father. If Vernon only knew that his bastard son had literally fucked his perfect, golden boy, favorite son. But that was my secret and Mark's guilt to live with. And it was guilt that had broken Mark. He kept his head lowered throughout Vernon's speech; Kathleen stood by Mark's side with her arm locked through his. The only emotion I felt for Mark was pity. Camera flashes recorded the end of an era.

The next day, Vernon's resignation from the board of Harris Construction was less public, but the same sacrifice had been made "for family."

"YEAH, I'M PACKING right now," I explained to Emma on the phone. "I have a flight out tomorrow."

"Want me to meet you at the airport? No, wait," Emma clicked her fingernails on the phone's mouthpiece, "I have to be in Sausalito for a catalog shoot. Well, I will see you when I see you. Will you be glad to get home?"

I sat on the bed among folded clothes and a half-packed suitcase and considered her question. "I don't know." The answer surprised me. Did I really want to go back to California? Ruby had begged me to stay, and so had Valerie. Gladys and I had become more at ease; she had actually hugged me when Vernon announced the end of his campaign. Mark was a lost cause, but Daniel wasn't. What did I have in California but a roommate and a cat? "Emma, I think I'm going to postpone the return trip again."

She sighed deep into the receiver. "I knew this would happen. It's that Daniel guy, isn't it?"

"No, not totally," I said. "Things have leveled out; my family is still totally fucked up, but not as bad as before I got here."

"Sounds like they need you," she teased. "You want me to box up your stuff and send it to... Where are you?"

"Charlotte, North Carolina," I reminded her, and then added, "home."

Greg Lilly is an author living in Sedona, Arizona. After 17 years as a Charlotte, North Carolina technology analyst and being warned that technical writing shouldn't involve characters and plots, he decided to leave the corporate life for the high desert. Greg is working on his next novel.

www.GregLilly.com

CPSIA information can be obtained at www.ICGtesting.com
Printed in the USA
LVOW061953081111

254071LV00003B/278/A